Catching Feelings in the End Zone

Dev Hahn

Fox Arrow Publishing

Also By Dev Hahn

<u>Standalones</u>
Beyond Broken Colors

<u>Bellwood Lady Baller Series</u>
Coming Out on the Sidelines
Catching Feelings in the End Zone
Tackling Temptations on the Line
Opposing Hearts on the Field, *Coming Fall 2025*

In loving memory of my grandmothers, Nancy and Sonja, who were the inspiration behind the character of Grams. This book is dedicated to them, for always showing grace, compassion, kindness and love. I wouldn't be the woman I am today if it wasn't for them.

Contents

Chapter 1

Colton

"What should we do?"

"I don't know, man. I've never seen him like this before."

My brain pounds against my skull with every word they speak. *How do I get them to shut the hell up?*

"Maybe we should call Payson?"

Payson ... Why does that name sound familiar?

"Nah, man. Her and Sadie are busy getting everything ready to head out to California soon. They have to get their dorms and stuff situated before their classes start."

"Okay, so no Payson and no Sadie. And we sure as hell can't call the parentals. What about Thea?"

"No! Absolutely not!"

Was that a dog snarl? And do the voices need to be so loud?

God, I feel like I'm in some kind of darkened abyss, with their voices vibrating off some unseen barrier.

"Damn, Z. Could you have shut that option down any faster? Any particular reason you don't want the smoking hot Thea—"

"Finish that sentence and so help me God I will knock your teeth down your throat," Zealand snarls.

Thea? Thea as in ... my sister? Wait ... I think I recognize these voices!

"Okay, okay. Let's all take a deep breath and calm down. We need to focus. Colton needs us to help him, *not* talk about his sister."

There's a reason he is one of my best friends.

"Jeremiah is right. The next asshole who mentions my little sister is going to get punched in the face," I grumble as I attempt to sit up. My head spins and nausea swirls in my stomach, so I drop back down onto the cool leather couch.

"Well, look who decided to return from the dead," taunts Rhett. "How are you feeling there, buddy?"

"Like shit," I groan. "What happened?"

"Well ... let's see. We went to that party at the Davenports' house, and you got wayyy trashed! Like, you were chugging so much alcohol, it didn't matter what was handed to you. You kept talking about wanting to drink away your heartache that Stace—"

"You had us worried, man." Zealand's concerned voice comes from close by, effectively cutting off Anthony. I would know for certain if it didn't hurt to open my damn eyes to check.

How long was I out if Z is so concerned about me?

"Here, man." Something hard and cold taps my hand. The coolness against my heated skin is a welcome reprieve. I grab the bottle, and it crinkles as I place it against my forehead. After a few moments, I finally open my eyes and take in my surroundings.

Once my eyes have adjusted to the blinding sunshine streaming through the shades, I recognize the room we are in. It's Jarrett Hastings's bedroom. Or it was before Zealand's older brother graduated two years ago and enlisted into the Army. Z's parents wanted to upgrade this space after he left so whenever Jarrett came home on leave he could have his own space to decompress from military life. It feels like not that long ago I helped move this couch in here.

Zealand stands in front of me with his hand held out like he has something to give me. "You're going to want to take these and drink that bottle of water. It's going to help with the nasty hangover I have no doubt you're dealing with right now."

I toss back the ibuprofen and chase them with the water, holding back the nausea that dares to takeover. "Thanks, man." We exchange fist bumps before he drops down onto the couch next to me.

The guys sitting around me are my best friends. Some I've known since kindergarten. Any other time we are together, there's laughter and jokes being made about each other. Right now, though? Nothing but silence and uneasy eyes directed at me.

"Why are you all staring?" I ask before I take a few sips of the cool water. *What I would give for a ginger ale to help with my stomach right now.*

Rhett rubs the back of his neck before he speaks. "The guys and I ... We are just ... You sure you're okay?"

This shit again?

"Apart from a little hungover, I'm good. Nothing to worry yourselves about." I try to keep my tone optimistic, not wanting them to know I'm the opposite of good. It takes so much effort to mask the anger and sadness that consumes me everyday, trying to hide it from my friends.

Did I let something slip last night I shouldn't have?

The thought of it has me irritated. My friends don't need to concern themselves with me, especially with us entering our last year of high school. They have far more important things to worry over, like SATs and choosing what college they want to go to or what they will do post graduation. My problems? What I'm dealing with? I will work through them on my own and get back to the old me—the me before my heart was shattered to pieces.

"Colton," Jeremiah speaks up. "You really expect us to believe that you're okay?"

"Yes, I do," I snip. My friends glance at each other, and I can tell they don't believe me. "Guys ... seriously. I'm fine! Okay? I've never been better! I'm just trying to live it up since it's our senior year! Isn't it a right of passage to get super drunk at a high school party? Are we not supposed to do these things?" My voice gets louder than I intended, not helping to prove my point.

"Take a breather, man," Rhett says in a calm tone. "It's not that we don't believe you. It's just ... you've never been one to drink alcohol. And last night? You literally were drinking a little bit of everything in sight. Had Jer and Zealand not noticed and cut you off, you would be in a hospital bed right now with alcohol poisoning. How would you explain that to your parents? To Payson?"

He's right. What I did last night doesn't sound like me. It's not who I am. I've never been one of those guys who need alcohol to have a good time. No wonder my friends don't believe me.

"I appreciate you guys, I really do, and I'm grateful you are looking out for me. But I promise you, I'm fine. I think I've just been playing it too safe for too long and it's our last year before we have to become adults in the real world. I just went a little overboard with the party. Trust me when I say I don't think I'll be doing that again."

My head throbs, and another wave of nausea has me ready to head toward the bathroom. *Yeah, never touching alcohol again.*

"You don't look so good there, Goldilocks," Anthony says. "You know what would help you feel better?"

"What?" I ask, leaning back on the couch and closing my eyes in hopes it will alleviate my headache until the meds kick in.

"A good hearty breakfast at Munson's Diner," he states.

"How the hell is food going to help? The mere thought of it going in my mouth makes me want to vomit."

"I don't know. I always heard that breakfast food is the cure to hangovers."

"I'll pass."

This new waitress is stunning. Caramel-brown hair pulled up in a messy bun on top of her head. Her skin is bronzed, like she spent her summer days lying in the sun every chance she got. If it wasn't for the dark-framed glasses and freckles dotting her face, I would have thought this was Stacey, my ex-girlfriend, standing before me.

And now I've lost my appetite.

"Excuse me? Miss? Not to be rude or anything, but, uh, what happened to blondie that was here a few moments ago?" Anthony asks.

"Really, Anthony?" Jeremiah shakes his head. "Please ignore our friend. He left his manners and some brain cells at a party last night."

"Uh ... well ... she kind of, sort of asked me to take your booth in exchange of taking my next customer," she says, staring at the floor instead of us.

"Damn, Colt. You better hope blondie doesn't mess with my food because you decided to piss her off."

This earns a giggle from our new waitress. "You won't have to worry about that. Promise. And honestly, this sort of thing happens quite a bit. Hollis ... She can be a bit hotheaded sometimes."

At that moment, the blonde waitress passes us on her way to approach customers who just entered the restaurant. "I am not hotheaded, Talia. I think the word you're looking for is bitch."

Talia's cheeks tinge pink. "I don't like cussing," she murmurs. She shakes her head, a soft smile upon her face. "Anywho, what can I get you guys started with?"

Talia goes around the booth, taking our order, as my eyes follow blondie as she greets the new guests and leads them to a booth a few seats down from us. She hands the couple their menus, gracefully placing them in their hands and discussing the options in a more pleasant tone from the one she used with us. Her eyes dart in my direction as if sensing me staring at her. I don't miss the smirk she gives before she clears off a nearby booth and takes the dirty dishes to the kitchen.

Is she—

"And for you, sir?"

"Hmm? Oh, sorry. I will just take some toast and a glass of water, please," I say before handing her my menu.

"You got it! I'll get those orders in for you, gentlemen." Talia heads to place our orders with the cooks. As soon as she's out of ear shot, my friends don't waste a second questioning my momentary distraction.

"Something, or maybe *someone*, catch your eye there, Colt?" Rhett teases.

I clear my throat. "Not at all," I say nonchalantly.

"You know what they say about those feisty girls, don't you? They are some of the freakiest ones in the sheets, ya know what I mean." Anthony waggles his eyebrows.

"Not interested, man. I think I'm going to take a page out of my cousin's handbook and do the no-dating thing this year. Put all my focus on senior year and figure out what I'm doing with my future."

"In case you forgot, or maybe it's because you're hungover but, uh, that plan didn't really work out for Payson. Now, did it?" Jeremiah says, his mouth quirking upward.

"Look, guys. You all know I love my cousin to pieces, but I believe I'm much more capable of following through on the no-dating rule than she did."

Anthony leans across the booth. "Care to make a bet, my dear friend?"

"Ooooohhh," the guys say in unison.

Anyone who knows me knows I'm a very competitive person. Bets? They're hard for me to resist.

"Go on," I urge him. I probably shouldn't be making a bet with Anthony while I'm hungover.

"Alright. If you can make it to graduation without dating or falling in love, the four of us will each pay you twenty dollars."

"So what I'm hearing is an easy one hundred dollars?"

"Hang on, now. You didn't let me finish. Should you break your own rule, and some girl has some magical coochy that makes you fall in love with her, you have to streak across the stage at graduation."

"I think I can manage that," I say.

"And I don't mean you in nothing but some tighty whities. I'm talking full ass, butt-naked-like-the-day-you-were-born streaking."

Cash money or streaking? Hmm ... I can take those chances.

Anthony places his hand in front of me. "Do we have a deal?"

A devilish smile spreads across my face as I grasp his hand. "You have a deal, my good friend. This is going to be the easiest one hundred dollars I'll make."

Chapter 2

Hollis

"Hey, Holls. Booth three is asking for you," Talia says as I scrape the plates and load the dishwashing rack with dirty dishes. "The one guy said he doesn't want anyone but *the pink-haired pixie*."

I drop my head and grit my teeth, releasing a small growl.

Great! Just what I want to deal with right before our Sunday brunch rush.

"You want me to tell them you're busy? I can take it over for you if you—"

"No! It's fine! I gave you the group of obnoxious jocks that are still out there hogging up my booth. I'll go take care of booth three." Only one person has ever called me pixie, and as much as I don't want to handle the request, I'm doing Talia a favor by keeping her far away from *him*.

"They're not obnoxious. Well ... the one might be a tad immature. But the rest of them have been very ... sweet."

"Sweet? Puh-lease. That's just their magical charm to lure in girls so they can get what they want before ghosting them. Hate to break it to you, Tal, but those guys are like any other jock. They only care about their sports, the parties, and getting laid."

"If you say so," Talia mutters before heading back into the dining area to check on her customers.

Talia likes to believe there is good in every person, and how could she not? She was raised in a home filled with love and parents who are still crazy for each other. Some of us aren't that lucky.

After ensuring my hands are clean, I stop at the kitchen door, taking a deep breath before making my way to the one person I have been trying to avoid these past few weeks—Rowan Hall.

Rowan is a junior at Ravenwood University, a decent college two towns over. He's well-known around campus for his social media presence but even more so for his house parties and side business. The side business that almost got me arrested and the reason I've been doing everything to steer clear of him. I guess my luck's run out if he tracked me down at my job.

With my pen and pad in hand, I steel my shoulders and make my way to where Rowan and his friend are sitting—two booths down from the jocks who are laughing a little too loudly. Except for the one who smells like a liquor cabinet and is wearing sunglasses inside. He doesn't seem to be in the mood, no doubt dealing with a massive hangover. Serves him right.

I stop in front of the booth with the curly-haired mullet blonde and his buddy, who eye-fucks the hell out of me as I approach them.

"Welcome to Munson's. What can I get you?"

"Hmm ... that is a good question. You know, I have never been here before. Just recently discovered this place," Rowan states.

"That's because it's way out of your way. What are you doing here?" I cross my arms over my chest, wondering what the real reason for him being here is.

"Why so hostile, Pixie? Can't a guy want to check out a new place for some good breakfast food?"

"You live in a small college town. I'm sure there was someplace much closer," I snarl.

"We've tried them all, and honestly, they're alright. Randall and I figured we would drive around until we found something new. Spotted this interesting place and figured a fifties restaurant has to have some bomb-ass breakfast food."

"Cut the bullshit. You're only here because you need me. Admit it."

"We are just two hungry college guys wanting a hearty breakfast." Rowan smiles, but I know a fake smile when I see one. "I'll take the steak and eggs breakfast platter. Cheese on the scrambled eggs. Make sure the hashbrowns are crispy, and regular bacon. Oh, and a glass of orange juice."

I glare at Rowan, trying to figure out his angle.

"You going to write my order down?"

Releasing a huff, I note his order before turning to his friend. "And for you?"

"Something that definitely is not on the menu," Randall says, licking his lips while looking me up and down.

"Hard pass," I say, glowering at him. "You're nowhere near my type."

"And what is your type, baby girl?" Randall smirks.

Gross.

"Big dick energy."

"Ha!" comes from the direction of the jocks, but I don't look that way.

Instead, I lean over to look under the booth and squint toward Randall's crotch. "And judging by the lack of bulge in your sweats, you ain't got that. So ... what will it be, Needle Dick?"

Laughter breaks out and someone shouts, "Damn," from two booths over. I glance in their direction, noticing the guy with sunglasses hiding his smirk. Seems Mr. Hungover must have overheard me. *Is he listening in on this conversation?*

I return my attention to the offended Randall.

"We can go into the bathroom if you want, and I'll show you just how little my dick really is." He smirks.

Opening my apron pockets, I act as if I'm searching for something. "Sorry, I don't have my magnifying glass with me today." I shrug.

"You little bitch," Randall snarls, and gets up from the booth. In a flash, an arm wraps around my waist and pulls me back, then a tall man stands in front of me, shielding me.

"You've got ten seconds to see your way out of here before I make you leave," the voice in front of me growls out.

"You're going to make me?"

What the fuck? I don't need someone to come to my defense. I can handle douchebags like Randall on my own.

I attempt to make my way around the man in front of me when his arm shoots out, forcing me back behind him. With a small whiff, I smell alcohol.

You've got to be kidding me.

"I don't need you to handle this!" I shout. "I have no problems manhandling little bitches like him."

"Who you calling a bitch, whore?" Randall snarls. The blonde-haired giant makes a move towards Randall but is stopped when another voice speaks up.

"Do I need to make a call to the sheriff's office to have you escorted out of my diner, gentlemen?" Beau Munson, my manager and one of the diner's owners, says from behind me. Looking over my shoulder, I spot Talia quivering by the kitchen door. Her dad, with his cell phone in hand, glares at the scene before us. All the jocks are standing right behind me, ready to have their friend's back.

"You know what? It's fine. We will find somewhere else to go," Rowan says. He gets out of the booth, all eyes on him and Randall. "Sorry everyone!" he says, raising a hand and giving off a fake apologetic smile.

"Here," he says, his hand stretched in my direction.

Mr. Hangover puts his hand out to stop him from coming in my direction, almost like a protector, not wanting Rowan near me.

"Relax, bruh. I'm just giving her a tip. It's the least I can do for the chaos my friend has caused."

"The chaos I've caused!? That little bit—" Randall shouts.

"Enough, Randall!" Rowan raises his free hand, cutting off his friend.

I snatch the tip from Rowan before he gives me a wink. Fucker. He grabs Randall by his shirt collar and shoves him toward the door, arguing as they go. Once they disappear into the parking lot, the diners return to their conversations, Talia disappears into the kitchen, and Beau returns to his office.

"You okay?" my human shield asks.

"Peachy," I state. I stare into the dark sunglasses covering his eyes, ready to have words with him. "You didn't need to do that. I could have handled him all on my own."

"I didn't trust that guy to not hurt you."

"So? He might have tried, but I can take it. I don't mind a little pain here and there. It's a reminder that I'm still alive." I shove past him to collect the menus off the table and return them to the stack by the register.

"My parents taught me that a man should never lay a finger on a woman. So excuse me for wanting to protect you from a potential threat. Did you even know him?"

"No," I say, annoyed by his presence.

"So how do you know what he is capable of doing?"

"I don't. I just take my chances. Like I said, I'm more than capable of dealing with people like him. Don't assume because I'm short, I can't handle myself."

"I-I wasn't insinuating that you couldn't, but can't a guy just want to help a girl out?"

"Help a girl out, huh?" I ask, stepping up to him. "Okay, you giant leaky distillery. Why don't you go back to your little group of friends and get the hell out of my way so I can work?"

He glares down at me, or at least I think he is glaring at me. The guy may be wearing shades, but I refuse to break his hidden eye contact. I could do this all day, but I need to make money since it doesn't fall from the sky when you beg or plead for it to.

"Sorry for trying to be a nice guy and helping you out."

"Nice guy? You copped a fucking attitude as I was about to take your table of goons' orders!"

"Only because you had the attitude first! Who slams menus down and rushes off?"

"A waitress who was running slightly behind and needed to clock in!"

"Maybe had you left, I don't know, earlier, you would have been on time!"

"It's not that simple!"

"Seems pretty simple to me."

Wait ... why am I arguing with this guy?

"You know what? You don't know me or what the hell goes on in my life. So why don't you take your hungover ass back to your table before I embarrass you in front of your friends."

I shove past him, making my way to the kitchen.

"Tal, I'm taking five," I say as I make my way to the back of the restaurant and out the door, in desperate need of some fresh air.

Can this day get any worse!?

Grabbing the stool one of our cooks uses when he takes his smoke break, I sit down and pull out the tip Rowan handed me. There is no way Rowan and his friend just happened upon this place. He must have done some digging into me to track me down, and I have a sneaking suspicion as to why.

As I unravel the cash, counting out the tens, fives, and few twenties, I spot it. A white piece of paper with Rowan's chicken scratch.

There's more green for you if you want it, Pixie. I can get you on the books for Friday night. Just holler at me.

Son of a bitch!

I blocked that piece of shit on everything I could think of, but I guess when you're the ultimate "dog" on campus and a rising social media star, you can get anyone to do your bidding, including tracking down your star fighter's place of work.

The money I'd won was fast, easy money and came in handy when I needed it. Not to mention, fighting became my outlet for all the aggression I've harbored ever since my parents decided to say peace out to their only kid.

If it wasn't for Grams, who knows where I would be.

Speaking of Grams …

I dial the number, hoping she answers her phone.

"Hello?" the sweetest voice says after the second ring.

"Hey Grams. I just wanted to check in and make sure you're doing okay."

"Oh, Hollipop. I'm fine! I'm just sitting here reading my romance novel in my chair. I've got to tell you, the guy in this story is really something. The things he says … Whew! I think I need to invest in a vibrator."

"Grams!"

"What? I may be old, but I'm not dead."

"Keep those thoughts to yourself. Please? I don't need the mental images." I groan extra loud so she knows how disturbed I am.

"Shouldn't you be working?"

"I'm taking a five-minute breather before the madness starts. Plus, I wanted to check in and make sure you're okay."

"I'm *fine*, sweetheart. Stop worrying so much about me before you gray and wrinkle from all the stress. Then people will think we're sisters."

I let out a chuckle; my Grams is always a jokester.

"Okay. But if you start to feel unwell or off, you better call me."

"Yes, *mother*. Now, how about you get back to work. These bills won't pay themselves or so you say."

"I love you, Grams."

"I love you infinitely, Hollipop."

I close my eyes and take a deep breath. Hearing Grams's voice and her silly personality in full force, reassures me she's okay. Her sugar levels were on the lower side this morning, and I wanted to make sure I got them back to where they needed to be before I left for work. I made her favorite breakfast—toast with butter, peanut butter, and brown sugar and cinnamon sprinkled on top—before checking her levels to make sure they were within range.

It's also why I was late to work, and when I'm late, it puts me in a foul mood. Every minute I'm not working is money I'm losing, and I need it to help Grams with the bills and her diabetes medicine.

After walking through the kitchen, I peek out the door window into the dining area. My eyes zero in on the jock who shielded me from Needle Dick. I don't miss the worry on the faces of his friends as they glance at him with his head resting on the table beside his untouched toast and glass of water.

He must really be suffering. Wait. Why the hell do I care?

"Don't you kind of feel bad for him?"

"Jesus, Talia!" I shriek. "Warn someone before you decide to sneak up on them next time."

"Sorry!"

"And no, I don't feel bad for him. He chose to drink, and now he's suffering the consequences of his actions."

"According to his friends, he's never been drunk before. It was his first time. And probably his last time, judging by how rough he looks."

"A high school athlete never been drunk before? I find that hard to believe."

Talia shrugs. "I believe it. Not all athletes are party boys. Take Theo, for instance."

"Doesn't count. He's your brother, and I've seen how your parents are with you guys. For Christ's sake, you can't even cuss."

She's about to retort when her name is called.

"Talia, your order for booth six is up!" Al, one of the cooks, shouts. She heads off to deliver the food to her customers, and I'm reminded I have my own customers to check on.

"Holls, I think your one booth is ready for their check."

"Thanks, Al." I ponder for a moment what Talia said about the group of athletes. If he has never been drunk before, he probably doesn't know how to help get over a nasty hangover, giving me an idea.

I go in search of the tea Mrs. Munson keeps on hand for some of the elderly ladies who prefer a particular tea with their meals. Once the peppermint tea has seeped enough, I swirl in some honey and place the mug on a small tray to carry out.

I'm not really sure why I'm even doing this. Maybe because I know Grams is okay, or it could be the ounce of guilt I have for my *attitude*, as he so eloquently put it. I make my way to the dining area, placing the tea next to the blonde head of Mr. Hungover.

His friends get quiet, their eyes bouncing from me to their friend.

"Here," I tell him. "You're going to want to drink that if you don't want to feel like shit anymore."

"What is it?" he asks, raising his head just an inch above the table.

"A peace offering," I state before walking away.

Chapter 3

Colton

I'm not sure what kind of tea the fervent waitress gave me or what she put in it, but I downed it in minutes. After a few sips, the nausea subsided and I was able to eat the toast I ordered, then felt more human than I did when we got there.

Anthony tried getting in my head, telling me he was certain she did something to my drink, but I highly doubted it. Despite her abrasiveness and cold demeanor, I have a feeling it's her way of disguising the real person underneath. Something I've been doing for most of the summer since I received that letter from Stacey.

Forget her. Don't even think about her and what she did to us.

I take a few deep breaths to calm myself, not allowing the anger and pain to consume me. That was the reason I overdid it with alcohol at the party to begin with, and I sure as hell don't plan to repeat it.

Lying in my bed, I urge my mind to think of something else, anything to take it off my ex-girlfriend. It goes to the moment in the diner when those two guys walked in. The energy in the room shifted when they entered. The mullet-haired one kept his eyes on Little Miss Sunshine as she went into the kitchen before he and his dickwad of a friend took a seat. A silent alarm bell went off in my head when he asked Talia for the blonde pixie. No one else who works there comes close to resembling a tiny mythical creature, but if I had to compare her to one, Tinkerbell would be the most befitting. Blonde hair, small stature, and the matching attitude to go with it. Yeah, she's practically a real-life Tinkerbell, and I have no doubt in my mind that she wouldn't like being compared to a Disney fairy.

I chuckle to myself, envisioning how red her face would turn if some random person called her that to her face.

"Why are you laughing to yourself, weirdo?" my sister asks from my bedroom door.

"I'm not."

"O-kay. I'll pretend like I just didn't see you do it a second ago."

"What do you want, Thea?"

"I came to tell you that Payson just pulled into the driveway. Wasn't sure if you knew she was coming over since you've been perched up here avoiding everyone ever since you got home. Are you still feeling like crap from all that *partying* you did last night?" She has a blonde eyebrow raised toward her hairline.

"How the hell did you hear about that?"

"Zealand told me."

"And why the hell are you talking to my friend?"

"Why do you automatically assume I'm the one who wants to talk to your friends? *He* texted *me*, so why don't you ask your friend about that." Thea rolls her eyes. "Anyway, he was worried about you and asked if I would check in on you for him. After about a hundred texts sparring with the doofus, I finally got him to tell me what you did that made him so worried."

"What did Colton do?" My cousin appears behind Thea a moment later.

"Mr. Good Boy, who *doesn't do anything fun*, got extremely wasted last night at the Davenport party, almost landing him in the hospital with alcohol poisoning had his friends not stepped in to stop him."

"Are you kidding me? Colton Reid Reynolds!" Payson spews my government name as if she is my parent. Judging by her face, she doesn't seem too pleased about it. Great. Just what I need. My cousin giving me a lecture about the dangers of drinking and putting toxic shit in my body, especially before football starts up.

"Thanks Thea," I grumble.

"You're welcome, big bro!" she says, clearly not apologetic about outing me, before leaving the two of us alone.

Payson pulls my desk chair to my bedside and sits on it backward. "Care to explain yourself?" she asks.

Payson is my cousin and first best friend. I can confide in her with anything, but this? This is something I'm just not ready to share with anyone, including my family. Especially when I can't even grasp my own emotions around it. I also didn't forget that Stacey is a good friend of Sadie's, and because Payson is in love with Sadie, that makes her a friend by association. I'm honestly not sure how they would take the news, but I know I don't want them to have any negative feelings toward someone who has had Sadie's back through everything that went down over their last school year.

"Colt, you know you can talk to me, right? Whatever it is, whatever you're going through, I would never judge you, in the same way you never judged me when I came out to our family. You made sure to have my back, and I just want you to know that I have yours."

"I appreciate that, Pace, I really do. It's just ... I'm not sure how to deal with my feelings right now, and I'm trying to process them."

"So drinking a shit ton of liquor is how you process your emotions?"

"I thought it would help," I state, avoiding the glare I have no doubt she's still giving me.

"And did it?" Payson asks.

"Absolutely not. I've never felt so sick in my life. I'm still not one hundred percent, but I'm a little better than how I was doing earlier. And don't worry, I'm not drinking ever again." I emphasize the not drinking part so she understands I mean it.

"You better. You're about to start football, and you don't want to be doing stupid shit, especially during senior year. This is *the* year! You need to be at the top of your game, preparing to go against your opponents, but most importantly, showcasing what you got for the college scouts."

"Yeah, you're right." That's something else I haven't talked to Payson about. Payson and I used to have this dream of being scouted to a top-ranking school, earning scholarships and one day being drafted into the NFL. It's still her dream, especially since she got into the college she wanted, along with the love of her life.

As for me? I'm not even sure that's the dream for me anymore. Football is great, and I love the sport, but as for college? The NFL? I don't believe I have what it takes. I'm not even sure if that is truly the dream I want for me. Don't get me wrong, the money those players make would be phenomenal. Being financially stable is definitely a goal of mine, but at what costs? Especially when you become a big name in the sport and millions of people know what you look like and your name. They'll dig into your past, looking for everything to expose you to profit off your name and character, and the last thing I want or need is for them to dig up anything in the letter tucked in my notebook on my desk. I cannot fathom the field day the media would have if that secret got out.

"Listen, I came by because I wanted to ask you something."

"What's up?"

"Coach Watson and I came up with a combine-like event for any girls who are interested in wanting to play football for the school."

"Glad he's had a change of heart about girls playing since you helped make us state champs." I chuckle.

"Yeah, yeah. Water under the bridge," she says. "Anyway, I'm trying to gather some of the guys from the team and see if they want to help out. Coach wants some extra eyes, see who would be an asset for the upcoming season. I figured you could get the guys to tag along?"

"Pace, you know if you just mention football with girls those guys will drop any plans to be there, right?"

"So is that a yes?"

"Yeah, I'll do it. What time does it start?"

At eight forty-five, I'm pulling up in the parking lot of Bellwood High School to head to the football field. After Payson left last night, I set my alarm, then I was out for the rest of the night. I woke up feeling a thousand times better and ready to get this day started.

Do I want to be around a bunch of girls who may be my teammates? Not really. However, this will be a good testament to my no-dating rule, solidifying my chances to win that bet.

I park next to Payson's yellow Jeep and head toward the entrance to the stadium, then I spot Anthony arguing with a girl who is the female version of him.

"You can't control everything I do. I'm not a little kid, Anthony!" Alora shouts at her twin brother.

"Hey, what's going on here, guys?" I ask as I walk up to them, hoping to defuse the tension.

"Trying to talk some sense into Alora—"

"He doesn't think I can play football," Alora cuts in, eyes filled with rage.

"It's not that I don't think you can. I just don't want you to!"

"Why is that? Huh? You intimidated by me, little bro?" Alora tilts her head, ready to go against her own flesh and blood.

"You're only older than me by ten minutes."

"Yeah, and what a wonderful ten minutes it was before your big head came into the world to ruin my life!" Alora shouts before storming off. Anthony stares after his sister, shooting imaginary lasers into her back until she disappears out of sight.

"You know, it's kind of messed up you don't want her to play the sport you love yourself," I say.

"Let me put it this way. If Thea were to show up right now telling you she wants to play football, how would you feel?"

I think about it for a second. "I say I'd be impressed, but cheerleading has been her thing—"

"But say she didn't feel like cheerleading anymore. What if she has, by some miraculous reason, decided to give it up to play football, putting her body on the line, being tackled by dudes bigger than her."

"Oh ... I get what you're saying, but you shouldn't tell her she can't do something because you're worried for her safety."

Anthony sighs, shoulders slacking before he runs his hands down his face. "I know, but I just don't want her to get hurt. Or to have to punch out one of our teammates for ogling her during practices."

He makes a valid point. I'd be the same way if it was Thea out there, but then I think of something, as if it was my sister, that would ease my friend's mind. "You're getting yourself worked up over something that may not even happen."

"What do you mean?"

"Think of today's event as a taste test. She's going to go out there, get a feel for the sport, and probably end up hating it. Then she won't even think about signing up for football, and you won't have to worry about knocking out anybody."

"I didn't think of it like that. She is absolutely going to hate getting all sweaty and stuff. No way is she going to want to play after today!" He smacks my chest. "Thanks, man!"

I rub the spot where his hand collided with my chest. "Don't mention it."

Anthony and I make our way to the field, heading toward the coaching staff where Payson stands.

"Hang on." Anthony smacks my chest with rapid taps.

"Dude, would you quit doing that!" I laugh, shoving his hand away.

"Look." He points toward my cousin. "Isn't that the hotheaded server from yesterday?"

My eyes follow his finger, and sure enough, standing next to my cousin is the waitress from yesterday.

What is she doing here?

I quicken my pace, with Anthony right on my heels.

"Oh, Colton," Anthony singsongs. "You sure seem awfully anxious to go to her for someone who is not interested in dating. Does this mean we get to see a Colton full moon at graduation?"

I pause in my tracks, remembering the bet we made and shook on. Fuck. Why am I eager to get to her?

I clear my throat, trying to be coy. "I'm not … It's not like that. I just want to ask her about the drink she made me. That's all."

"Mm-hm …" I ignore him and continue making my way toward her.

"Hey," I say the moment I step up to the lifelike Tinkerbell. *She probably doesn't like to be called that.* Right.

"Colt!" Payson says as she grabs my hand and pulls me in for a hug. "Thanks for coming to help out today."

"Always happy to help, cuz," I state.

Little Miss Sunshine's vibrant blue eyes bounce between Payson and me, with an eyebrow quirked.

"Cuz?" she asks.

"Right. Sorry. Hollis, this is my cousin, Colton. Colton, this is Hollis," Payson says.

I extend my hand, but Hollis just stares at it.

"It's called a handshake," I tease her.

"Yeah … We've already met," she says, keeping her arms folded across her chest.

"Wait, you two know each other?" Payson questions, probably trying to figure out how we met, but my brain is trying to do the same. How the heck does my cousin know this girl that I've never seen or met before yesterday?

"It was brief," I state.

"He came into my job hungover and smelling like a bar. I was a bit of a bitch to him since he was being an ass. Then he got in my business—"

"That guy almost put his hands on you and would have had I not stepped in the way!" Is she seriously still pissed off about that?

"And like I told you, I can handle douchebags like him on my own," she snarls, stepping into my space, pressing her chest into mine. The softness of her breasts and the warmth emanating from her body send a sensation through me, like a tiny electric energy zapping around my body.

"Whoa ... hold up. Time out," Payson says, making a T with her hands. "*This* is the tall blonde brewery guy you were talking about?"

"Yep," Hollis says, putting emphasis on the p.

A smile slowly makes its way across my face. "You were talking about me? Wait. How the hell do you two know each other?"

"Nathan told me he gave my number to a waitress with stellar hand-eye coordination, said she was intrigued that our team had a girl on it, but he wasn't sure if she would reach out or not. Then I found out Jenna met her when she showed up at the studio about looking into a session, but couldn—"

"Ahem," Hollis says, shaking her head no.

"She couldn't paint," Payson finishes. I don't miss the little eye conversation between the two of them. "Since it seemed like a few people close to me knew of her and I never got a text or phone call, I decided I would go to her. Took Sadie to the diner, made sure we sat in Hollis's section, and we talked. She had questions about Bellwood and the football program, so I've been giving her what information I can, and we have been in touch since then. Recently, I was talking to Hollis about how I was thinking about putting together some sort of event for girls who would be interested in playing football to get a feel for the sport and see if it's something they want to pursue. She seemed pretty interested, so I snagged her up and brought her here."

"I said I was vaguely interested," Hollis states, trying to be stoic.

"Sure. We'll go with that." Payson smirks.

"So, you're good with your hands?" I ask, not realizing the innuendo in that question, but Hollis does.

"Oh, I'm amazing with my hands." She smirks before walking off.

"Whoo! Did you feel that?" Anthony asks Payson, stepping to stand beside her. I almost forgot he was still around.

"Feel what?" I ask.

"Oh, just the chemistry between you and Hollis." Payson smiles.

"Psh, there is ... not ... There is definitely no chemistry there."

"I don't know, man," Anthony says. "You could just feel the tension."

"Sooo much tension," Payson says, giving me a pointed look.

"You guys can say or assume whatever you want. I promise you, there is *nothing* between that girl and me."

Chapter 4

Hollis

I head toward the middle of the field, where some girls who arrived before me are standing but keep my distance from them. Some may say I'm antisocial, but I prefer to call it anti-people. How can anyone hurt you when you don't allow anyone to connect with you?

"Are you as nervous about this as I am?" a girl with copper hair asks me. She's curvy and fair skinned with a touch of red like she spent a little extra time in the sun and forgot to reapply her sunscreen. Freckles adorning her cheeks and eyes, unsure if they are blue or gray, stand out against her coppery tresses. She's slightly taller than me, but when you're five foot two, a majority of the public is.

I shrug and look out around the field, acting like I'm searching for someone to avoid a conversation with the girl. I don't do the whole small-talk thing.

"I'm Maisie, incoming senior. This is my first time trying football. What about you?" the redhead asks.

"Porkenstein!" A shrill voice screeches through the quiet morning air. "What are you doing here? Did old farmer Higgins let you out of the pig pen today?"

"I think the real question, Charmin, is what are you doing here? Aren't you afraid you may break a nail?" Copperhead fires back.

Okay, so the redhead has bite to her. I didn't expect that.

"It's *Charmaine*! And don't be ridiculous! You could never catch me breaking a sweat or putting on that gaudy uniform," a girl with long golden-blonde hair says. She looks like a young version of Paris Hilton. "For your information, I'm here to drop off my sister, Corrine."

A quiet girl who looks almost identical to the stuck-up, primpy princess stands behind her.

These two seem like polar opposites of each other.

"Now, if you'll kindly move your lard ass, I need to speak to whoever is in charge of this thing," Charmaine says.

"Oh, this big ol' thang?" Maisie turns to her side so she is looking at her ass. "Yeah, I'm surprised it took you so long to notice, considering your *boyfriend* hasn't stopped staring at it since I got here."

"Dylan's here!?" Charmaine shrieks, searching the field until her eyes land on one of the guys standing in the group. "Dylan! Dylan!" Charmaine yells as she storms off, her sister following close behind.

Once the pair are out of earshot, Maisie turns with a mischievous smile. "He hasn't been looking. I just knew it would piss her off."

We both laugh as we watch pompous Barbie go off on her clueless boyfriend, feeling slightly bad for him.

I raise a fist toward Maisie, who gladly reciprocates my fist bump. "Respect. Got to say, Red, that has to be the highlight of my Monday."

"Well, when you're the victim of Charmaine's constant bullying for as long as I have been, you tend to get tired of all the fat jokes and just have to fight back."

"Fair point," I state. "So, what's the deal with those two?"

"Charmaine Summers is the mean girl of our class. She only cares about her hair, how she looks, all things designer, and making sure she's the center of attention. Her parents are, for the most part, loaded and have spoiled her into the snobby little brat she is today. Her ego's been inflated since her cousin Lydia got pregnant and had to leave school when she started showing, so she became Bellwood High's newest mean girl. Corrine Summers is her younger sister."

"They're not twins?" I ask.

"Charmaine wishes, as much as she has tried to get Corrine to dress and act like her. If anyone doesn't know them, she says they are because of the attention it gives her. Like I said, Charmaine loves the spotlight." Maisie rolls her eyes, clearly annoyed about this girl I'm forming a distaste for. "I think they are, like, thirteen months apart? So more like Irish twins than actual twins."

"So does Corrine just follow her sister around? Or is she her own person?"

"She's been in Charmaine's shadow for as long as I've known them, even more so since Charmaine's rise to popularity. I'm not sure if it's because of her sister or if people just avoid her for the sake of staying away from Charmaine's evil wrath."

A whistle blows and the group of coaches and Payson gather the small group of girls at the fifty-yard line.

"Huddle up, ladies," the rounded belly old guy shouts. "I'm Coach Watson, Bellwood's head football coach. The gentleman next to me is Coach Harbaugh." He points to the guy, a tall gentleman, with salt and pepper hair with the matching beard and mustache. He seems fairly fit too, a real silver fox as Grams would say. I'm sure all the single moms flock to this guy the moment they see him around the school. He would have the attention of mine if she'd bothered to stick around.

"The other two gentlemen are my offensive and defensive coaches, Coach Freeman and Coach Wells." He points to the two darker-complexion coaches, one who looks like Dwayne Johnson's doppelgänger, and the other a little shorter and not as bulky but still a fairly good-looking guy. I bet a lot of moms attend these football games for the eye candy on the sidelines. "Depending on if you decide to continue with football and what position you are strongly suited for, you will be working with one of them. We are going to get started on some drills, but I want to take a moment to introduce you to the young woman behind today's camp, Miss Payson Moore."

The girls around me clap, and I hear some whistling and hoots from the small group of guys close by. Mister tall, blonde, and annoying seems to be the loudest of them all.

Could he be any more intolerable?

"Thanks, Coach," Payson says as she steps in front of the coaching staff. "Some of you may know me, but for anyone who doesn't, I'm Payson. I recently graduated from Bellwood this past May and will soon be leaving for California for USC. It was just about a year ago my family and I moved to Bellwood after my father retired from the military. Having to leave my friends sucked, but I think what sucked even more was leaving my old school and former teammates.

"I took our football team to the California state championship games not once but *twice* and busted my ass to earn the respect from my peers and coaches, being one of few girls to play the game of football. Moving here, it felt like I had to start all over again, proving my worth on the field to a whole new staff of coaches and a bunch of guys I would call teammates. Down here, football is taken seriously, and being a girl in football? Well ... let's just say I really had to make an impression on these guys. Just ask Coach Watson. Pretty sure I earned it though when our team brought home the trophy and title of South Carolina state champs!"

The guys get loud again, clapping, whistling, and shouting, "State champs" until Payson gets them to simmer down.

"I'd like to think that what I did for Bellwood High opened their eyes in more ways than one. Are there still people who feel some type of way about me? Absolutely. Are there people who don't think girls should play in a sport dominated by boys? Without a doubt. I would like to think that when I took on the quarterback position and led this team to its rightful victory, each win garnering more support, I opened this small town up to see the beauty that not everything is blue and pink. Which leads me to today. I wanted girls who never thought they could be a part of a physical and aggressive sport like football simply because they are female to have the opportunity. I want other girls to see that they can do anything they want, be a part of a male-dominated team and show them that we are just as equally capable as they are. Today is about empowerment and depleting gender stereotypes."

This time, the girls clap and whistle, exposing their inner warrior from Payson's impassioned speech.

Once the girls quiet down, Payson continues speaking.

"In case you didn't notice, I brought some of my former teammates along to help out today. It is their job to be an extra set of eyes, to see what position is best suited for you as you go through the different drills. If at any point you don't feel like this is something meant for you, that's okay. There is no shame in that. You came out and gave it your best, and that in itself means more to me than you could possibly know. With that said, how about we get started?"

Payson leads us to the first station. Two orange cones sit on the goal line, with another pair down the field.

"Alright, ladies. This station we are going to see how fast you can run. Speed is needed on both offense and defense. On offense, if you're a wide receiver or tight end, you're going to want to get out in the open as fast as you can to get the ball from your quarterback and obtain as many yards as possible. Same can be applied to running backs. On defense, you want to be quick to catch up to any offensive player on the opposing team who gets past your defensive line. You're going to start here at the goal line and run as fast as you can to the other cones on the forty-yard line. The two gentlemen down at the other end are Zion and Kai. They will be recording your speeds for the coaches. Anyone here want to go first?"

For a moment, none of us seem to want to go until a tall girl with thick curly hair pulled back in a high ponytail steps up to the starting line.

"Alright, I'll go first. Alora Lewis," the girl tells Payson.

"Lewis?" Payson cocks her head to the side. "Any relation to Dom and Anthony?"

"Yeah. I'm the older twin to the one who's pouting on the side over there." She nods toward who I can only assume is the brother she is referring to.

Payson shakes her head, smiling. "Yeah, Anthony can be a crybaby sometimes."

"I heard that!" a masculine voice shouts from the sidelines.

"Well, Alora, I've got to say, your brothers are impressive on the field. I can't wait to see how you top them. Are you ready?"

"Absolutely," Alora states.

Payson counts down from three before she blows her whistle, and the girl takes off at record speed. I don't think I've ever seen anyone run as fast as her.

"Four-point-six-two!" the Asiatic gentleman with short, spiky black hair recording our speeds shouts. "Anthony, I believe your sister just destroyed your run time, dawg."

"Shut up, Kai!" Anthony yells.

"Don't be such a sour puss, little bro. You just hate that I'm showing you up and proving I'm going to be better than you on the field."

The siblings banter back and forth until one of the coaches separates them. If this girl actually makes the team with her brother, these coaches will have their hands full with the competitive rivalry they clearly have between them.

"Who's next?" Payson shouts, putting our attention back on the drill.

This time, I head to the starting line, ready to get this thing over with as I wait for Payson's signal. As soon as the whistle is blown, I run down the field as fast as my short legs allow.

Within what feels like seconds, I cross the forty-yard line, and one of the guys shouts my time.

"Four-point-nine-one seconds!"

"Is ... that ... good?" I pant out as I try to gather my breath. *Damn, I really need to start running more.*

"Considering that the elite time for women athletes is under five-point-two seconds, I'd say that is impressively good," Mr. Tall, Blonde, and Annoying says as he comes to my side wearing a big stupid grin on his face. "But not as good as my running time."

Is he suggesting he's faster than me?

I glare up at the nuisance, trying to think of the perfect comeback when—

"What's your name, shortcake?" a guy with warm, bronzy skin and brown curls on top of his head asks.

"Shortcake?" I snarl. "Let me make something very clear to you. One, just because I'm short, it doesn't give you a right to call me something you think is cute or adorable in reference to my size since you don't know my name. Okay? And two, I'm the furthest thing from sweet. Quite the opposite actually, so if you think about calling me any other stupid little pet name, you're going to see exactly how unsweet I can be."

He adjusts the clipboard in his hand, raising his pen with a trembling hand. "O-o-okay. No pet names. Got it. Wh-what is your name?"

"Hollis."

"Last name?"

"For me to know and for you to never figure out," I say before walking away so the other girls can do this drill and we can move forward with the rest of this camp. The sooner we make it through this thing, the faster I can get out of here and call my boss to see if I can pick up another shift. Since I turned eighteen, my boss has been more lenient about me taking on more hours whenever I can. More hours mean more money to help the only woman who has ever cared about me. Bills don't pay themselves, and Grams's diabetic medication won't pay for itself either.

Chapter 5

Colton

This wasn't how I envisioned my Monday morning, but when your cousin asks you to help with one of her ideas, you do it. I've got to applaud Payson for putting this camp together and giving these girls an opportunity she didn't have. She's such an incredible person, and when she makes it into the NFL, because I have no doubt she will make it, I hope it inspires more girls to go out there and fight for their dreams, gender norms be damned.

I have to admit, I'm surprised at the turnout we got today. Nineteen girls showed up, inspired by my cousin, and damn if that doesn't make me even more proud to be related to Payson Moore. I didn't think that many girls wanted to put the pads on and go toe to toe against guys bigger than them. It's clear we were all mistaken.

Nineteen girls, yet only one keeps stealing my attention from the rest. The one who seems to despise my very existence, for reasons unknown to me. Or maybe she isn't a fan of the male species, seeing as how she nearly chewed off Zion's head over a simple nickname.

Blonde hair with pink in it that makes her stand out in a crowd. Blue eyes that sparkle when the sun shines on them. A body, although short in stature, that is toned and fit of an athlete. Makes you wonder what other sports she's played. Softball? Volleyball?

Hollis ... a name you don't hear often. Kind of makes me think of holly and Christmas time, a season full of jolly people. The irony in that is hilarious.

I wonder what her last name is and why she didn't want to tell Zion? Is it an embarrassing one, like Dickson or something?

Hollis Dickson? That would be a name the guys would get a kick out of.

I chuckle to myself before I feel like I'm being watched. Glancing around the field, I lock eyes with a pair of blue ones.

If looks could kill, I would be a dead man. I don't know what I did to deserve her disdain, but I wonder if I'm able to get on her good side? I mean, I'm pretty funny, and I like to think of myself as charming.

I give her my best smile before blowing an air kiss in her direction to see how she will react. Hollis rolls her eyes before raising her hand until it's at eye level with her face. Slowly, her middle finger goes up. Her perfectly pink lips mouth what I can only assume is *Fuck off* before she returns her attention back to the group.

"Okay, what is going on between you two?" Payson asks as she comes to stand beside me while we watch the girls go through some tackling drills with some of the defensive players.

"What are you talking about?"

"Don't think I haven't noticed what's happening around here. I'm a quarterback, remember? It's my job to observe my surroundings, and clearly, there is something between you and Hollis. Neither of you can seem to keep your eyes off the other."

Hollis keeps looking at me? Wait ... why does that excite me?

"Like I said before. What are you talking about? There is nothing between that girl and me. I barely know her! And maybe you want to get your eyes examined, dear old cousin, because that girl has done nothing but hate my guts since we've met. Have you not seen the dirty looks?"

"So, what did you do to piss her off?"

"What did I—Are you serious?" I never thought my cousin would assume *I* did something to upset a stranger.

"Walk me through what happened yesterday, and I'll pinpoint where you fucked up."

"I'm not the one who fucked up."

Payson glares at me. "Ugh, fine." I take a deep breath and do my best to recount everything that went down from the moment I sat down until the guys and I left the diner.

"Just as I suspected. You fucked up and need to apologize," Payson states.

"Why?"

"Instead of losing your cool when she got to your booth, you could have been more polite and shown her a little grace."

"I was hungover and feeling like shit. Do you know how loud things are when you're recovering from a shit ton of alcohol?"

"No, not really, but it didn't give you the right to react to her with ignorance the way you did. You're better than that, Colt." She takes a moment for herself before speaking again. "Look, some people don't always get dealt a great hand in life, not like us. We have been very fortunate with the people who love us. But for some people? Sometimes, they have a bad morning or things don't go according to plan, so yeah, they can come off as rude when they're going through some personal stuff. However, *we* were raised to always show kindness to others, no matter how they respond to us."

"A little bit of kindness goes a long way," Payson and I say in unison. It's been one of those sayings our moms hounded into all of us growing up.

"Maybe an apology will help smooth things over." She pats my back, putting a little extra force into it. *Ow*. "Now, if you will excuse me, I need to go check and see how the girls are doing." She walks toward the group of young women, then turns to face me as she walks backward. "For what it's worth, I like that she's bringing a bit of the old you out. It's kind of been missing since ... well, you know."

Payson turns back around and jogs away from me, leaving me to my thoughts.

Have I allowed myself to stray from the person I used to be?

We finally make it to the last drill for today, and the energy coursing through me is kinetic. To say I'm pumped is an understatement. This one specifically focuses on the best position one can be on a football team.

Wide receiver.

"This drill focuses on running routes, a great drill for wide receivers and tight ends."

Okay, I guess the top two positions in football.

"What's the difference?" one of the girls asks.

"The wide receiver's job is to run out and catch the passes from the quarterback. They need to be fast and get as far away from the defense to get open. This allows you to get closer to the end zone as long as the wide receiver catches the pass. Tight ends are a combination of a wide receiver and lineman. It is their job to either run out and catch a pass or they help block the defense, offering another layer of protection to the quarterback or running back. Dylan here is the varsity quarterback for the upcoming season. He and Zion are going to demonstrate a few routes for you first, then we'll have you ladies try them out," Payson explains.

Dylan and Zion run through some basic routes first—slant, curl, and go routes. The girls seem to pay close attention, especially Hollis. Her eyes are laser focused on their footwork and hand positioning.

"Alright, who wants to give it a try first?" Payson asks.

To my surprise, Hollis steps forward without hesitation. "I'll go."

Payson grins. "Perfect. Let's start with a simple slant route. I want you to run straight for about five yards, then cut diagonally across the field to try and catch a pass from Dylan."

Hollis nods and gets into position. At the coach's whistle, she takes off like a shot.

She dashes down the field, her short legs pumping as she runs the route exactly as demonstrated. As she makes her cut across the field, Dylan launches a perfect spiral right on target. Without breaking stride, Hollis extends her arms and snags the ball out of the air, tucking it securely against her body as she continues sprinting.

"Holy shit," I mutter. I don't think I've seen anything as impressive—or hot.

Hollis jogs back, tossing the ball to Dylan.

"Nice catch, Hollis!" Payson exclaims, exchanging a quick high-five.

There's a hint of a smile on her face, the first I've seen all day.

"That was textbook," I say as she passes by. "You've clearly done this before."

She pauses, eyeing me disapprovingly. "Maybe I have, maybe I haven't. I've been told I have stellar hand-eye coordination."

She leers at me and walks to the back of the line, allowing the next girl to go.

Once the girls make their way through the routes, Payson decides to switch things up on them.

"Not bad, ladies. Now we are going to shake things up a bit. I'm going to have you each go against Zion or Colton. Zion, Colt you'll play defense against the girls running routes. Let's see how they do in a more gamelike scenario."

The girls nod, with a mix of nervousness and excitement. I catch Hollis's gaze and wink at her, and she narrows her eyes at me.

We run through the drill with each girl. Some struggle to keep up with my speed and agility, while others show surprising natural ability, and I find myself eagerly anticipating Hollis's turn.

"Alright, Hollis you're up next," Payson says. "Let's have you run a go route straight down the field as fast as you can. Colton will be covering you."

My smirk widens, and I jog over to line up across from Hollis.

"Ready to eat my dust, Sunshine?" I tease, unable to resist riling her up.

Her blue eyes flash dangerously, her gaze locked on me with a hint of malice. "Bring it on, Golden Boy. I just hope you're ready to see how a real athlete plays."

At the whistle, I take off running, and to my surprise, Hollis matches me stride for stride, staying right on my hip. I try to juke left, then cut right, but she anticipates my moves, mirroring me perfectly.

Dylan launches the ball high in the air. I leap up to intercept it when a small body collides with mine as my hands knock the ball downward. She reaches up to deflect the pass, the ball bouncing off her fingertips, and I watch in disbelief when Hollis twists midair, snatching the ball before it hits the ground. She lands gracefully on her feet, cradling the ball against her chest.

For a moment, I'm too stunned to speak. Hollis just outplayed me on a drill I've run hundreds of times.

She turns and smirks at me, tossing the ball up and catching it. "What was that about eating your dust?"

I laugh, shaking my head in amazement. "Okay, I'll admit, that was impressive. Where did you learn to play like that?"

"Like I said. Stellar hand-eye coordination," she says before walking back toward the group of girls.

I watch her go, feeling a mixture of admiration and something else I can't quite name. One thing's for certain: there's more to Hollis than meets the eye.

"Alright everyone, gather round!" Coach Watson calls out. "That's it for today's drills. I want to thank you all for coming out and giving it everything you got. You ladies showed a lot of heart and determination out there today. I have to admit, I'm impressed with the skills and athleticism I've seen.

"Now, for those of you who are interested in joining the team this fall, we'll be holding official tryouts next Monday afternoon. That will give you a week to think it over and decide if football is something you want to pursue. For anyone who decides this isn't for them, I commend you for coming out and giving it a shot. No matter what you choose, you should be proud of yourselves for stepping outside your comfort zone. Thank you, ladies."

As the girls disperse, Hollis hangs back with a contemplative look on her face. At that moment, I decide to seize the opportunity to talk to her one-on-one.

"Hey," I say, approaching her cautiously. "You did great out there today. Are you thinking of trying out for the team?"

Hollis looks up at me, her blue eyes guarded. "I'm not sure yet. I've got a lot to consider."

"Well, for what it's worth, I think you'd make an awesome addition."

"Thanks, I guess. But I don't need your approval or anyone else's. I'll make my own decision."

I hold my hands up. "Hey, I didn't mean to overstep. I just wanted to give you a compliment. You've clearly got talent."

She narrows her eyes, studying me. "What's your angle here? Why are you being nice to me all of a sudden?"

I sigh, running a hand through my hair. "Look, I wanted to apologize for how I acted at the diner yesterday. I was hungover and grumpy, not to mention I felt like death, and I took it out on you. That wasn't cool of me."

Hollis raises a blonde eyebrow. "Did your cousin put you up to this?"

"She may have suggested it," I admit with a sheepish grin. "But I am truly sorry. I was raised better, and if my mother ever found out, I don't want to imagine the punishment she would have lined up for me."

I chuckle, but she doesn't seem amused. If she only knew how my mother dishes out punishments, she would find it hilarious, especially considering how painfully embarrassed I would be.

"Look, I appreciate the compliment and the apology, but I'm not sure football is in the cards for me. I've got a lot of other responsibilities to consider."

Her words pique my curiosity. "Like what?" I ask, genuinely interested.

She narrows her eyes, as if trying to determine whether my interest is sincere. "Not that it's any of your business, but I work a lot. I don't know if I can commit to practices and games on top of that."

I nod, understanding dawning. "That's why you work at the diner. To help support yourself?"

"Something like that," she mutters, looking uncomfortable with the turn of the conversation.

Sensing her unease, I decide to change tactics. "Well, if you do decide to try out, I'd be happy to help you practice this week," I offer. "No pressure or anything, just if you want some extra help before tryouts."

Hollis squints at me. "And why would you want to do that?"

I shrug. "Because you've got talent, and I think you could really help the team. Not to mention, I kind of owe you for being a jerk yesterday. Plus, it might be fun to have someone challenge me for a change," I add with a grin.

She crosses her arms. "Uh-huh. And this has nothing to do with trying to get in my pants?"

I laugh at her bluntness. "Wow, you really don't pull any punches, do you? Look, I promise this isn't about anything like that. I just genuinely think you've got potential and would be an asset to the team."

"Look, I'll think about it, okay? But don't get your hopes up, Goldendoodle."

I chuckle at the nickname. "Fair enough, Tinkerbell."

"Call me that again and you'll be singing soprano for a week," Hollis growls, her blue eyes flashing with anger.

I hold my hands up in surrender, trying not to laugh at her fierce expression. "Okay, okay. No Tinkerbell or fairylike nicknames. Got it."

I can't believe I was right with the whole Tinkerbell pet name.

She glares at me for another moment before deflating slightly. "Look, I appreciate the offer to help me practice, but I really do need to think about whether I can even commit to this. I've got a lot on my plate."

What responsibilities could a high school girl have that would make joining the football team such a big decision? I can tell she's not ready to open up about her personal life, so I don't push.

"I understand," I say. "Well, if you change your mind or want to toss the ball around sometime, let me know. No pressure either way."

Hollis nods, her expression softening slightly. "Thanks. I'll think about it."

As she turns to leave, I can't help but call out, "Hey, Hollis?"

She pauses, looking back at me with a raised eyebrow.

"For what it's worth, I really am sorry about yesterday. And I meant what I said, you've got talent. I hope you at least give tryouts a shot."

I see a flicker of something in her eyes, maybe gratitude or appreciation, but it's gone as quickly as it appeared, replaced by her usual guarded expression.

"We'll see" is all she says before walking away.

As she leaves the field, a mix of emotions swirl inside of me. There's clearly more to her story than she's letting on, and a part of me wants to pursue it further, to try to crack that tough exterior and figure out what makes her so intriguing. But I know I need to be careful, for her sake and my own.

I made a bet with the guys about not dating this year, and I intend to keep it. The last thing I need is to catch feelings for someone, especially someone as prickly and complicated as Hollis. Still, I can't deny that something about her draws me in.

Maybe it's the challenge she presents, so different from the jersey chasers who throw themselves at football players. Or maybe it's the glimpses of vulnerability I've seen peeking through her tough facade. Whatever it is, I hope she decides to try out for the team, if only so I can spend time with her, and maybe, we can at least be friends. Friendships are something I can manage. Relationships? I'm not sure I could go through one again, at least for awhile.

Chapter 6

Hollis

I drag myself through the front door, careful not to make too much noise so I don't wake up Grams.

It's almost midnight, and Grams is no doubt tucked into bed, sound asleep. The last thing I want to do is wake her when she deserves all the rest she can get.

I pick up the romance novel she's been reading from her recliner and set it at her usual seat at our small dining table. That way it's ready for her when she wakes up at the crack of dawn as she drinks her coffee and eats her toast.

Making my way around the living space, I tidy up before going into the kitchen to wash the little bit of dishes Grams left in the sink, probably a chore she planned to do in the morning. I may have pulled a ten-hour shift after that grueling three-hour camp, but no way should Grams have to worry about it. Once the dishes are done, I wipe down the kitchen counters before grabbing the stack of mail.

I plop down on the couch, turning on the small lamp next to me, and flip through the pile of mail, and my stomach sinks lower with each envelope. Electric bill, water bill, mortgage statement, medical bills … The pile of expenses seems never-ending. I pull out my phone and open my banking app, wincing at the meager balance. Even with picking up extra shifts at the diner and Grams's social security, we're barely scraping by.

I lean back on the couch and close my eyes, exhaustion settling deep in my bones. Between work, taking care of Grams, school starting up soon, and potentially adding football to the mix, I don't know how I will juggle it all.

As tempting as it would be to join the team, I don't know how I can afford to lose those precious hours at work. Grams needs me, and she has to come first.

Still, a small part of me can't help but feel a pang of longing. Being out on the field today, running and making plays, I felt more alive in a way I haven't in a while. The last time I felt that kind of rush was my last underground fight, which nearly took me away from the only woman who has stood by me. For a few brief hours, I'd been able to forget about all my responsibilities and just … play.

Thinking about football brings Colton's face to mind. His offer to help me practice was unexpected, and I'm still not sure what to make of it. Part of me wants to believe he was being genuine, but experience has taught me to be wary of people's motives. Especially tall, handsome football players with easy smiles.

I shake my head, pushing thoughts of Colton aside. Nope! I don't have time to think of boys. I've got bigger things to worry about than some guy's questionable intentions. Like how I will stretch this paycheck to cover all our bills and still have enough for basic necessities.

With a heavy sigh, I open my banking app once again. Time to see how creative I can get with budgeting this month. I move a small amount from my limited savings to cover the most pressing bills first. The electric company isn't messing around—that needs to be paid ASAP, or we risk getting our power shut off. The water bill can probably wait another week or two. I'll have to call the doctor's office again and see if we can set up a payment plan for Grams's latest round of tests.

As I'm juggling numbers, trying to make everything work, my phone buzzes with a text notification from an unknown number.

UNKNOWN

> Hey Hollis, it's Colton. I hope you don't mind but I got your number from Payson. I just wanted to say great job at camp today and the offer to practice still stands if you want. No pressure though!

I stare at the text, conflicting emotions swirling inside me. Part of me wants to snap back with some snarky comment, telling him to leave me alone, but another part—a part I try to keep locked away—feels a little flutter at his reaching out.

I shake my head, pushing that feeling aside. *No boys, Holls!*

Football is a pipe dream I can't afford to entertain, no matter how tempting it might be. Dreams don't pay the bills, and Grams needs me, no matter how many times she swears she can do things on her own without my breathing down her neck all the time. Her words, not mine.

Ignoring Colton's text, I refocus on the bills in front of me. After another hour of creative budgeting and some careful planning, I get things sorted to where we can scrape by for another month. It's not ideal, but we'll make it work. We always do.

As I finally crawl into my bed in the early hours of the morning, exhaustion weighing heavily on me, my mind drifts back to football camp and the rush I felt making plays and outmaneuvering Colton on that last drill. For a moment, it didn't feel like the world was on my shoulders. I was simply able to be a normal, regular teen.

Can I really afford to lose more hours though? I'm already going to miss out on hours once school starts up. Can I afford to lose more for practices? Games?

At that moment, I realize with a heavy heart what my answer is.

No, I can't.

Football will just have to be another want that gets pushed to the side because I can't afford the distraction or time commitment. Taking care of Grams and working—those are my priorities. There isn't room for anything else.

"Oh, fiddlesticks!"

I pop up out of my bed so fast I tumble to the floor.

"Ow," I grunt when my body smacks the hardwood.

Scrambling to my feet, I race out of my room toward the kitchen where Grams's voice came from. As I round the corner, I find her standing by the sink, a broken mug in pieces on the floor.

"Grams! Are you okay?" I ask, quickly moving to her side, ensuring I don't step on any of the broken pieces.

She waves me off. "Oh, I'm fine, dear. Just these old hands of mine not wanting to cooperate this morning. Slipped right out of my grasp."

I breathe a sigh of relief, glad she isn't hurt. "Here, let me clean that up for you. Why don't you go sit down, and I'll bring you a fresh cup of coffee?"

"Hollipop, I'm perfectly capable of cleaning up my own messes," Grams says with a hint of exasperation.

"I know you are, but humor me, okay? It'll make me feel better," I say, already grabbing the broom and dustpan.

She sighs but relents, moving to sit at the kitchen table. As I sweep up the broken ceramic, I can feel her eyes on me.

"You got in late last night," she states as I sweep up the broken pieces.

I keep my eyes focused on the task at hand, not wanting to meet her gaze. "Yeah, I picked up an extra shift at the diner. We were short-staffed."

"Mm-hm." I can hear the skepticism in her voice. "And how about yesterday morning? You left awfully early for a Monday, knowing it's your one day off and you take full advantage of sleeping in."

I dump the broken mug pieces in the trash and grab a fresh mug from the cabinet. "Oh, that. I, uh, I went to help out at a thing. For school."

"A thing for school? School doesn't start for another two weeks." Grams raises an eyebrow at me as I pour her coffee.

I sigh, knowing I can't keep anything from her for long. "Okay, fine. There was a football camp for girls interested in trying out for the team this fall at Bellwood, you know, since I'll be going there for senior year."

"A football camp?" Grams perks up, interest clear in her voice. "I didn't know you were interested in playing football."

I shrug, trying to downplay it. "It was just a one-time thing. My friend Payson put it together. She wanted girls to have an opportunity to play the sport for their school if they want to since it's like a rarity for girls to play."

"And?" Grams prompts. "How did it go?"

"It was fine," I say, dumping the last bit of the broken mug in the trash.

"Just fine? That's all you have to say about it?"

I sigh, turning to face her. "What do you want me to say, Grams? It was fun, but it's not like I can actually join the team or anything."

"And why not?" she asks, raising an eyebrow at me.

"You know why," I say, gesturing vaguely around us. "I don't have time for extracurriculars. I need to work."

Grams's face softens, her eyes filled with understanding. "Oh, Hollipop. Is that what you think? That you can't do anything for yourself because you need to take care of me?"

I bite my lip, avoiding her gaze. "It's not just that, Grams. We need the money. The bills—"

"Are not your responsibility. I appreciate everything you do for me, sweetheart, more than you possibly know, but I don't want you sacrificing your whole life just to take care of me."

"But—"

"No buts," Grams says, holding up a hand to stop me. "You're young! You should be out there living your life, trying new things, having fun with friends, and dating hot boys. Not working yourself to the bone and worrying about bills. That's my job!"

Tears prick my eyes. "How are we supposed to manage without my income?"

"Tell me something. Did you enjoy playing football yesterday?"

I hesitate for a moment before nodding reluctantly. "Yeah, I did. It was way more fun than I expected, and I think I may even be pretty good at it."

A smile spreads across Grams's face. "Then that's all that matters. If this is something you want to pursue, then you should go for it."

"But what about work? And who will help you around the house?" I protest.

Grams takes my hand in hers. "Honey, I managed just fine before you came to live with me. I promise you we will figure it out together. Besides, I don't want you to look back years from now and regret not taking chances or pursuing your passions. You're only young once. I mean, look at me." She gestures at herself with a chuckle. "I'm old and gray, and my joints creak like a worn rocking chair. But you? You've got your whole life ahead of you. Don't waste these years worrying about things that should be my responsibility."

More tears well up in my eyes. "But Grams, I just want to help. You've done so much for me ..."

"And I'd do it all over again in a heartbeat," she states. "But the best way you can repay me is by living your life to the fullest. If that means playing football, then by golly, you go out there and play football!"

I laugh at her enthusiasm. "You really think I should try out?"

"Absolutely!" Grams exclaims. "And when you make the team, I'll be right there on the sidelines, cheering you on at as many games as I can."

"I love you, Grams," I say before giving her the best hugs one could ever get—a grandmother hug.

"Oh, I love you too, Hollipop." She squeezes me before pulling away. "Now, tell me. Are there any hot guys on this team?"

"Grams!"

"What? I just want to know if any of them may have an influence on you joining the team."

"No, there are no boys influencing me to join the football team. I don't even bother talking to boys, let alone dating."

I make my grandmother her usual breakfast and set it down in front of her.

"I will say, there is plenty of eye candy on the coaching staff for you to ogle at if I make the team."

"Are any of them single and in need of a sugar mama?"

"Oh my gosh, Grams!"

"What? I think I still got it. What's the saying you young kids say these days? Shots fired?"

"You mean shooting your shot?"

"Yeah. I think I'm going to shoot my shot and get you a new granddaddy."

Chapter 7

Colton

I glance at my phone for what feels like the hundredth time, willing it to buzz with a response from Hollis, and like every other time I've checked, there's nothing but my unanswered text from last night staring back at me.

"Dude, what's got you so focused on your phone?" Rhett asks as he grabs the spare game controller and plops down next to me on the couch. "Are you waiting on a text from a girl or something?"

I quickly lock my screen and shove my phone in my pocket. "What? No. Just checking the time."

Anthony snorts. "Uh-huh. You've got that dopey look on your face. It's definitely a girl."

"It's not a girl," I protest, but I can feel my ears turning red.

"Sure it's not," Zealand chimes in. "So, who is she? Someone from camp yesterday?"

"Spill it, Reynolds. Who's got you all worked up?" Jeremiah asks.

Anthony's kicker misses the field goal in the Madden game we are playing, so he passes me the controller for my turn.

I hesitate, debating whether to tell them about Hollis. On one hand, they're my best friends and I usually tell them everything, but I'm not sure how to explain my interest in her without them getting the wrong idea.

I sigh, knowing there's no point in keeping it from them. "It's ... it's Hollis."

"The blonde waitress from the diner? The one who nearly took Zion's head off yesterday?" Anthony's eyes widen.

"Yeah, her," I admit grudgingly. "I texted her last night offering to help her practice if she decides to try out for the team, but she hasn't responded."

Anthony lets out a low whistle. "Man, you've got it bad already."

"I do not," I say, with as much conviction as possible. "It's not like that, I swear!"

"So, tell us what *is* it like?" Zealand asks.

I run a hand through my hair, trying to find the right words to explain my fascination with Hollis without it sounding like I'm into her romantically. "Look, it's not what you guys think. I just ... I don't know, I guess I'm intrigued by her. She's different from most girls around here."

"Different how?" Rhett asks, raising an eyebrow.

"Well, for starters, she doesn't seem impressed by the whole football player thing. If anything, she seems annoyed by it. And she's got this tough exterior, but I get the feeling there's a lot more going on beneath the surface."

"So you want to crack that tough exterior, huh?" Anthony wiggles his eyebrows.

I roll my eyes. "Not like that, man. I just ... I don't know, I guess I want to figure her out. Why is she always on the defense? Plus, she's actually really good at football. I mean, you guys saw her at camp yesterday. She could be a real asset to the team if she goes through with tryouts."

"Uh-huh," Jeremiah says. "And this has nothing to do with the fact that she's hot and feisty and clearly gets under your skin?"

"No!" I protest, perhaps a bit too forcefully. "I mean, I'm not blind, okay? Yes, she's attractive. But that's not why I'm interested in her. I made that bet with you guys, in case you forgot. No dating this year, remember? I'm just trying to help recruit a good player for the team."

"Riiight, for the team. It has nothing to do with you wanting to spend more time with her or why you're obsessively checking your phone every five seconds," Anthony teases.

I groan, flopping back against the couch cushions. "Whatever, you guys. Think what you want to think, and don't believe me. There's just ... something about her. I can't quite put my finger on it."

"Sounds like you want to put your finger on something," Zealand mutters.

I chuck a throw pillow at his head. "Shut up, Z!"

"Oh, fellas. Looks like we hit a nerve!" Anthony's big mouth shouts.

"Whatever. Screw all of ya'll!" I grab my gaming controller and get back to playing the game, pretending to ignore my friends.

It's been a few days and still no response from Hollis. I'm starting to think I miswrote the cell phone number and texted the wrong person, but I'm sure if that was the case, whoever I sent the message to would have the courtesy to tell me. Right?

She must be ignoring me. It's the only logical explanation.

While driving down Main Street, I see the diner, and an idea sparks in my mind. I don't even second-guess as I pull into a parking spot.

If she won't respond to my text, then I guess I will have to resort to seeing her in person.

But what if she isn't working?

Only one way to know for sure.

Making my way inside, I spot her cleaning up a booth and stacking all the dirty dishes onto an empty tray. She grabs the tip from the table to count out the money, her jaw tense, and releases a heavy sigh. How can someone going into her final year of school be so stressed over finances?

My eyes follow her as she makes her way into the kitchen with the tray and disappears behind the door, before I'm greeted by an employee.

"Welcome to Munson's Diner," an elderly woman approaches me. "Would you like the countertop or a booth?"

I glance at the woman's name tag. "Hello, Janet. Is it okay if I request a booth in Hollis's section?"

"Right this way," Janet says, and escorts me to one of the clean booths. "You're a brave soul to want to take on that one. She can be a bit intimidating."

"Well, Janet, I particularly like a little challenge," I say, giving her one of my flashy smiles. "May I ask what kind of mood she's in today?"

"Let's just say ... proceed with caution." She smirks before walking off.

I look over the menu when a petite, delicate hand with black nail polish smacks the table, grabbing my attention.

"What are you doing here?" Hollis scowls.

"What's it look like? Trying to decide what I want to eat. After all, it is lunch time."

Hollis crosses her arms. "You still have about thirty minutes."

"Well, I'm starving, and an athlete's got to eat." I pat my stomach for emphasis. "What do you recommend?" I pull my gaze away from her, something I find slightly difficult but try not to read too much into, and look back at the menu.

Out of the corner of my eye, she continues to glare at me before finally relenting and raising her pen and pad to take my order.

"Will it be just you today or can I expect your posse to join you? Maybe your flavor of the week?"

"No. Just me today. The guys are either working, at the gym, or sleeping. And I don't get down like that. My mama raised me to respect women, not use them."

I don't miss the flicker of emotion in her eyes before she reverts to her signature stone-cold face.

"Well, then. I would recommend the breakfast sampler. It covers the protein and carbs you need as an athlete."

"Sounds perfect. Can I get some orange juice and a side of fruit with it?"

"Sure," she answers curtly, taking the menu from my hands, and walks off to place my order.

I glance around the diner, noting the few customers eating, assuming this is typical for a Thursday.

My phone vibrates on the table with an incoming text.

MOM

> Dinner tonight at 6pm at your aunt and uncle's. They want us all together for one last family meal before Payson heads out tomorrow.

COLTON

> I'll be there.

A moment later, a glass and bowl are placed in front of me. "Girlfriend?"

"Uh, no. My mother, actually. Just letting me know about family dinner since Payson leaves tomorrow for college."

She turns away from me, glances at the floor, then quickly masks her sadness. Makes me wonder—

"The rest of your food will be out soon. I'm going to go check on it," she says, her voice slightly cracking as she starts to walk away.

"Hollis, wait!" She pauses. "Can you sit for a minute?"

"I can't. I'm really busy—"

"Doesn't seem that busy to me," I state, motioning around at the near empty diner. "I think you can spare me at least a few minutes of your time." I add on a 'please' for good measure, hoping she knows I'm not trying to be a dick.

Rolling her eyes, she plops down in the booth, taking a seat across from me. "I'm seated. What do you want?"

"I texted you the other night and you never responded back."

"Yeah, well … I've been busy."

"It takes like two seconds to reply."

"Look. I appreciate your willingness to help, but I'm really not sure if I can commit the time to football."

"How come?"

"Not really any of your business now, is it?" she snaps.

I hold my hands up in surrender. "You're right, I'm sorry. I didn't mean to pry. I just … I guess I was hoping you'd give football a shot. You've got real talent, Hollis, and we could really use someone like you on the team."

She sighs, her shoulders slumping slightly. "It's not about talent. I've got responsibilities, okay? I can't just drop everything to play a sport."

"I get that," I murmur. "But don't you think you deserve to do something for yourself too? To have some fun?"

She lifts her head, and a glimpse of vulnerability flashes in her eyes before her walls fly back up.

"Fun doesn't pay the bills."

Before I can respond, Janet calls out from behind the counter. "Order up, Hollis!"

Hollis jumps up. "I've got to get back to work. That's probably your food now."

Before I can stop her, she rushes off. *Damn.* So much for that idea working. I finish my meal and stack my dirty dishes to make it easier for Hollis to deal with, then head to the register to pay my bill.

After she dropped off my meal, I didn't see her again. She was most likely avoiding me since our small conversation.

"How was everything?" Janet asks as I hand her the money.

"Delicious and filling. Thank you," Disappointed I didn't get to speak with Hollis, I decide to lay on the charm and see if her co-worker could maybe give me some insight. "Can I ask you something, Janet? You seem like the kind of lady who knows a thing or two about everyone in this place."

"Maybe I do," she says slyly. "What's your question, sweetie?"

I hesitate for a moment, wondering if I should pry into Hollis's personal life, but my curiosity gets the better of me.

"I was just wondering ... Does Hollis always work such long hours? She seems to be here a lot."

Janet's expression softens. "That girl works harder than anyone I've ever seen, especially for someone her age. She's here almost every day, picking up extra shifts whenever she can."

"Do you know why?" I ask, trying to keep my tone casual.

Janet glances around, then leans in closer. "Well, I probably shouldn't say too much, but ... let's just say Hollis has had it rough. She lives with her grandmother, a sweet lady named Nancy. From what I understand, Hollis pretty much takes care of everything: the bills, the house, her grandmother's medical needs. It's a lot for a teenager to handle."

My heart sinks as I process this information. No wonder she's is so guarded and stressed all the time. She's carrying the weight of the world on her shoulders.

"That's ... Wow. I had no idea," I murmur.

Janet nods. "She's a tough cookie. She has some anger issues, probably from all the stress. You know, she's been kicked out of her high school because she got into one too many fights? Nancy had to put her in one of those online classes so she could keep up with her grades, last I heard."

"And it sucked monkey balls," Hollis says coming from the kitchen. "Janet, stop gossiping about my life with the customer. Al needs you in the back."

"Who says I'm gossiping? The handsome boy was just asking about you. He's pretty cute, don't you think?" Janet wiggles her eyebrows, causing Hollis to roll her eyes. "You have a nice day, young man."

Once Janet disappears into the kitchen, Hollis turns her angry eyes on me. "What the hell do you think you're doing? Snooping for information about me? What are you trying to find out?"

"Relax, Sunshine. It's not like that. I was curious about how often you work."

"Why?"

"I'm just trying to help you. Look, if you're really interested in football, which I suspect you are, then I think you can manage both, without sacrificing your job."

"How so?" she asks, crossing her arms, her interest slightly piqued.

"Well, I've been a part of the Bellwood football team for the past three years. I know that we practice right after school on Tuesdays, Wednesdays, and Thursdays for about two hours. I'm going to assume on those days, you get busy around dinner time, correct?"

She nods.

"Okay. So I'm also going to assume you drive, right? You could come in right after practices. The high school isn't too far from here. Game days are typically Friday nights—"

"Friday nights are busy for us. I tend to make some of my best tips those nights," she states. "So, there? See? It's already a no-can-do."

"You do realize the majority of this town shows up for our games, right?" I give her a cocky smile. This town loves their hometown football team, especially after we brought home the state champs title last year.

"Well … I wouldn't know that. I only started here last October, and I don't exactly follow sports."

"Okay, well, all I'm saying is I think you can swing it. C'mon Sunshine. I really think you could make the team and help us get to the championship game again."

She tilts her head, taking in everything I said. Her tongue darts out, wetting her pretty, soft lips. "I'll consider it, but don't get your hopes up. Okay?"

"Would it help if I begged?" Her eyes light up, as if the mere image of me on my knees and begging her brings her joy.

Damn, I think I like the imagery myself.

"You'll beg? Like on your hands and knees, literally pleading for me to try out?"

"If that's what it takes to get you to come." I pause, thinking about what I said and how it came out, and a slight heat flushes my cheeks.

Hollis moves away from the counter to stand in front of me. "Okay. Prove it. Get on your knees for me, like a good boy," she orders, and damn if I don't feel a bit turned on.

Judging by the look on her face, she doesn't believe I will follow through. Locking my eyes with hers, I slowly drop to my knees, raising my hands up as if I was praying.

"Hollis, whose last name I don't know, I am begging you with all of my pride for you to show up and try out for our football team. You are a phenomenal athlete whose skills kick ass. We need you on the team. So I beg of you, please, please, *please* come try out?" I do my best puppy-dog expression, hoping it will be convincing enough for her.

"Wow. You really want me there, don't you?" She smirks and taps a finger against her chin, thinking it over. "I thought it over."

"And?" I ask, hopeful, quickly getting back on my feet.

"I guess you'll just have to wait and see come Monday," she says before walking away from me.

Chapter 8

Hollis

Janet locks the door to the diner and flips the open sign to close before making her way over to close out the register as I sweep the floors.

"You know, that young man sure seemed smitten with you," Janet says as she counts the money.

"What boy?" I ask as if I'm clueless to who she is talking about, but I'm no dumb blonde.

"Oh, don't be so coy. You know the one. Tall blonde with the gorgeous eyes. He was asking about you. You should consider asking him out."

"Yeah ... that's not going to happen."

"Oh, why not? He's handsome, and I think the two of you would be cute together. Not to mention, he can tolerate your snarky behind."

"I don't date, Janet. I don't have time for boys and their nonsense."

"Well, if you ever do, I think you should take a chance on that one. He's a good kid. Comes from a very loving, respectable family."

My heart pangs with hurt and jealousy. What I would give to have a loving family. Then maybe I would be living a normal, teenage life like the rest of the kids my age. All I have is Grams, but she showers me with enough love to make up for the ones who left me behind.

"Oh, I almost forgot. He left you this," she says, holding out an envelope with my name on it. I grab the envelope and open it slightly to see the tip inside.

"Thanks," I say, pocketing it in my apron before going back to sweeping.

Once the diner has been cleaned and locked up, I say goodbye to my manager and Janet and head to my car. It's an early 2000s champagne-colored Toyota Camry. Grams gave it to me when I got my license at sixteen, and surprisingly, it's held out this long.

I turn the key in the ignition, but it doesn't turn on.

What the fuck!?

I try it again a few more times, and the damn thing doesn't start.

"No! No, no, no. Please don't do this. Not right now!" A few more attempts and the car refuses to do anything. "I don't need this shit right now!"

Slamming my fist into the steering wheel, I release my frustration at the financial burden this will put me in or the fact this interferes with me making money. How the hell am I going to get to and from work without a car? I can't just ask for a ride from friends, because the sad truth is, I don't have any.

I grab my cell phone and look at the few contacts I have. Can't call Grams; she's in bed at this hour, and I have our only vehicle.

I shoot off a text to the one person I have somewhat bonded to, hoping they respond.

A few moments later, the bubbles pop up.

I contemplate saying no thanks, but what other option do I have? It costs money to take an Uber, and I need every cent to get by this month now that my car wants to give me problems.

While I wait for whoever is coming to get me, I pull out the envelope Janet gave me after closing. As I pull the money to count it, a piece of paper falls out.

*I'm sorry if I somehow upset you. That wasn't my intention. Hopefully this tip helps out in some way. –
Colton*

"What the hell?" He left me a fifty-dollar tip. That's almost triple what his meal cost! I count and recount to be sure, in disbelief this guy would tip me so much.

Is his family rich?

The thought alone irritates me, making me feel like he sees me as a beggar.

A tap on my window jerks me from the internal spiel, making me scream.

"Sorry! I didn't mean to spook you!"

Think of the devil and he shall appear.

Just who I wanted to see. Colton.

Of course, he is who would come to my aid, of all people.

After shoving my door open, I get out of my car and push him.

"Do you think I'm some sort of charity case?"

"Excuse me?"

I grab the envelope from the car and smack it to his chest. "I don't need you to feel sorry for me. Okay? I can manage my money just fine!"

Colton grabs the envelope and opens it. "That's ... that's not what ... I don't feel sorry for you. I tipped you that money because I wanted to help you."

"I don't need your help! Or anyone else's. Okay? I've got it handled; I always do!" I shout. Reaching back into my car, I grab everything I need before locking it up. Brushing past Colton, I start walking down the darkened street, not wanting to be near him.

"Where are you going, Sunshine?" Colton asks, right on my heels. Damn him and his long legs.

"Home. Where else?" I retort.

"Look, I don't know where you live or how far away it is, but you can't walk home by yourself. It's not safe. It's late, not to mention it's too dark, and anything could happen to you."

"In case you didn't hear me when I told you before, I'm very capable of handling people myself. Just because I'm short and female, doesn't mean I'm weak."

"Didn't say you were. But could you … just … let me give you a ride. Please?"

I stop at the pleading in his voice. Looking around at how dark it is and knowing I live a good twenty-minute drive away means I won't get home until well after one in the morning. I'm exhausted and in need of a shower before I can crawl into bed.

When I turn around to face him, his blue eyes are practically begging for me to appease his request. "Fine. You can give me a ride home, but that is it."

A smile crosses his face, a dimple making an appearance. "After you, m'lady." He gestures for me to go in front of him as we make our way to his car.

I slide into the passenger seat of his white Honda, trying to ignore how clean and new it smells compared to my old beater. As he gets in on the driver's side, I can't help but feel a twinge of resentment. Must be nice to have parents who can afford to buy you a nice car.

"So, where am I taking you?" Colton asks as he starts the engine.

I hesitate for a moment, not wanting him to know where I live, but I suppose I have little choice at this point and my bed is screaming my name.

"Fourteen-twenty-three Willow Lane," I mutter, staring out the window.

Colton nods and pulls out of the parking lot. We drive in silence for a few minutes before he clears his throat.

"Look, about the tip … I really didn't mean to offend you," he says. "I just thought … Well, I know you work hard, and I wanted to show my appreciation."

I sigh, feeling some of my anger deflate. "It's fine. I shouldn't have snapped at you like that. I just … I don't like feeling like a charity case."

"That's not how I see you at all," he assures me. "I think you're incredibly strong and capable. I wasn't trying to make you feel any other way, Sunshine. I swear it."

I turn to look at him, his blue eyes are earnest, his expression open and sincere. It makes something twist uncomfortably in my chest, and I don't like it.

"I may have overreacted a bit. It's just … I'm not used to people helping me without wanting something in return."

Colton nods slowly. "I can understand that, but I hope you know not everyone has ulterior motives. Sometimes people genuinely just want to help. Is that so wrong?"

"Easy for you to say, considering you don't look like you ever had to worry about anything in your life."

Colton chuckles softly. "You'd be surprised. My life isn't as perfect as you might think."

I scoff. "Oh, please. Nice car, clearly well-off family. What could you possibly have to worry about?"

He's quiet for a moment, his grip tightening on the steering wheel. "Money isn't everything, Hollis. And having it doesn't mean life is easy."

Something in his tone makes me glance over at him. His jaw is clenched, a shadow passing over his features. For a moment, I glimpse … something. Pain? Sadness? But before I can place it, his expression clears.

"Look, I'm not trying to compare our situations or anything," he says. "I know I've been fortunate in a lot of ways. I just … I guess I want you to know that I'm not some spoiled rich kid who's never faced any hardship. We've all got our own battles to fight."

I study his profile as he drives, trying to reconcile this more serious version of Colton with the happy-go-lucky jock I thought he was. Maybe there's more to him than meets the eye.

"I suppose you're not wrong there."

We ride in silence again, apart from the directions I give him to get me home. When he pulls into the driveway, I realize I need to figure out what to do with my car.

"Fuck," I mutter.

"What's wrong?" Colton asks, not expecting him to have heard me.

"It's nothing. I just realized I don't know how I'm going to get to work tomorrow or what to do about my car." I massage my temples, the stress and exhaustion setting in, giving me a migraine.

"What time do you have to be at work?"

"No, you've already done more than enough for me. In fact, here." I pull out the money he tipped me and hold it out toward him.

"That's your money."

"Yeah, and now I'm giving it back as gas money for the ride home. So here. Take it."

Colton wraps his big hands around my small one, pushing it back toward me. He leans forward, our faces within inches of each other. His scent—a cologne that mixes citrus with notes of ocean and amber—envelops me, making my head spin slightly.

"Keep it," he mutters. "I meant what I said earlier. It's not charity, Hollis. And I'm not looking for anything in return. I just want to help you anyway I can."

I swallow hard, trying to ignore the way my skin tingles where his hand touches mine. His blue eyes bore into mine, and for a moment, I feel like I'm drowning in them.

"Why?" I whisper. "Why do you care so much?"

Colton's gaze flickers briefly to my lips before meeting my eyes again. "Because ... because I think you're worth caring about."

My breath catches in my throat. No one has ever said anything like that to me before. For a split second, I lean in slightly, drawn by some invisible force ...

Then reality comes crashing back. I jerk away, my walls slamming back into place.

"I should go," I say abruptly, fumbling for the door handle. "Thanks for the ride."

I start to open the door, but Colton's voice stops me. "Hollis, wait. Let me help you with your car tomorrow. I can come by in the morning and give you a ride to work, then we can figure out what's wrong with your car after your shift. I actually know someone who works on cars and would be able to help."

I hesitate, torn between my pride and the practical need for help. "I don't know ..."

"Please?" he says. "I promise, no strings attached. Just one friend helping another."

Why am I sucker to his begging?

"Fine. I need to be at work by ten, and my shift ends at three."

"I'll be here around nine thirty," he says with a smile.

"Later, Goldendoodle," I say before shutting the door, then head to my front door. I make my way inside, turning to close the door, and Colton is still sitting in my driveway.

After motioning for him to leave, my cell phone alerts me to a text, so I pull it out of my pocket.

UNKNOWN

Not leaving until you're safely locked inside.

I do my best annoyed expression, unsure if he can see it, and give him the middle finger before closing the door and locking it. A moment later, another text comes through.

UNKNOWN

That wasn't very nice, but I'll let it slide. See you in the morning, Sunshine.

Peeking through the blinds, I watch Colton pull away until I no longer see his taillights. For a moment, a pang of sadness courses through me.

The sound of the floor creaking jolts that ounce of sadness away. My heart is racing so fast it feels like it could beat its way out of my chest. Turning around, I see Grams standing in the doorway.

"Bejesus, Grams! You scared the crap out of me. Wh-what are you doing up?"

"Well, I was having a very *romantic* dream date with a young George Clooney when I woke up needing a glass of water."

"Oh, God."

"That's what I told him too just as I was about to—"

"Please, stop! Do *not* finish that sentence."

Grams chuckles softly before she takes in my attire.

"Are you just getting in?" she asks.

"Yeah. I worked until closing time. I'm sorry, I meant to call to tell you."

"It's alright. You're home safe and sound. That's all that matters to me." She smiles, opening her arms for a hug.

Wrapping my arms around her, inhaling her baby powdery scent, I squeeze the one woman whose love I've never had to question.

"Hollipop?"

"Yeah, Grams?"

"I love you to pieces, but honey, you stink!"

"Yeah, that stench is called sweat-and-diner dior." I chuckle as Grams laughs. "I'm about to take a shower and call it a night."

"I'll see you in the morning. I love you."

"I love you too, Grams." I kiss her on the forehead before making my way to the bathroom, ready to wash the stench and stress away.

The next morning, I'm busy finishing getting ready for work when there's a pounding on the front door.

"I've got it, Hollipop!" Grams shouts from down the hall. After grabbing my apron and ensuring I have everything I need for work, I head down the hallway into the living room and spot Colton standing in the middle of it.

"Hollipop, this young man says he is giving you a ride to work," Grams says, and I don't miss the glint in her eye at the prospect of a boy picking me up for work.

"Yeah, uh that was our arrangement. And no, don't read too much into it. We are just acquaintances."

"Awe, Sunshine. You kill me," Colton says, slapping his hands over his heart. "Here I thought last night we decided we were finally friends."

"Mm-hm ..." Grams glances between Colton and me as if she doesn't believe it.

"I've got to get to work. Grams, I will call you later to check in." I grab my small backpack and give Grams a hug and whisper in her ear where only she can hear me, "You've got to stop reading so many romance books. They're putting ideas in your head that don't need to be." I pull away and make for the front door.

"It was a pleasure meeting you"—Colton reaches out a hand to Grams to shake it—"Mrs. ..."

"Ellsworth. But please, call me Nancy."

Colton gently shakes her hand. "Have a good rest of your day, Nancy."

"Alright, Goldendoodle, let's go," I state before grabbing the tall blonde by his shirt and dragging him out the door. "I don't want to be late for work. You of all people should know how I act when I am."

Work was slow until the lunch rush hit, then it was nonstop go, go, go. I made out decently in tips, but it still doesn't feel like enough to help with the bills.

I asked Mr. Munson if I could work the dinner shift, but he said he couldn't offer me more hours and that I had to clock out at my usual time.

Three o' clock on the dot, Colton walks into the diner looking like the perfect model for a beach boy magazine in his cargo shorts and muscle tank, showcasing sun-kissed toned arms. Only this time, he's not alone. A guy who looks vaguely familiar is with him, but I don't know where I recognize him.

"You clocked out yet?" Colton asks as they approach the countertop.

"I'm about to ..." I glance between him and the guy standing next to him.

"Sorry. Uh, Nathan, Hollis. Hollis, this is Nathan. He's the guy I know who works on cars."

"Yeah, we've met before," Nathan says. "I'm the one who gave her Payson's number months ago when I was here. You dumped water on a guy's lap and saved my friend's face from a flying burger. You also had purple in your hair at the time, I believe."

"Right. I was in my lavender phase." I had switched to pink shortly after that incident. "Sorry, I didn't recognize you. So ... any chance we can figure out what's up with my car?"

"Lead the way," Colton says, his arms out in front of him as if I'm royalty.

I clock out of my shift, leading the guys out to my car before giving the keys to Nathan. He pops the hood to look at the engine while Colton sits in the driver's seat. At Nathan's direction, Colton attempts to start my car, but it doesn't turn over. They try a few more times, and sadly, no change.

"I think you need a new alternator," Nathan states.

"Great. How much do those cost?" I ask, irritation in my voice because this is another stress I don't need in my life.

"For your car? You're looking at anywhere from four hundred seventy dollars to a little over six hundred."

"What!?" I shriek. "Are you fucking serious!?"

"Hey, hey. Calm down, Sunshine."

"Don't tell me to calm down!" I yell at Colton. "How the fuck am I supposed to calm down when that's money I don't have! Can't just pull that out of my ass."

"I understand, but Nathan? He's great about this sort of thing. He can help you."

"How? Wait. No. Let me guess, I got to do some sketchy favors? Steal a car? Break into someone's car and take theirs?" I cross my arms over my chest, scowling at them. "Or do you prefer blowjobs?"

"Hollis, I'm not that kind of guy. I have a girlfriend, one that I love very much, and she is the only woman I want," Nathan says. "I also happen to be the son of a cop who respects the law. What Colton is trying to tell you is I work with my uncle at the shop down the road. One of our policies is ensuring our customers can afford to have their cars fixed. We can do a payment plan, something that works for you without affecting your other finances. I'll order the part and get it fixed as soon as possible so you can have your car back. You just may need to find a ride until I can get it fixed."

"And how long is that going to take?" My voice comes out shaky as I force back the meltdown I'm on the verge of having right in this moment.

"Well, I can message my uncle to put the order in today, but it could take anywhere from a few days to maybe a week before the part arrives. Good news is it doesn't take really long to replace. About an hour or two tops."

Ugh ... I do not need this right now but what can I do?

"Fine. Whatever you have to do."

Nathan pulls his phone out and quickly types out a message. After a few moments, he gets a reply. "Alright, the part has been ordered. My uncle says it should be there anytime between Monday and next Friday."

"Thanks, man," Colton says, clapping Nathan's hand in that handshake thing most guys do.

"No problem." He looks between Colton and me with a smirk on his face before he gets in his car.

Why does everyone keep doing that?

After Nathan leaves, I follow Colton to his car and get in so he can take me home.

The car ride is quiet until Colton speaks up. "If you want, I can pull some money from my savings account to give you for the part."

"No! Absolutely not!"

"It's really no big deal—"

"To you, it's no big deal! To me? To me, it's money I don't have. It's money I didn't bust my ass working for, and it will be hanging over my head everyday until I pay you back every dollar and penny."

"You won't have to pay me back. Consider it an advancement on work tips."

"And how the hell am I supposed to get to and from work without a car? Huh?"

"You can ask for rides?"

"I don't have any—" I stop myself from continuing that sentence, not wanting him to have pity for me. "You know what? Just forget it. I will figure this out, so you don't have to lend me anything."

Colton pulls into the driveway, putting his car in park before turning to face me, but I jump out before he can open his mouth.

I make a dash for the door, quickly closing it behind me, then head to my bedroom. Plopping down on my bed, I place a pillow over my head and scream into the mattress, releasing all my frustrations.

"Hollipop?" Grams knocks on my bedroom door. "You all right?"

"Yeah, Grams. Just a rough day at work, but I'm good!" I call out.

"Okay. Just remember. A rough day doesn't equal a rough life."

My life is a series of rough days.

I wait until I hear the floorboards creak as Grams heads down the hall to the living room. The last thing I want to do is worry her with my stress.

Sitting on my bed, I contemplate what I will do about the car. How the hell am I going to get that much money fast?

Well ... there is one way ...

Without thinking about it, I go onto my social media account and unblock Rowan, sending him a message.

A few moments pass before he responds.

Great. Now all I gotta do is figure out a way to get there.

Chapter 9

Colton

I can't get Hollis out of my head as I drive home. The look of panic and frustration on her face when she found out how much the car repair would cost is burned into my mind. I wish she would let me help her, but I understand her pride and reluctance to accept a helping hand.

As I pull into my driveway, I see Zealand's Bronco is already here. Weird, he usually doesn't come by when I'm not home. I head inside, calling out as I enter.

"Z, you here?"

I make my way to the kitchen to find Zealand rummaging through my fridge. "Dude, what are you doing here? And why are you raiding my fridge?"

Zealand straightens up, a slice of pizza hanging from his mouth. He takes a bite and swallows before answering. "Your mom let me in. Said you'd be back soon and to make myself at home."

I roll my eyes. "Of course she did. So what's up? Why the impromptu visit?"

Zealand leans against the counter, taking another bite of pizza. "Can't a guy just want to hang out with his best friend?"

I raise an eyebrow. "Sure, but you usually text first."

"I did. Several times, but you weren't responding."

I pull out my phone, realizing I left it on silent. Sure enough, there are several texts from Zealand.

"Sorry, I was helping Hollis with her car troubles. What's going on?"

Zealand's eyebrows shoot up. "Hollis? As in the diner girl?"

I roll my eyes. "How many girls do you know with that name? Her car broke down, and I got Nathan to look at it, knowing he would know what the issue was, before I gave her a lift home. Now, what did you need?"

Zealand's expression turns serious. "Have you heard about the underground fights at Ravenwood University?"

I shake my head, encouraging Zealand to continue.

"I overheard some guys at the gym talking about it. Apparently, there's a big match tonight, and some of our friends want to go check it out. What do you say? You in?"

"I don't know, man. Isn't that shit illegal? And what if the cops get wind of it, busting the joint?"

Zealand shrugs. "From what I heard, they've been running these fights for years without getting caught. Apparently they move locations frequently and have some system to avoid police raids. C'mon, man, when's the last time we did something exciting, aside from you getting blackout wasted?"

I hesitate, weighing the risks. On one hand, it does sound intriguing and a bit thrilling. On the other hand, if we got caught, it could jeopardize my football scholarship.

"I don't know, Z. It seems pretty risky. What if someone recognizes us?"

"That's the beauty of it; everyone wears masks. It's like this whole secret underground society thing. Plus, I heard the fights are intense. Real knockdown, drag-out brawls. No rules, no refs. Just raw combat."

I have to admit, my interest is piqued. "And you're sure it's safe? We won't get arrested or anything?"

Zealand grins. "As safe as an illegal underground fight club can be. Look, if you're not comfortable, we don't have to go. I just thought it might be fun to check out. Get our adrenaline pumping a bit before the season starts."

"Who else is going?"

"Anthony and Rhett for sure. I think Jeremiah might come too if his parents don't make him babysit tonight."

I run a hand through my hair, still uncertain.

"I just figured it would help take your mind off Payson leaving for college today."

I have been feeling down, but helping Hollis kept me distracted from the hurt of my cousin moving across the country. I mean, we were used to being apart when her dad was active in the Army, but having her here for her senior year? It was great having my best friend home.

"Alright, fine. I'm in. What time do we leave?"

Zealand grins. "That's my boy! I'll message the guys to let them know. Fight starts at ten. I'll pick you up around nine."

As Zealand heads out, I can't help but feel a mix of excitement and nervousness. I've never really done anything remotely risky or rebellious. Except drink my weight in alcohol and black out.

I head upstairs to shower and change, my mind drifting back to Hollis. I wonder what she's up to tonight? Probably spending time with her grandmother since she's stuck at home.

You could text her and ask to tag along.

I could, but then that would raise suspicions from my friends. Besides, after the way she refused to accept my help, I doubt she wants to see me, let alone speak to me.

I push the thought aside and get ready for a night out with the guys.

The underground fight club is nothing like I expected. We pull up to an abandoned warehouse on the outskirts of town, following a line of cars down a dirt road. Guys in dark hoodies stand guard, checking IDs and collecting cash before waving people through.

"You sure about this?" I ask Zealand as we approach the entrance, adjusting the simple black mask covering the upper half of my face. I'm grateful for the anonymity it provides. Zealand was right; everyone here is wearing some kind of disguise.

He grins, slapping me on the back. "Too late to back out now, bro. Let's do this."

The atmosphere at the underground fight club is electric. Inside, the place is packed, bodies pressed tightly together as everyone jostles for a good view of the makeshift fighting ring in the center.

Graffiti covers the walls, the air thick with cigarette smoke and the smell of sweat. A DJ in the corner blasts heavy bass music that vibrates through my chest.

"Damn, this is insane!" Anthony shouts as we push our way through the crowd, earning glares and muttered curses from the people we squeeze past.

"I know, right?" Zealand grins, clearly thrilled to be here. "C'mon, let's try to get closer to the ring."

As we near the front, I see two fighters already in the ring—a huge, muscular guy with tattoos covering his arms, and a smaller, leaner opponent in a black hoodie with the hood pulled up. I can't make out their faces, as they, too, are wearing dark masks.

"Looks like we made it just in time," Rhett says. "The fight's about to start."

A guy who I assume is the announcer, steps inside the ring. "Alright, you degenerates! Are you ready for a show?"

The crowd roars in response, the energy in the room palpable.

"In the red corner, weighing in at two hundred and twenty pounds, is the current reigning champion, Titan!"

The tattooed behemoth raises his fists, eliciting cheers from the crowd.

"And in the blue corner, challenging him tonight, making a return from their hiatus, weighing in at just one hundred and four pounds, and folks, don't let the size fool you, this little firecracker packs quite a punch. Give it up for Pixie!"

The smaller fighter in the black hoodie raises a gloved hand but remains otherwise still and silent. I can't help but feel like there's something familiar about their stance.

There are some cheers but also quite a few jeers and boos. Clearly, the crowd doesn't have much faith in the smaller fighter's chances.

"Pixie? What kind of name is that for a fighter?" Anthony scoffs.

"Alright, fighters, you know the rules, and that is ..." There's a momentary pause before the announcer, along with the majority of crowd shouts, "There are no rules!" The crowd goes berserk before the announcer gets them to calm down. "The last fighter standing wins. Titan, are you ready?"

The big guy nods.

"Pixie, are you ready?" He points at the smaller fighter, who also nods their head.

"Fighters, get into your stances, and let's get ready to rumble!" he shouts like he's on WWE.

A bell rings, and the two fighters circle each other warily. Titan lunges first, swinging a meaty fist at Pixie's head, but Pixie is fast, ducking under the punch and landing a quick jab to Titan's ribs.

The crowd goes wild as the two exchange blows. Titan clearly plans to use his size advantage to overwhelm his opponent, but the smaller fighter is quick, darting in and out to land a few quick jabs before dancing away from Titan's reach.

"Damn, that little one's fast," Anthony comments, clearly impressed.

I nod in agreement, my eyes glued to the action. As Pixie moves around the ring, dodging Titan's powerful swings with impressive agility, I can't shake the feeling that I've seen those quick movements before. The way they pivot and duck, using their smaller size to their advantage ... It reminds me of someone, but I can't quite place who.

Titan lands a solid blow to Pixie's midsection, causing them to stumble back. For a moment, it looks like the smaller fighter might go down, but they quickly regain their footing.

"Finish them off!" someone in the crowd yells.

Titan charges forward, clearly thinking he has Pixie on the ropes, but at the last second, Pixie ducks low and sweeps Titan's legs out from under him. The big man crashes to the mat with a thunderous thud that reverberates through the warehouse.

Before Titan can recover, Pixie is on him, raining down a flurry of quick punches. The crowd goes absolutely wild, shocked to see the smaller fighter gaining the upper hand.

"Holy shit!" Zealand exclaims. "Did you see that move?"

The fight continues, and Titan grabs Pixie's arm, using his superior strength to throw the smaller fighter off.

Both fighters scramble to their feet, circling each other warily. There's a brief pause as they size each other up. Suddenly, Titan grabs Pixie in a bear hug, lifting them off their feet. The crowd roars, as it looks like the fight might be over, but Pixie doesn't give up, instead driving their elbow repeatedly into Titan's temple until he's forced to release his hold.

As Pixie stumbles back, their hood falls, revealing a flash of blonde hair with pink streaks before they quickly pull it back up.

My heart stops. No. It can't be ... Can it?

My mind races as I try to process what I just saw. It can't be Hollis, can it? But the more I watch Pixie move, the more certain I become. The quick footwork, the agile dodges ... It's like how she outmaneuvered me on the football field.

"Dude, you okay?" Zealand nudges me, pulling me from my thoughts. "You look like you've seen a ghost."

I shake my head, trying to refocus on the fight. "Yeah, I'm fine. Just ... intense, you know?"

The fight continues, both fighters showing signs of fatigue. Titan's movements are slower, his punches lacking their earlier power. But Pixie—Hollis?—is still light on their feet, darting in to land quick jabs before dancing away.

Finally, Pixie sees an opening, and as Titan swings wide, leaving himself exposed, Pixie ducks under his arm and delivers a devastating uppercut to his jaw. The big man's eyes roll back, and he crumples to the mat like a fallen tree. The impact is audible even over the roar of the crowd.

The warehouse erupts in chaos as people realize the underdog has won.

"Holy shit!" Anthony yells, shaking my shoulder. "Did you see that? That was insane!"

I nod numbly, my eyes still fixed on Pixie. They're standing over Titan's prone form, chest heaving with exertion. The announcer returns to the ring and raises the victor's arm.

"Our new fighting champion ... Pixie!" The announcer points at the small fighter, raising their arm.

After a few moments, Pixie attempts to yank their arm free, as if to get away from the announcer who seems reluctant to let them go. He pulls the fighter closer to him, seeming to tell them something.

My instincts have me charging toward the ring, alarm bells going off like that day at the diner. I'm close when Zealand yells my name.

"Colton!"

The fighter, Pixie, locks eyes with me, sparkly blues piercing me through the dark mask for a moment before retreating.

"Colton, where are you going? We got to go!" Zealand appears with Rhett and Anthony behind him. "Someone swore they heard sirens closeby. C'mon!"

My friends and I waste no time getting back to the car and hitting the road back to Bellwood. Not sure if the police coming was true or not, but we were not sticking around to find out.

As my friends discuss the fight, my mind can't let go of Pixie. There's no way it could have been Hollis, could it? I mean, her car is stuck at the diner, at least until Nathan can tow it to the shop. Ravenwood is a good fifty minutes away from Bellwood. How would she get here?

The weekend passes in a blur, and before I know it, it's Monday. I hop up out of bed, throw on some workout clothes, wanting to get a run in before I head over to the football field to watch the tryouts.

I send a text message to Hollis, asking if she will need a ride to tryouts before I take off. An hour passes before I return to the house, and still no response.

I sent her several messages over the weekend, asking if she needed a ride to work, but I never got a response. I thought about dropping in but figured she was still upset about our last conversation, so I gave her some space.

But not hearing from her? It's driving me crazy.

What is this girl doing to me?

After I shower and change, I head over to the school, finding a spot in the bleachers to watch tryouts.

With my eyes focused on the entrance to the stadium, I wait for blonde hair with pink in it.

When it looks like there is no one else coming, Coach Watson blows his whistle to get the girls' attention to go over the tryout protocols.

With Hollis nowhere in sight, a sinking feeling in my chest along with disappointment settles in like a heavy fog. Was it because of the car? Or was this the final straw for her? I couldn't help but wonder what else had gone wrong, or if maybe my persistence was the final nail in her football-playing coffin.

Chapter 10

Hollis

I groan as I roll over in bed, every muscle in my body screaming in protest. The fight on Friday night took more out of me than I expected. I'd forgotten how brutal those matches can be after taking a break for so long.

Slowly rising, I wince at the pain in my ribs where Titan landed a nasty blow, then catch sight of myself in my full-length mirror. A large purple bruise has bloomed across my cheekbone. *Shit. How am I going to explain that?*

I dig through my makeup bag, hoping I have enough concealer to cover it up. The last thing I need is Grams asking questions or finding out exactly where it came from.

After mostly hiding the bruise and throwing on some clothes, I head to the kitchen. Grams is already up, humming to herself as she makes breakfast.

"Morning, Hollipop!" she says. "Are you ready for today?"

"Ready for what?" I ask, unsure what she is talking about.

"Football tryouts."

Oh, right.

"Yeah ... about that, Grams. I'm not going to go."

Grams sets a plate of eggs and bacon down in front of me before taking a seat beside mine. "Why not?"

I take a bite of the crispy, greasy bacon and ponder how to explain to my grandmother to where she'll understand.

"Honestly? I just don't have the time for it. If I miss work, I miss making money for bills and your insulin. I'm basically having to choose between doing something for me or jeopardizing your life, and you can't expect me to choose my happiness over your life. Not when you've been the only person to ever give a damn about me!"

Emotions clog my throat, the mere idea of losing my grandmother is my biggest fear. It takes everything in me to not shed the tears so close to falling.

Grams grabs my face, her light-blue eyes staring into mine. "Hollis, listen to me very carefully. I appreciate everything you do for me, but I can't allow you to keep sacrificing what you want to do for my sake. Your happiness matters more to me than anything else in this world. More than bills, more than insulin, more than my own life even."

I try to look away, but she holds me firmly. "I know you've been working yourself to exhaustion trying to take care of everything. And I love you for it, I truly do. But sweetheart, you're young. You should be out there living your life, not worrying about an old lady like me."

"But Grams—"

"No buts. Now, I've been talking to the nice lady at the pharmacy, and it turns out there's a program that can help cover some of my insulin cost, and we can also look into some of those assistance programs the social worker told us about. There's no shame in getting help when you need it."

My throat tightens. "I don't want to be a burden on anyone."

Grams sighs, pulling me into a hug. "Oh, Hollipop, you could never be a burden. Accepting help doesn't make you weak. It takes strength to admit when you can't do it all. Tell me something and I want you to be honest. When you were at that camp, how did it make you feel?"

I felt free in a way I hadn't in years. The adrenaline rush, the satisfaction of making a great play—it awakened something in me I thought was long dead. The way fighting used to be before I was nearly apprehended.

"It felt like all my troubles went away and I didn't have to think about anything else."

"It sounds to me like you need to play football, Hollipop. You need to go to that tryout and show them what you're capable of and make that team!" She has so much belief in me that I will make the team, but the question is … can I?

"But what if something happens to you? What if you need me and I'm not here because of practice or a game?"

Grams smiles. "Honey, I'm old, not helpless. I managed just fine before you came to live with me, and I can manage now. Your job is to be a teenager, to live your life to the fullest. My job is to support you in that, not hold you back."

I open my mouth, ready to say something back, but Grams raises a hand, stopping me before I get the chance to speak.

"You're going to finish your breakfast, then you're going to go put something a little more comfortable on for tryouts and get yourself down to the football field!" she says firmly.

"Yes, ma'am."

There's no arguing with Grams when she puts her foot down. After I finish eating, I change into clothes a bit more appropriate for football tryouts. Now all that is left is to figure out how I'm getting to the field.

Talia pulls to a quick stop outside of the stadium entrance. I'm cutting it close, thanks to the stupid slow ass train holding us up.

"Thanks, Tal! I owe you!" I say before slamming her car door and running as fast as I can to the field. Not so easy when your body is sore from taking a beating like I did.

I spot the coaches and the girls who made it on time and do my best to get there. Coach blows his whistle, so I pick up the pace even more.

"You're a minute late," Coach says when I finally make it to the group.

"Yeah ... sorry," I say between breaths. "I had to get ... a ride from ... someone, and then we ... got stuck by ... the slowest ... train on the planet."

He eyes me for a moment. "Yeah, it's the slowest fucking train in the whole dang country." He turns his focus back to the rest of the group. "Alright, ladies. Let's see what you all got."

Colton

I perk up as a flash of blonde hair sprints toward the field. Hollis made it after all. Relief and excitement flood through me as she joins the group, apologizing to Coach Watson for being late.

As tryouts begin, I can't take my eyes off her. Even though she seems slower than she was at camp, favoring her left side slightly, her natural talent still shines through. She runs routes with precision, catches passes effortlessly, and even manages to juke past some of the other girls during scrimmage drills.

"Damn, that little blonde is something else," one of the other coaches says.

Coach Watson nods. "She's got real potential. Raw talent like that doesn't come along often."

Pride swells in my chest at hearing them praise Hollis, even though I have no real claim to her success. As tryouts wind down, Coach Watson gathers the girls for a final talk. I strain to hear what he's saying and only catch bits and pieces.

"…impressed with what I've seen today … decisions by the end of week … check your emails …

Once the girls are dismissed, I make my way over to Hollis. "Glad you could make it."

"Yeah … well, Grams kind of, sort of threatened me with punishment if I didn't."

"Really? What kind of punishment?"

"Believe me, you don't want to know."

I let out a chuckle. "Fair enough. So … what have you got planned for the rest of the day?"

She squints at me. "Why do you ask?"

I shrug, trying to appear casual. "Just curious. Thought maybe we could hang out or something if you're free."

She raises an eyebrow. "Hang out? You mean like … friends?"

"Yeah, why not?" I say, flashing her a grin. "Unless you've got better plans than spending time with the Jolly Green Giant."

To my surprise, a small smile tugs at the corner of her mouth. "Well, as tempting as that sounds, I actually have to get to work. My shift starts in an hour."

"Oh," I say, trying not to sound too disappointed. "Well, how about I give you a ride? Save you from having to bum one off someone else."

She hesitates for a moment, seeming to weigh her options. Finally, she sighs. "Fine. But only because I don't want to be late and risk losing my job."

As we walk to my car, I can't help but notice she's moving stiffly, favoring her left side. "You okay?" I ask. "You seem a little sore."

Hollis tenses at my question. "I'm fine," she says quickly. "Just ... pushed myself a little hard, that's all."

I'm not entirely convinced, but I decide not to push it. We get in the car and head toward the diner, my mind wandering back to the underground fight on Friday night. The way Pixie moved, the flash of blonde hair ... Could it really have been Hollis?

She has a faint discoloration on her cheekbone that looks like a partially concealed bruise. My suspicions grow stronger, but I'm not sure how to bring it up without potentially pushing her away.

"So," I say, trying to keep my tone casual, "what did you get up to this weekend? Anything exciting?"

Hollis shrugs, staring out the window. "Not really. Just worked and hung out with Grams. You?"

"Oh, you know. The usual. Hung out with the guys, watched some movies." I hesitate for a moment before adding, "Actually, we went to this ... event on Friday night. It was pretty intense."

Hollis stiffens at my words, her eyes darting to me briefly before looking back out the window. "Oh, yeah? What kind of event?"

I hesitate, debating how much to reveal. "It was ... well, it was this underground fighting thing near Ravenwood University."

Hollis goes still, her face carefully blank. "Huh. Sounds dangerous, especially for someone like you."

"It was pretty crazy," I say, watching her reaction closely. "There was this one fighter, they called them Pixie. Small but incredibly fast and agile. Took down this huge guy twice their size."

Hollis swallows hard, her fingers tightening on the strap of her bag. "Is that so?"

I nod, pulling into the diner parking lot. "Yeah. It was impressive. Almost reminded me of someone I know."

As I park the car, Hollis turns to face me, her blue eyes hard. "What exactly are you trying to say, Colton?"

I meet her gaze steadily. "I think you know what I'm saying, Hollis. Or should I call you Pixie?"

For a moment, I think she might deny it or lash out at me, but her shoulders slump.

"Fuck," she mutters. "How did you figure it out?"

"I wasn't sure at first," I admit. "But the way you moved in the ring … It reminded me how you outmaneuvered me on the football field at camp. And then I saw your hair when your hood fell back."

Hollis runs a hand through her hair, looking frustrated. "Damn it. I knew I should have dyed it a different color or at least worn a wig."

"Why are you doing this, Hollis?" I murmur. "Those fights are dangerous. You could get seriously hurt."

She laughs bitterly. "You think I don't know that? Here's a newsflash for you. Sometimes, you gotta do what you gotta do to survive."

"What do you mean?"

Hollis sighs. "Look, it's complicated, okay? I don't exactly have a lot of options. Those fights pay well, a lot better than waiting tables." Grabbing her small bag, she scrambles out of my car.

"Let's face the facts, pretty boy. We come from two very different worlds. You were just dealt a better hand than I was. So don't judge what you don't understand. Okay?"

She slams the door and dashes inside. Meanwhile, I'm trying to figure out how the hell I got on her bad side *again*, and why does that bother me so much?

Chapter 11

Hollis

I t's been over a week since tryouts, and football conditioning has commenced. Receiving the email that I made varsity was probably the best news I ever received in my life. Second to Grams pulling me from that lame ass online school to get me registered as a student at Bellwood High.

The weather has been brutal, your usual hot and humid South Carolina summer. As I jog around the track with the rest of the team, sweat pours down my face and back. My muscles ache from the intense workouts, but I continue to push through. I can't afford to show any weakness. Making varsity was no small feat, and I'm determined to prove I deserve to be here.

I'm not the only girl on the team. Maisie Jorgensen, Alora Lewis, and Corrine Summers have all made the cut, and I can admit, I'm impressed. It will be so badass having the four of us playing with the guys, kicking all our rivals' asses.

Coach Watson blows his whistle, signaling us to gather around. "Alright, we are going to break off into groups. If you are on the line, whether that is offense or defense, I want you practicing your blocking on the fifty-yard line. The rest of the offense, I want you on one end of the field practicing passes and running routes. The rest of defense, I want you working on your footwork, coordination, and reaction time. Eagles on three. One, two, three … Eagles!"

We all clap and go off to our perspective drills.

I jog over to join the offensive players for pass and route practice. As I approach, I see Colton already there, tossing a football back and forth with our quarterback, Dylan. My stomach does an annoying little flip at the sight of him, which I promptly ignore.

I've been avoiding Colton since he confronted me about the underground fights. He wouldn't understand my desperation for the money to get my car fixed. Not with the privileged life he lives.

Colton's eyes meet mine as I approach, and he gives me a small nod. I return it stiffly before turning my attention to Coach Freeman, who's explaining the drill to the group.

"Alright, we're going to work on some route combinations. I want to see crisp cuts and clean catches. Reynolds, you'll be running with the first group. Whitlock, you'll go up next."

Some of the guys murmur at the mention of my last name, but I choose to ignore them.

As Colton runs his routes, I can't help but admire his form. His cuts are sharp and precise, his hands sure as he plucks the ball out of the air. It's clear why he's one of the starting receivers on the team.

When it's my turn, I channel all my focus into running the routes perfectly. I push myself to make each cut as sharp as Colton, each catch as clean. By the time we finish the drill, I'm breathing hard but feeling satisfied with my performance.

"Nice work out there, Sunshine," Colton says as we head to get water.

"Thanks. Yours could use some improvement."

Colton chuckles. "Always with the insults. You sure know how to make a guy feel special."

I roll my eyes. "Don't let it go to your head, Golden Boy. Your ego's big enough as it is."

We grab our water bottles and take long gulps, the cool liquid a welcome relief from the scorching heat. As I lower my bottle, I catch Colton studying me with an intense look in his eyes.

"What?" I ask, suddenly self-conscious.

He shakes his head slightly. "Nothing, just … you're really good out there, and I'm glad you made varsity."

The next round of drills, Coach Freeman has us running routes where one receiver will block us or intercept the ball. Colton and another guy go first. Colton manages to block the pass, swatting the ball to the ground.

"Nice attempt, Weedon. I think we will have to work on your timing a little bit, though. Great defense, Reynolds." Coach glances down at the clipboard. "Alright, Colton, you're offense, and Whitlock, you're defense."

I take my place on the defensive side while Colton lines up across from me as a receiver.

"Your last name is Whitlock?" Coltons asks.

"Trying to make small talk to distract me isn't going to help you, you know?"

The quarterback snaps the ball, and I immediately move into position, trying to anticipate Colton's movements. He runs a quick slant route, and I follow him closely, keeping my hands ready in case he catches the ball.

Colton fakes a catch and takes off running toward the linemen where they are doing their drills. I quickly change direction and sprint after him, determined not to let him get away with the ball. I push myself harder, my fingers within reach when I stumble on the turf, my foot catching unexpectedly.

The momentum sends me crashing into Colton's back, and we both go down hard, tumbling across the field in a tangle of limbs. When we finally come to a stop, Colton lands on top of me, our faces merely inches apart.

For a moment, time seems to stand still. I'm acutely aware of every point of contact between our bodies: his chest rising and falling rapidly beneath mine, the smell of sweat and his cologne mixed, the warmth of his breath on my face. His blue eyes are filled with an intensity that makes my heart race even faster.

"You okay, Sunshine?" Colton asks, gripping my waist.

I swallow hard, trying to ignore the flutter in my stomach at his touch. "I'm fine," I say, my voice coming out huskier than I intended. "Just … lost my footing."

My heart races, and I'm not sure if it's from exertion or our proximity.

Some of the guys whistle and some shout, "Get it, Reynolds," bringing me back to reality.

"You can get off me now," I snarl.

"Right. Sorry about that!" Colton's cheeks flush as he scrambles to his feet. He holds out a hand to help me up, which I reluctantly accept.

As he pulls me to my feet, I try to ignore the tingling sensation where his hand touches mine. I drop his hand and step back, putting some distance between us.

"Whitlock! Reynolds! You two all right?" Coach Freeman calls out as he jogs over.

"We're fine, Coach," Colton responds. "Just a little collision. No harm done."

Coach skeptically looks us both over. "Alright, if you're sure. Take five to catch your breath, then I want you both back in the drill. And try to stay on your feet this time."

As Coach walks away, I feel Colton's eyes on me. I pointedly avoid his gaze, brushing off any turf debris from my clothes. My skin still tingles where his body was pressed against mine, and I'm fighting to regain my composure.

"I don't need to take five," I mutter, more to myself, and make my way back for the rest of drills.

Colton

As Hollis jogs back to rejoin the group, I can't shake the feeling of her body pressed against mine. The scent of her floral shampoo, the softness of her skin where my hands had gripped her waist—it's all seared into my memory.

I shake my head, trying to clear my thoughts. *Focus, Reynolds. This is football practice, not some kind of wet dream.*

I take a deep breath, willing myself to focus. I can't afford to be distracted, especially not by someone who is my teammate.

As I make my way back to the group, I can't help but steal glances at Hollis. The way she moves with such determination and grace, her blonde ponytail swinging as she runs her routes. Even covered in sweat, she's breathtaking.

Stop it! You made a bet. No dating, remember? Besides, Hollis doesn't seem to be interested in you, anyway. Or anyone for that matter.

For the rest of practice, I throw myself into the drills with renewed intensity, channeling my confusing emotions into physical exertion. By the time Coach blows the final whistle, I'm exhausted but feeling more centered.

"Great practice, everyone. Make sure you're here tomorrow. Same time. Locker rooms are open if any of you want to hit the showers. Otherwise, go home. Get some rest. You're all dismissed!" Coach Watson calls out.

We gather our things, and I stare at Hollis as she takes off toward the stadium exit in a hurry.

"You're staring," Zealand whispers in my ear, breaking my attention. "Something going on between the two of you?"

"Hm? What? No!"

"C'mon bro. I'm not blind. There is clearly some sort of tension happening between you and her. It's okay if you're developing feelings for her. Just make sure it doesn't steal your focus from the game."

"The tension is that she despises me and I'm just trying to be nice to her. She's dealing with a lot for someone our age."

"Well, why not try spending time with her? Plan something for you guys to do that allows her to let her guard down."

"Like a date? Because that sounds an awful lot like a date."

"Not a date. Just ... two teammates hanging out who just so happen to be male and female."

"Still sounds like a date, my guy." I pat his shoulder as we head out to our vehicles.

Later that evening, I browse the internet for the name Whitlock. Coaches have a habit of calling us by our last names. The only time they call you by your first is if you share the same last name with someone else on the team.

The moment I press enter, news articles pop up about an NFL player named Weston Whitlock. I knew the name sounded familiar!

Weston Whitlock, a highly paid NFL wide receiver, used to play on the same team as Russell Thomas, Brady's dad. I scour the articles, looking for any indication he had a family, trying to see if Hollis has any ties to him. *Could that be why she didn't want to share her last name?*

The closest I got to anything was a sketchy celebrity news website claiming that the once best friends had a falling out because Weston had an affair with Russell's wife. *Brady's mom? Wait! Would that mean ... Brady and Hollis are ... half siblings?*

I close my laptop, my brain analyzing what I discovered. No way that could possibly be true. Could it? I mean, I could ask Hollis, but I have no doubt she would just keep me in the no-friend zone.

I think over what Zealand said. What if the best way to help Hollis break down her defenses is by hanging out and showing her the kind of person I am?

Pulling out my phone, I send her a message.

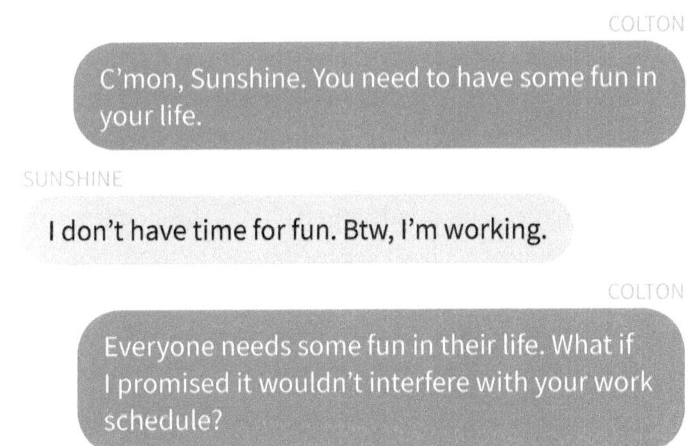

I stare at my phone, surprised she actually responded.

I wait anxiously for her response, hoping she'll give me a chance. After what feels like an eternity, my phone buzzes.

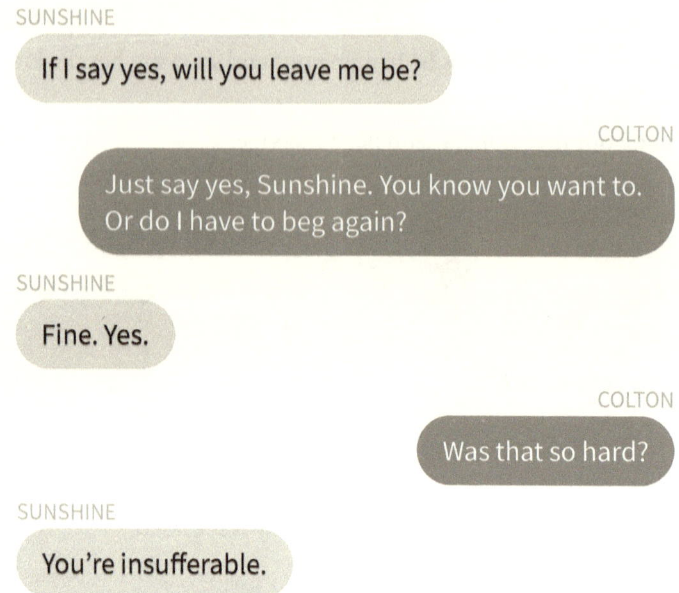

I place my phone on the charger and crawl into bed, already planning different ideas in my head. I'm determined to show Hollis there's more to life than just work and responsibilities. And maybe, just maybe, I can get her to let her guard down a little.

As I drift off to sleep, my mind keeps replaying the moment we fell on the field—the feeling of her body against mine, the way my body reacted to hers.

My dick jumps at the memory, and I quietly groan as I feel myself harden.

There's no harm giving in to the fantasy, is there? Who's going to know?

I reach into my sweatpants, gripping myself and slowly start stroking. I picture Hollis beneath me, with her breasts on display for my mouth to suck and blow on, begging me to slide inside her and fuck her until she's floating, releasing her from all the tension weighing her down. I imagine how tight she would feel, her heat gripping me, and pump faster and harder, and within in moments, I come all over my hand.

"Fuck!" I mutter as I come down from my orgasmic high. The last time I got myself off was the night before I gave my virginity to Stacey over spring break.

I wanted to ensure I would last so she would come before I did. We had been dating since homecoming, and it just felt like the right time. We were both ready, and Stacey made sure I didn't feel like a pathetic loser after I told her it was my first time. She was more than excited that I was whole for her.

Looking back, I guess it wasn't that meaningful for her when she broke things off, using the guise of college. The truth is, I got her pregnant, and she was planning to hide it from me so she could give the baby up for adoption, but then she ended up aborting it.

Memories of our relationship and that letter she left me, consume me, and the anger I thought I had finally overcome, washes over me like a raging ocean wave.

I go into my bathroom and clean myself up before heading back to bed. Before I can think it over, I grab my phone and send off a text to Hollis.

COLTON

Look, how about you don't worry about the plans. I shouldn't push you into doing something with me. You'd clearly rather avoid me, so I won't bother you again. I'm sorry.

It's for the best. If I avoid building onto whatever feelings she stirs in me now, I prevent things from developing any further with her, sealing my bet win and not having to worry she will break me the way Stacey did.

It's all for the best.

Chapter 12

Hollis

I glare at the message I got from Colton last night.

> Look, how about you don't worry about the plans. I shouldn't push you into doing something with me. You'd clearly rather avoid me, so I won't bother you again. I'm sorry.

I'm a bit baffled and confused. Why did he change his mind so fast? I'm not sure if I should be relieved or … upset? Angry?

Something, no doubt, happened between us yesterday when we collided. I'm not a relationship type of girl, preferring one-night stands over anything long term. You're less likely to be let down by the other person.

Yet I know something was there. I saw it in his eyes, in his reaction. I didn't miss the slight bulge forming in his shorts before he quickly adjusted himself either.

"Everything okay?"

I look up at Talia, who's holding open the back door to the diner.

"Yeah. Peachy," I state. "What's up?"

"We're starting to pick up in here. Thought you would like to know."

"Coming," I say, pocketing my phone. Time to go make this money.

"Hollipop!" Grams knocks on my bedroom door. "Time to get up! You don't want to be late for your first day of school!"

"Ugh, give me five more minutes?" I groan.

"Not unless you want me to unenroll you from that school. You know, the one you practically begged me to put you in. I'm sure there's still time to have you back into that online school you *loved* so much."

"Fine. I'm up! I'm up!"

Crawling out of bed, I make my way to my dresser. I throw on a pair of ripped, loose-fitting jeans along with a baggy black band tee, tying it into a knot in the front, showcasing a little skin.

After applying some eyeliner and mascara, I run my brush through my blonde and now, baby-blue locks. I decided over the weekend to ditch the pink and go blue. New school, new year. Why not add in new hair?

Not to mention the annoying emotions I have been dealing with since Colton decided to finally adhere to my requests to leave me be.

I grab my bookbag and head into the kitchen, snagging the waffle Grams set on the table for me.

"Bye, Grams. I'll see you later. I love you!" I place a kiss on her cheek and head for the door.

"I love you too. Have a wonderful day!" Grams shouts as the door closes behind me.

I get in my car, tossing my bookbag into the passenger seat. "Please start up for me," I whisper.

The money I won in my fight against Titan was just enough to cover the new alternator. Nathan received the part a few days after he ordered it and got it fixed for me. I was so relieved, but now I have anxiety every time I get in.

With a turn of the key, my car turns on, and I shout yes in my head before driving off to school.

Twenty minutes later, I park in the student parking lot and head into my new school, the nerves slowly kicking in.

I take a deep breath as I walk through the main entrance of Bellwood High. The hallways are already bustling with students reuniting after summer break, their excited chatter echoing off the lockers. I grip the strap of my backpack tighter, steeling myself for what's to come.

I make my way to the front office to pick up my schedule and locker assignment. As I wait in line, I overhear snippets of conversations from the other students.

"Did you hear about all the new girls on the football team? They've added like five on varsity."

"Yeah, I can't believe Coach Watson actually let them join."

"Are they actually any good? Or are they all just wannabes because Payson took us to state? Like, get real. No way that many girls can play, let alone be interested in football."

I clench my jaw, resisting the urge to turn around and tell them off. The last thing I need is to get kicked out for fucking up a bunch of kids on my first day in a new school. Instead, I focus on the task at hand and step up to the counter when it's my turn.

"Name?" the secretary asks without looking up from her computer.

"Hollis Whitlock," I reply. "I'm new here."

She types something into the computer before printing out my schedule and handing it to me along with a small slip of paper. "Here's your schedule and locker information. Welcome to Bellwood High, Ms. Whitlock."

I mumble a quick "Thanks" before turning away, studying my schedule as I walk. I'm not paying attention to where I'm going when I collide with someone.

"Hey! Watch where you're going!"

Looking up, I recognize it's the pompous Barbie from football camp. What was her name again?

"Oh my gosh! Charmin! How was your summer?"

"It's Charmaine!" she shrieks, causing many students in the hall to stop and stare.

"Yeah, I don't really care. So sorry, but not sorry for bumping into you. Got to find my first class. See ya!"

I go to bypass her when she latches onto my arm. A mistake on her part. My glare moves from her hand, up her arm, before making eye contact with the Paris Hilton doppelgänger.

"Unless you want me to break every manicured fingernail and fracture your hands an orthopedic surgeon won't even know how to fix, I'd suggest you remove it from my arm."

"Puh-lease. As if a little shrimp like you could do anything—"

With my quick reflexes, I snap one of her manicured nails in half. A blood-curdling scream fills the hall, forcing those within proximity to cover their ears.

"You little bitch! I will fucking ruin you!"

"Ms. Summers, is everything all right?" Coach Harbaugh appears from one of the classrooms, looking around the hall, then to Charmaine and me.

She points to me, then shows him her disfigured manicure. "That heathen broke my nail!"

I shrug. "No idea what she's talking about. I'm just trying to find my first class when she bumped into me."

"Oh no. Charmin! I told you the sketchy nail salon you go to is a fraud. You need to go to a higher end one," Maisie says, causing Charmaine's face to turn even more red than it was a second ago.

"I ... you ... gahh!" Charmaine screams before storming off to who knows where.

"Alright. Scene's over. Everyone, let's get to class!" Coach Harbaugh says as he ushers some students away.

"That ... was ... awesome!" Maisie exclaims once the halls return to their chatter. "I've never seen anyone lay a finger on Charmaine. She's one of those girls who likes to use her father's name to get away with just about anything."

"Great," I state, glancing around at the numbers on the doors and the school map, trying to figure out where the hell my first class is and what direction I need to go in.

"You need help?" Maisie asks, noticing my frustration. "What do you have?"

"Chemistry with Mr. Feeser," I say.

"Oh, that's in the hall where all the science classes are," she says. "My first class is on the way there. I'll walk with you."

"Thanks," I say, following Maisie as she leads the way through the crowded hallways.

"No problem," she says with a friendly smile. "Us football girls have to stick together, right?"

I nod noncommittally, not used to the camaraderie. As we walk, Maisie chatters about classes, teachers, and the upcoming football season. I half-listen, still taking in my new surroundings and trying to mentally note how I'll find my way around this monstrosity of a school.

We turn a corner and nearly collide with a group of guys in letterman jackets. My stomach does an annoying flip when I recognize Colton is among them.

"Whoa, ladies. Our bad. We weren't paying attention. Please excuse us," one of the guys says. "Wait ... diner girl?"

Colton's eyes meet mine briefly before he looks away. *So, I see we're still at this.*

"It's Hollis," I snarl. "You might want to remember that next time you come in and get seated in my section. I'll be sure to remember this moment and, I don't know, mess with your order." I give him one of my devilish smiles, the one that says do not test me.

"I'm sorry. I didn't mean for it to come off like that. It's just ... I was used to the pink hair, and it took me by surprise seeing that you changed it up. Digging the blue, though," he says with a corny grin, giving me two thumbs-up.

"You'll have to ignore Anthony. His brain doesn't know how to function on the first day of school," Dylan says. I don't miss the way he glances toward Maisie with a twinkle in his eye or the way her cheeks turn a shade pink.

"Whatever. I need to get to class." I turn to Maisie and thank her for her help before walking through the door to my chemistry class.

Morning classes go by fairly quickly: the usual syllabus and classroom introductions, what your teacher expects from you, blah, blah, blah. Soon enough, the lunch bell rings, and I'm ready for a reprieve from the awkwardness that is the first day.

I'm here before the majority of the senior class and take full opportunity at selecting a table toward an area that looks secluded enough from everyone else.

The cafeteria's volume gradually increases as more students enter and find friends to sit with and catch up on what I can only presume is gossip or how their classes are going.

As I scan the cafeteria, I note the typical high school social hierarchy playing out before my eyes. The jocks and cheerleaders dominate the center tables, laughing loudly and drawing attention. The band kids cluster together near the windows, instrument cases piled around them. The artsy types have claimed a corner, sketchbooks open as they pick at their lunches.

My eyes land on Colton sitting with his football buddies at one of the prime center tables. He's smiling and joking around, but he's scanning the cafeteria every so often. Is he looking for someone? For me?

I quickly look away when his gaze drifts in my direction. The last thing I need is for him to catch me staring at his handsome face.

"Mind if we join you?" Maisie is there with her lunch tray, along with the other two girls from the football team—Alora and Corrine.

For a moment, I consider telling them no. I'm not here to make friends, but something in Maisie's friendly smile makes me hesitate and I can hear Grams in my mind, lecturing me about how I need to make some friends.

I shrug. "It's a free country."

Maisie takes the seat beside mine while Alora and Corrine slide into the seats across from us.

"So, how's your first day going so far?" Alora asks, popping a fry into her mouth.

"It's school," I state. "Nothing special, but it sure as hell beats online schooling."

"Online schooling?" Corrine asks.

"Yeah. I got kicked out of my old school for fighting, and my grandmother had me do some virtual school stuff so I wouldn't fall behind. She wants to make sure I graduate when I'm supposed to."

"What school did you go to?" Alora asks.

"Wimbleton," I say. I don't miss the disgusted looks the girls give each other at the mention of my old school.

"What?" I ask.

"Wimbleton is our big rival school. They're basically our enemy," Maisie explains. "Di-did you not know that?"

"Sorry. I wasn't into school sports. I was too busy fighting douchebags who thought they could just get away with touching you inappropriately, and the principal doesn't do shit about it but blame the female students."

"What!?"

"Excuse me?"

"You're joking?"

"Not something I would joke about," I deadpan.

"Who was—" Corrine starts to ask, but she gets interrupted by a girl I've come to despise.

"What the hell are you doing sitting over here, Corrine? You're supposed to be sitting with me and the rest of our group." Her angry hazel eyes glare at each of us until they land on me.

"Charmaine, those people are not—"

"I will not allow you to sit with these losers, especially with the likes of *her*! Get up! You're sitting with me."

"I'm perfectly fine sitting right here. What's the big deal?"

"You're sitting with the girl who broke my perfectly manicured nail," Charmaine whines. She lifts the finger with a tan Band-Aid wrapped around the nail. "And my nail lady won't be able to fix it until Friday, so now I have to have ugly nails until then."

"Awe, you poor thing," I coo. "If you want a matching set, I can arrange that for you so the school doesn't have to hear you cry about it."

Charmaine's nostrils flare, her eyes flashing fear.

Good. You should fear me, bitch.

"Corrine, let's go!" Charmaine demands, grabbing her sister's arm in an attempt to pull her out of her seat.

"Listen, Charmin. Your sister clearly doesn't want to sit with you, and honestly, I don't blame her. So why don't you leave her alone," Maisie speaks up.

"Why don't you mind your business, porkenstein. Shouldn't your fat ass be nose deep scarfing down your lunch?" Charmaine says a little too loud, causing the cafeteria to get quiet.

"Hey!" Alora stands, putting herself in Charmaine's personal space. "You got a lot of room to be talking for someone who's going to end up with all sorts of plastic surgery in her future. You will be made of so much plastic you will be a lifelike Barbie. Only, no man will want to play with you."

The surrounding students "Oooo" at Alora's comment, which I admit was a good comeback.

"You little—" Charmaine starts, but Corrine jumps between them.

"Stop! Stop!" She looks at Alora. "I don't need you getting in a fight with my sister. Coach will sit you for our first game if you do, and we can't afford that on defense." She turns to face her sister. "Let me grab my lunch," she grits out. Corrine grabs her tray and follows behind her pathetic sister to her table.

As I watch Corrine take her seat next to Charmaine, I notice the freeing expression she held here is replaced with a somber one.

"What is up with that?" I nod in their direction once Alora returns to her seat, the cafeteria back to being loud as everyone returns their attention to their friends and eating.

"Charmaine puts so much pressure on Corrine to be just like her, but Corrine just wants to be her own person."

"So why doesn't Corrine tell her sister to fuck off?" It can't be that hard to do.

Some people aren't as abrasive as you are. Oh, right.

"I'm not sure. I guess Corrine doesn't know how to? The girl needs to grow a backbone and tell her sister to kiss her ass."

The girls change the topic from Corrine to something to do with one of their classes. Meanwhile, my attention goes back to Corrine picking at her lunch. I can't imagine what's going through her mind, but judging by her lack in appetite, she's hurting. I know that kind of hurt, having lived with it for years. Family shouldn't have the power to make you feel less than who you are.

My eyes drift over to where the football team is sitting, and I catch Colton staring in our direction. For a moment, our gazes lock. His blue eyes seem to soften slightly as they meet mine with a flicker of something. Concern? Curiosity? Then he quickly looks away, turning back to laugh at something one of his teammates said.

I feel a strange twinge in my chest at the dismissal. Which is ridiculous. I'm the one who told him to leave me alone. Isn't this what I wanted? For him to stop pestering me, stop trying to be my friend or whatever it was he was doing?

So why does it bother me so much to see him acting like I don't exist?

"Earth to Hollis!" Maisie's voice snaps me out of my thoughts. "You with us?"

"Huh? Oh, yeah. Sorry, just ... zoned out there for a sec," I mumble, forcing my attention back to the girls at my table.

"I was asking if you wanted to come hang out with us after school today since we don't have practice," Maisie says. "We can go to the mall, maybe get smoothies. What do you say?"

"I wish I could, but I can't. I have work after school."

"Oh. Okay. Maybe another day?"

"Yeah, sure." If only I could tell them there won't be an opportunity for us to hang out. Now that school has started and I'm on the football team, I'll be working all evenings and available weekends I can get.

Good-bye free time.

The lunch bell rings, so I quickly gather up my trash, dump it in the nearest can, and make way for my next class.

Chapter 13

Colton

I'm such a fucking idiot!

Seeing Hollis outside of football and her work attire in normal street clothes makes it nearly impossible to ignore her. The blue in her hair caught me off guard, but it suits her, bringing out the vibrant blue of her eyes.

As Hollis hurries out of the cafeteria, I decide I'm tired of fighting whatever feelings she stirs within me, bet be damned, and I need to make this right. Trying to ignore her and putting distance between us has done nothing but make me think about her more, driving me crazy.

With my long legs, I'm able to fall in step with her as she makes her way down the hall.

"Hey," I murmur.

"What do you want?" she asks, not slowing her pace.

"Look, about that text ... I shouldn't have sent that. I was dealing with some personal stuff and felt like maybe it was best to finally give you what you wanted."

"Yeah, thanks for that."

"I know sarcasm when I hear it." I smirk at her, hoping to ease the fiery attitude she's directing at me.

"Wow, you're a real genius," Hollis says. "Is there a point to this conversation, or are you just here to state the obvious?"

I take a deep breath, steeling myself. "Look, I know I've been all over the place lately. And I'm sorry for that. The truth is ... I realized that pushing you away isn't what I really want. I like you, Hollis."

She stops abruptly, turning to face me with wide eyes. "What?"

"I like you," I repeat, my heart pounding wildly in my chest. "And I know you probably don't feel the same way, but I needed to be honest with you. That's why I've been acting so weird lately. I have been trying to fight these feelings you stir in me, to keep my distance, but I don't think I can anymore."

She stares at me, her expression unreadable until she lets out a stifled laugh. "You're joking, right?"

"I'm not, Hollis. What I'm feeling for you? I haven't felt this way with anyone before."

She shakes her head. "You don't even know me, Colton. Not really."

"Then let me get to know you. Give me a chance to prove to you that I'm not as wishy washy as I have been. That way when I ask you on a date, you'll be able to say yes, no questions or doubts in your mind."

"It's not that simple. I've told you, Colton, I don't do the dating thing, but if you want to fuck me out of your system, then that's something I'd be up for."

"W-w-wait, what?"

Did I hear her correctly?

"If you need to have sex with me to get me out of your system, just let me know. Otherwise, you're going to be waiting around forever for me to want to say yes to a date with you."

She picks up the pace, walking away from me as fast as she can.

I'm left standing in the hallway, thinking over what she said. I mean, sex would be amazing, but it's not what I want from her. It's the last thing I care about with Hollis. There are so many admirable qualities to her; how could anyone not see her? I only question what or who has made her so defensive and guard her heart. I want to show her how amazing she is, to heal what someone else broke.

Getting Hollis to date me will be a challenge, but one I gladly accept.

As part of Bellwood football tradition, Coach doesn't have us practice on the first day of school.

Normally, the guys and I hit the gym after school on our non-practice days, but Thea and I had dentist appointments after school.

"What's on your mind, big bro?" Thea asks on our drive home from our appointments.

"What makes you think I have something on my mind?" Who am I kidding, I'm easy to read when it comes to my sister.

"You're not as chatty or hounding me with a hundred million questions about my classes or what boys are giving me problems. It's none, by the way."

When I don't say anything, Thea reaches across, placing her hand on my forehead. "Are you feeling okay?"

"Yeah. Why?"

"Well, when I said no boy has bothered me today, you didn't say something like *Good! Better keep it that way!* Or some other offhand remark about me being a lonely old woman who will forever be a virgin unless her protective older brother moves away so this girl can finally get d—"

"Jesus, Thea. I'm fine! Alright? It's …" I contemplate if I should even be discussing this with her.

"Yes?" she asks, the ever-persistent little sister she is.

"Just … It's a girl."

"Finally!" Thea raises her hands in the air, praising the heavens.

"What's that supposed to mean?"

"It *means* you finally can start moving forward with your life and stop being so hung up on Stacey. You haven't been the same since she dumped your behind to go off to college. We've all noticed, Mom and Dad included."

I didn't realize they could tell. "How come you guys didn't say anything?"

"We've just been letting you go through the emotions, even though Mom wanted to baby you there a few times." We laugh, probably at the imagery of Mom coddling me. "You do know there are plenty more girls in that school who would love to be with you. Trust me, I hear it all the time. It's gross."

"Thea, there was more to it than just a breakup. Alright? I didn't just give her my heart. I gave her parts of me that I never gave to anyone else."

Thea's jaw drops. "Oh … my … god! Did you give her your virginity!? Wait … don't answer that. I think I may barf!"

"That's not the point. There was more to the breakup than just the distance. Things I'm not quite ready to share with you, or anyone." I keep my eyes on the road, unwilling to let my sister see my pain. "Not even Payson knows," I mutter.

"It must be serious if you didn't share with her." Thea reaches over and places her hand on top of mine. "Whatever it is, just know I'm here for you, big bro."

"Thanks, Thea."

"Anytime," she says, squeezing my hand to show her support. "So … about this girl. What is bothering you so much about her? Maybe I can give you some advice. I mean, I am a girl, after all."

She makes a valid point. "So ... I fucked up. I messaged her, asking her if she would like to make plans to hang out and stuff, in a nonromantic way. Just wanting to get to know her. I've been getting these feelings though, feelings I've been trying to ignore so I don't lose the bet—"

"You made a bet!?" Thea scowls. "Do you know how offensive that is? You know if she finds out she's a bet, you can kiss any chances with her goodbye, because no girl wants or deserves to be a bet. Have you not seen *She's All That*!?"

"Calm down, sis. The bet wasn't even about Hollis at all! I simply made a bet with the guys that I could pull off the no-dating rule that Payson didn't."

"Okay. Well, first thing you need to do is text your homeboys the bet is off, because when you get the girl, the last thing you want is for your friends to find out and one of them, *cough* Anthony *cough*, blab about it, then you not only lost your bet, you lose the girl."

I glance at my sister and back on the road a few times. "So you're saying I'll get the girl?" The corner of my mouth tips up at my sister believing this could actually work out for me.

"That's what you took out of that?"

"I heard you, sis. I'm just surprised you have that much confidence in me."

"You're a great guy, Colton, and I have a feeling you will find a way to charm this girl."

"Thanks, Thea. That means a lot to me."

"Colton?"

"Yeah, baby sis?"

"Call off the bet. ASAP!"

Once we get home, I make my way into the kitchen for a snack before heading upstairs to my bedroom. I set my book bag on the floor and drop down onto my bed, exhaling the day away.

"Call off the bet. ASAP!" My sister's words echo in my head.

No time like the present. I pull my phone from my shorts pocket and select our group chat.

COLTON

The bet's off.

ANTHONY

What!? Colton Reynolds doesn't quit a bet!

RHETT

You serious, man?

COLTON

Dead serious.

ZEALAND

Something you want to share with the class?

COLTON

Guys … I think you've had your suspicions.

JEREMIAH

Maybe …? But please, do explain it for us.

COLTON

I've developed some feelings for Hollis. Okay? I've tried to ignore them, tried avoiding her, but I can't do it. Anytime she's nearby, I have to look at her because my body automatically seeks her out. Only, now I'm not sure if I can get her to take me seriously. Plus, she's strongly against dating, which is going to be a problem.

ANTHONY

Hmm … What's that smell? Could it be the smell of a new bet coming?

COLTON

No! Absolutely no bets.

JEREMIAH

I'm with Colt. If word got around we were placing a bet on Colt getting Hollis to date him? The consequences would not be pretty. That devastates a girl's ego.

COLTON

Not sure she would be devastated as much as she would be pissed off. She would come for me, and you guys would be out a wide receiver.

ANTHONY

Dude, she's like a foot shorter than you. What damage can she possibly do? lol

COLTON

Not sure if I should tell you guys this, but you remember that fight we went to?

ZEALAND

Of course. It was mad crazy!

JEREMIAH

No, because I was on babysitting duty :/ Or did you all forget?

RHETT

Dude, the whole show was crazy!

COLTON

Hollis is Pixie.

ANTHONY

Ain't no way, man! You're fucking with us.

COLTON

I wish I was, but she is. She took out Titan.

ZEALAND

How can you be so certain?

COLTON

I called her out on it after I gave her a ride home from tryouts. She was trying to mask her injuries from the fight. I still don't know how she made it through football tryouts.

RHETT

Is this chick the same one who broke Charmaine's finger today?

JEREMIAH

It wasn't her finger, nitwit. It was her fingernail. Snapped it pretty good too. Heard that hurts like a bitch.

ANTHONY

Colton, you sure you want to go for this girl? I mean, I'd be a little scared.

ZEALAND

That's because you're not man enough to handle someone like her.

ANTHONY

Hey! I think I'm plenty of man to handle any woman.

COLTON

Sure. Whatever you say. But just so we are clear, stay away from Hollis. That woman is mine!

A text from my mom comes through, so I close out of the group chat to see what she wants.

MOM

Hey sweetie. I'm going to be in the office a little later than I expected, and Dad called saying he isn't going to be home in time for dinner. You and Thea are okay on your own?

COLTON

Yeah. We can find something to make I'm sure.

Just then a thought came to mind.

COLTON

Actually, would it be cool if we went out to eat for dinner?

"Thea!" I yell for my sister, who's probably next door in her bedroom. A few moments later, she appears in my doorway.

"You know you could have just walked over, right?" She crosses her arms and leans into my doorframe. "What do you want?"

"Mom just texted that her and Dad won't be home 'til later. What do you say we go out for dinner? My treat." I wiggle my eyebrows.

"If it means I don't have to dip into my babysitting money, I'm all for it. Where are we going?"

"Munson's Diner."

We make our way across town to the old fifties-themed diner. As I pull into the parking lot, I exhale the relief I feel at her car still being in the lot.

Why not get the closest thing to a home-cooked meal and use my sister to help me get bonus points with the fiery girl who won't leave my thoughts?

The bell above the door chimes, alerting the employees new guests have entered.

"Welcome to Munson's. How many will it ... be?" Hollis greets us, her eyes bouncing from me to Thea and back, and her pretty blonde eyebrows furrow.

"Hey, Sunshine. It'll just be my sister and I tonight. Preferably a booth in your section?"

Her eyebrows relax, relief washing over her face before she turns into the pleasant hostess.

"Of course. Right this way." She gestures for us to follow her.

We take our seats in the booth as Hollis gently places the menus down on the table, and her pink lips tilt up on one side when she glances at me.

I return her smirk with one of my own, knowing full well she's being a smart ass.

"What can I get you guys to drink?" she asks.

"I'll take a Coke, please," Thea says.

"Make that two, thanks."

"Coming right up," Hollis says before walking off to get our drinks.

"Is that her?" Thea leans slightly in, keeping her voice down so Hollis doesn't overhear.

"Yeah. That's her," I state, glancing to where Hollis is filling our cups.

"She's beautiful and seems pretty nice. Why were you so worried?"

I chuckle. "Oh, you haven't seen the real her yet."

Hollis returns to our table, gently placing our drinks on the table. "Are you ready to order or do you still need a moment?"

"Hmm ... I can't decide between the steak dinner or the cheeseburger. I think I will go with the steak."

Hollis starts writing it down before I say, "Actually, the burger and fries sounds pretty delicious. I've changed my mind. I'll take the burger."

Hollis's jaw clenches, her nostrils flaring as I aggravate her last nerve.

"Oh, you know what? The steak would actually be—"

"Oh, for fuck's sake, Golden Boy. Would you make up your damn mind before I jam my pen into your hand, and you won't be able to catch anymore footballs in the foreseeable future because the nerves in your hand would be so fucked up you won't be able to use them properly!"

I can't help the grin that spreads across my face as Hollis leans in close, our noses practically touching. Her blue eyes flash with irritation, daring me to push her further. "The next dish that comes out of your mouth is what you're getting. So, what. Will. It. Be?"

"Well, since you asked so nicely, I think I'll go with the cheeseburger. Medium, with extra pickles."

Hollis narrows her eyes at me before straightening up and jotting down my order. She turns to Thea, her expression softening slightly. "And for you?"

"I'll have the grilled chicken sandwich, please," Thea says, looking between Hollis and me with a mixture of amusement and confusion.

"Coming right up," Hollis says, snatching our menus and stalking off toward the kitchen.

As she walks away, I can't help but watch, admiring the confident sway of her hips.

The moment she's out of earshot, Thea leans across the table. "Oh. My. God. I see what you mean now," she whispers excitedly. "She totally has a thing for you!"

Chapter 14

Hollis

"So who's the chick with your boo?" Janet asks when I grab a customer's order from the window.

"Okay, first, he's not my boo. And second, it's his sister." Janet opens her mouth to say something, but I cut her off. "I know what you're going to say, and yes, I'm one thousand percent certain it's his sister. You can clearly see the familial similarities. *You* can't tell because you only see the back of her head."

I take the food order to the family of four sitting two booths down from Colton and his sister and ensure everyone has what they need before I check in with the siblings.

"Everything good here?" I ask, mentally noting they may need a refill on drinks soon.

"Actually, no," Colton's sister speaks up. "You see, my dear old brother here has the brain cell of a panda. What's he got to do for you to go on a date with him?"

Colton chokes on his drink, nearly spraying the table with his Coke. "Thea! What the hell are you doing?"

"Helping," she says with a devilish smile. "Anyway, my brother clearly likes you, soooo ... what do you say?"

I raise an eyebrow at Thea's bold question, then glance at Colton who looks like he wants to sink into the booth and disappear. Part of me is amused by his embarrassment, but another part feels a twinge of ... something. Sympathy? Guilt?

"Look, I appreciate the effort, but I've already told your brother I don't date. It's nothing personal against him, it's just not my thing."

Thea opens her mouth, likely to argue, but Colton cuts her off. "Thea, drop it. I told you it's complicated."

I give Colton a small nod of thanks for shutting down his sister's matchmaking attempts. "Anything else I can get for you two?"

"No, we're good. Thanks, Hollis," Colton mutters.

I turn to head back to the kitchen, but Thea's voice stops me. "Wait! Can I at least get your number? You know, in case I ever need help kicking my brother's butt."

I chuckle at her persistence. "Is that really why you want my number? Or is it your way of trying to convince me to take your brother out?"

"Can't it be both?" she asks.

"I'll think about it," I say, appreciative of her honesty, and go about my duties.

Nearly two hours pass before Colton and his sister finally get up to leave.

"Here." Colton drops his keys into his sister's hand. "Go start the car while I pay for this."

"Okay, but if you're not out there in ten minutes, I'm driving home."

"You better not—" Thea is out the door before he can finish his sentence.

"Sisters, am I right?" he asks, looking at me.

"I wouldn't know. I'm an only child." I shrug, feeling slightly jealous that he has at least a sibling to keep him company, even if they get on each other's nerves. Not sure those two actually do. I've been watching from a distance, and it's clear they have a good relationship with each other.

"Oh. I'm sorry, Hollis. I—"

"No need to apologize. Anyway, that will be twenty-nine fifty."

Colton hands me his money, and I ring him up, ensuring I give him the correct change.

"Here you go," I say, and place the money into his palm. The warmth of his hand sends tingly sensations into my arm. Before I can pull away, Colton closes his hand around mine.

"Keep it. You've earned it, especially putting up with my little sister."

"She wasn't that bad. A bit persistent, but obviously, she cares about you. You guys seem very close." I try to hide the sadness from my tone, not wanting him to see how much it affects me.

"If you're going to keep holding my hand, I'm going to assume you want me as much as I want you, Sunshine," he says, his mouth slowly curling until he's flashing me his pretty, white teeth.

Pulling my hand away, I pocket the tip into my apron, scoffing at his comment. "Psh. Only in your dreams, Golden Boy."

"Then I'll guess I'll be waiting," he says. "Good night, Hollis."

I watch him walk out the door before I head to clean off their booth and start wrapping silverware for tomorrow.

"Oooh, child. That boy is so smitten with you. How are you going to turn a handsome young man down like that?" Janet asks as she helps me.

"Easy, by rejecting him over and over until he gets the message. It's easier to turn people away when you know what it's like when they leave you."

"But how do you know who will stay if you don't give them the chance? Look, I'm not telling you what you should do or how to live your life, but just know not everyone is set out to hurt you."

"I wish it were that simple," I mutter to myself.

The next few days go by in a blur of classes, football practices, and work. It feels like there are never enough minutes in the day to accomplish everything plus sleep, and I'm starting to feel it. *Man, I'm exhausted!*

As the bell rings to dismiss us for the weekend, I grab my things from my locker and make my way toward the football field. Typically, we don't have Friday practices, but with our first game of the season quickly approaching, Coach Watson wants us to scrimmage against a team from some town about an hour away.

My phone chimes with a text message.

I laugh to myself, imagining the confusion on his face. Got to give it to him, though, since the night he and his sister came into the diner, he's asked me that question at least once a day. That family really embodies the definition of persistence.

"Hey Hollis!" Maisie calls out as I enter the locker room. "Ready for the scrimmage?"

I nod, heading to my locker to change. "As ready as I'll ever be. Are you nervous?"

Maisie shrugs. "A little. But mostly excited. It'll be good to see how we measure up against another team before the actual season starts." Maisie has been killing it on the defensive line, holding her own against some of the biggest guys on our team. I have no doubt she will excel against this team we are facing, giving her an added boost to her already confident self.

As we change into our practice gear, ensuring our shoulder pads are on nice and tight, Alora joins us. "Did you guys hear? There's a big ass party out near Ravenwood tonight. A bunch of the guys on the team are going and asked if we wanted to tag along. What do you say?"

"Hard pass for me," I state as I do a quick French braid in my hair to ensure my helmet fits comfortably on my head. "I've got work early in the morning."

"Ah, that's a bummer." Alora pouts. "I really was hoping all us girls could get dolled up and have some fun. Together."

"My sister's forcing me to go," Corrine says, adjusting the belt on her practice pants. "Where there's a party, Charmaine must be in attendance, and where she goes, I go. Honestly, I think she's only going to make sure Dylan doesn't cheat on her."

"Dylan's not the cheating type," Maisie states. "That boy is loyal to a fault."

"You would know, wouldn't you?" Alora asks, wiggling her eyebrows before putting her focus back on Corrine. "Corrine, have you ever considered putting your foot down and telling your sister to fuck off?"

"I'm not sure I can. Charmaine holds grudges, not to mention she can find the dirt on just about anyone and use it against them to get what she wants." Corrine refuses to look up, and I have to wonder if Charmaine has something on her own sister.

We tighten our laces on our cleats, then make our way to the field. Excitement along with nervousness runs through my veins. The anticipation of going against an actual opponent, not our own teammates, has me pumped.

The sun is glaring down on us on the home team's sideline, and once again, the South Carolina humidity is unbearable, even more so with the football equipment on.

How do these guys tolerate this heat in pads?

As we line up for warm-ups, the opposing team is arriving on the field in their crimson and gold uniforms. They're bigger than I expected, with some of their players looking massive—easily over six feet tall and built like tanks. I push down the flicker of doubt trying to creep in. Size isn't everything in football; speed and agility are just as important.

Coach Watson gathers us around for a quick pep talk before the scrimmage starts. "Alright, Eagles. This is our chance to see where we stand before the season kicks off. I want you to treat this like a real game. Give it your all out there, and show these boys what Bellwood is made of!"

Then we break from the huddle with an enthusiastic "Eagles!"

As we take our positions on the field, the adrenaline starts pumping through my veins. This is what I've been waiting for—a chance to prove myself against real competition.

A few of their players are whispering and snickering to each other. I clench my jaw, determined to prove them wrong about us girls.

"Hey. Don't let them get in your head," Colton says, coming to stand beside me. "We've got this."

I nod, appreciating his encouragement even if I'd never admit it out loud. "Oh, I'm not worried. I just hope they're ready to get their asses handed to them by a bunch of girls."

Colton grins. "That's the spirit, Sunshine."

The whistle blows and the scrimmage begins. It's intense from the start—hard hits, fast plays, the satisfying smack of pads colliding. I'm playing as a slot receiver, and on our first offensive drive, I shake my defender and catch a fifteen-yard pass from Dylan, securing a first down.

"Yes!" I shout to myself.

"Nice catch, Sunshine," Colton says, giving me a high-five with his gloved hand. "Let's see if you can do it again."

"Oh, I'm planning on it," I state.

The next play, Dylan hands the ball to Corrine, our running back, who squeezes through the hole our offensive line created and runs about twenty yards before going out on the sidelines.

"What the hell are you doing, Sanders? Make the fucking tackle!" their coach yells to the player covering Corrine.

"But ... Coach, she's a girl, and I was raised to never hit a girl!"

"She's wearing pads, for fuck's sake! She signed up for the sport knowing damn well tackling is a part of it. Now, stop being a baby and make some fucking tackles!"

"You trying to get my mama to whoop my ass," the player mutters as he gets back into position.

I laugh at the scene. The guy looks intimidating, but he seems to be more of a gentle giant than anything.

I wonder how many times this will happen in our season?

We take the field again, and this time, I line up wide, across from a cornerback who towers over me by at least six inches. He smirks down at me, trying to be an intimidating fucker. He clearly doesn't know who I am.

I stare back at the cocky cornerback, refusing to be intimidated by his size.

He leans in close, his voice dripping with condescension. "You sure you're in the right place, little girl? Cheerleaders are supposed to be over there." He jerks his thumb toward the sidelines. "Or in your case, at home playing with your baby dolls."

I narrow my eyes at him, a familiar fire igniting in my chest and a dangerous smile playing on my lips. "Oh, I'm exactly where I need to be. Why don't you worry about covering me instead of running your mouth?"

The ball is snapped, and I explode off the line, using my speed to my advantage. The cornerback tries to jam me at the line, but I slip past him, cutting sharply to the inside. I run a post route, cutting toward the middle of the field, and glance back to see Dylan winding up to throw, his eyes in my direction.

The ball spirals through the air, and I track it, adjusting my speed. Time seems to slow as the ball soars, my legs pumping to get into position. When I feel him reaching out to try and deflect the pass, I time my jump perfectly. I leap up, stretching as far as I can and snatching the ball out of the air just beyond his fingers.

The moment my cleats touch the turf, I hit the ground running, my legs pumping as I race toward the end zone. Cleats pound behind me as the cornerback gives chase. He's fast, but I'm faster. I push myself harder when I sense him closing in on me. Just as he's about to make contact, I cut sharply to the left, leaving him grasping at air as I cross the goal line.

The sidelines erupt in cheers, and I spike the ball, feeling like I'm on top of the world as my teammates rush me.

"That's what I'm talking about!" Zion shouts, smacking the top of my helmet.

"Way to kick ass, Sunshine," Colton says, his eyes sparkling with admiration.

"Thanks."

I jog back to the rest of my team and can't resist throwing a smirk at the cornerback who's still picking himself up off the turf. "Not bad for a little girl, huh?" I coo at him. "Maybe you're the one who's in the wrong place."

He growls, clearly not amused by my taunting.

Approaching the bench, I remove my helmet and grab the nearest water bottle, ensuring to quench my thirst before dousing some on my head. Between the humidity and the helmet, I'm sweating profusely and in desperate need of a cold shower.

"Excellent job, Whitlock!" Coach Watson praises. "Keep playing like that and I have no doubt college scouts will seek you out."

Scouts? Meaning, colleges could offer me money to attend their school? I never put much thought past getting my diploma. If I can get into college, I could actually make something of my life. Get a career with benefits, make money. I could really help Grams out with that.

"Thanks, Coach," I say, soaking in his praise.

"That was incredible!" Colton says, coming to stand next to me. "You're such a badass on the field ... I-I-I have no words."

Colton smiling at me, so warm and full of pride, makes butterflies swarm my belly. *Crap!*

"What do you say? We shake things up a bit. Are you a betting woman, Sunshine?"

"Oh, I don't know. You tell me, Golden Boy."

His eyes from head to toe, slowly, as if he's truly taking me in. My cheeks warm before he locks his blue eyes on mine.

"The next touchdown I make, you have to go on a date with me."

"I'm sorry, did you say the next touchdown? Because I don't recall you making a first," I tease him.

"Are you saying I need to make two touchdowns?"

"Yup," I say, putting extra emphasis on the p. "Two touchdowns, and I will go on a date with you."

His long arm extends, his hand waiting to shake mine. "Do we have a deal, Sunshine?"

I place my hand in his, giving it an extra tight squeeze to affirm my seriousness. "Deal. Think you can manage two?"

"Psh, I *know* I can." His eyes sparkle with excitement, and he picks up his helmet and straps up. "You better be ready."

"Yeah, we'll see about that."

The rest of the scrimmage was a tough battle, but we came out on top, winning twenty-seven to twenty-four, with two of the touchdowns coming from Golden Boy himself.

Looks like I have a date to get ready for, and I'm not sure if I'm more annoyed or nervous.

Chapter 15

Colton

Yesterday's win against the Winfield Commanders is nothing compared to getting to take Hollis on a date to get to know the girl who stirs the craziest feelings in me.

Looking in the mirror, I apply some hair wax to my golden locks, styling it to the side just a bit. I apply deodorant and spritz a little extra cologne, making sure I smell good for my sunshine.

Double-checking that I have my wallet, I make my way downstairs to let my parents know I'm heading out for the night.

"Well, don't you look so handsome." My mom's smile is big and bright as she admires me.

"Got a hot date tonight?" Dad asks. "A little dressed up for a night out with the guys."

I'm about to tell him when Thea walks into the room and speaks for me. "Sure does. A hottie who scored one of the touchdowns in yesterday's scrimmage."

Dad's eyes widen. "She plays football?"

"Wide receiver," I say with so much pride. "She's phenomenal too!"

"Oh, so some common interests." Mom smirks. "Is the coach okay with you two seeing each other? I mean, teammates dating could be detrimental to the team if the two of you break up."

I didn't think about that.

"Coach doesn't know. It's more like a first date, get to know each other a bit sort of thing."

"She didn't even want to go on this date," Thea says. "She's only going because bozo here made a bet with her."

I glare at my sister, wishing like hell I had laser vision to fry her to a crisp.

"Oh, honey. You must be smitten if you did all of that. I hope it goes well for you." Mom leans in and places a kiss on my cheek.

"Thanks, Mom."

"Remember your manners and treat her like the young lady she is."

"Yes sir." I salute my father before giving him a hug and heading out the door to go pick up Hollis.

Twenty minutes later, I park out front of the rickety small white house with black shutters. One of them is loose, barely hanging onto the side of the house.

I wonder if I could fix that? ... Focus, Colt!

The nerves are settling in now that I'm here, and I'm getting distracted. I take a moment to breathe and calm my racing heartbeat.

"You've got this. It's just a date with a really pretty girl."

A pretty smoking hot girl who can ball.

Right.

I head up the stoney walkway onto the tiny front porch and knock three times on the black front door. A few moments later, it opens, and I'm greeted by a short elderly woman with white-blonde hair to her shoulders who has the same baby-blue eyes as my sunshine.

"Good evening, ma'am. I'm here to pick up your granddaughter," I say, giving her my best charming smile.

"Oh, stop it! It's Nancy. So nice to see you again, handsome. Please, come on in and make yourself at home." Nancy opens the door wide, gesturing for me to enter.

"Thank you, Nancy. It's nice to see you again too."

I step inside the living room, taking in the cozy atmosphere this time. The walls are adorned with framed photos, many of them showing a younger Hollis with her grandmother. There's a comfortable-looking floral couch and a recliner facing an older model TV. The whole space has a warm, lived-in feel.

"Hollis! There's a handsome young man here for you!" Nancy calls out, then turns with a warm smile and a twinkle in her eye. "Why don't you have a seat? Hollis should be ready any minute now. That girl takes forever to get ready when she actually puts in the effort."

"Grams!" Hollis's voice comes from down the hall, sounding mortified. "I can hear you, you know!"

Nancy smiles and winks at me. "Must be a special occasion."

I take a seat on the edge of the couch, my hands clasped in my lap. "I hope so. I'm really looking forward to our date."

"I think Hollis is too. Though, she won't admit to it. She's been fussing over what to wear for the past hour. I haven't seen her this worked up over a boy since ... Well, ever!"

A flutter of excitement fills me at her words. Maybe Hollis is more interested than she lets on.

"So, Colton," she says, "tell me a bit about yourself. What are your intentions with my granddaughter?"

Before I can answer, Hollis's voice rings out. "Grams! You don't need to interrogate him!"

"Well, where's the fun in that? I'm just looking out for you, Hollipop! It's not like your Uncle Mikey is around to threaten him with gardening shears."

"I can take care of myself, thanks!" Hollis yells back.

Nancy chuckles, so much warmth and love wrapped up in this little woman. The love she has for Hollis just shines through. Meanwhile, I'm fearful of whoever this Uncle Mikey guy is, and why does he have shears?

Clearing my throat, I give the only answer I know to reassure Nancy her granddaughter is in great hands this evening. "Well, ma'am ..." Hollis's grandmother gives me a pointed look. "I mean, uh, Nancy. My plan is to treat your granddaughter with the utmost respect and have her back in time for bed so she is plenty rested for her shift tomorrow."

"Good answer," Nancy says, patting my knee.

Just then, footsteps come down the hall. I turn toward the hallway just as Hollis emerges, and my breath catches in my throat.

Her dark skinny jeans hug her curves perfectly and are paired with a flowing off-the-shoulder top in a deep blue that brings out her eyes. Her blonde hair falls in soft waves around her shoulders, and she's applied a touch of makeup to enhance her natural beauty. She looks stunning, and I'm practically speechless.

"Wow," I breathe out. "You look amazing, Sunshine."

Hollis rolls her eyes, but I catch the faint blush on her cheeks. "You don't need to do that."

"The boy likes what he sees, Hollipop." Nancy walks over to Hollis, taking her hand in hers. "You've got to stop letting your past bleed into your present and future. Take the compliment." Nancy pulls Hollis in, kissing the top of her head.

I watch the two for a moment, analyzing the love and respect that is abundantly there. For once, I'm seeing a side of Hollis I haven't seen before, her guard down completely.

"Ready to go, Hollipop?" I ask, breaking the loving moment. Only, I may regret it with the way Hollis's eyes would murder me if looks could kill.

"You don't get to call me that. That nickname is reserved for Grams and Grams only. You have Sunshine."

"So you like me calling you that, do you?"

"Actually, I find it stupid because I'm the least sunshine-y person to exist."

"Exactly."

Her brows furrow, not quite getting why I keep calling her that.

"Anyway … Grams, I'll be back as soon as I can. If you need me, call me, and I'll make sure Golden Boy gets me back to you, pronto. Do you need—"

Nancy raises her hand, effectively silencing Hollis. "I'm perfectly capable of being home alone. You, my sweet girl, need to go have some fun. Go be a teen for once, will ya?"

"Are you sure?"

"Unless you two want to stay here. I mean, I would love to talk about the latest romance novel I'm reading. There's this scene where the lead lady has two gentlemen penetrating her at the same time—"

"Oh, god. Stop! We're leaving! We're leaving!" Hollis darts toward the front door and leaves just as fast, with Nancy laughing behind her.

"Two men, you say? That sounds like you're in for a fun evening, Nancy."

"Don't I know it." She winks. Her expression morphs from playful to concerning. "Colton, before you go, there's something I think you should know about my granddaughter."

I nod to indicate I'm listening. Anything pertaining to the girl sitting in my car is important, and I want to learn everything there is about her.

"I'm not sure if you noticed, but Hollis can be very standoffish. She's got a lot of trauma from her youth that she hasn't quite worked through. I've been trying to get her to seek help, to work through those emotions. Art therapy wasn't in the budget, therapy costs way too much. It's one of the reasons I pushed her to try out for football. I'm hoping this could be a way for her to channel that aggression she holds onto all the time and let it go. All of that to say this. That girl's been through more than most folks twice her age. She works hard to take care of me, on top of managing good grades in school. She never complains, just puts her head down and does what needs to be done. Be patient with her. Show her that people can mean what they say, and they will stay."

Damn, I hadn't expected all of that, but I'm grateful for Nancy telling me. A moment later, a car's horn blares outside, reminding me that I have plans.

"I promise you, your granddaughter's heart is in good hands." I lean down, giving Nancy a hug to help ease her mind before heading out the door for my first date with Hollis Whitlock.

Hollis

"So where are we going?" It's been a quiet car ride, a clear indication how awkward I am at dating.

"Well, I figured we could play a round of mini golf before we go eat dinner, and then maybe a movie afterward?"

"Isn't that the typical cliché of first dates?" Not that I would know because I don't do dating, but I'm certain that's how they do it in those lame ass teen drama movies.

"I was thinking more along the lines of simple." He shrugs and gives me that big dopey grin of his, but I respond with an eye roll, folding my arms over my chest, then stare out the window.

We finally arrive at Sweets N Swings, the local mini golf course. The way it's designed and set up makes me think of Candyland, but bigger and in 3D.

We approach the associate at the entrance, a young guy who looks to be around our age, with big glasses and a slight wheeze when he speaks. "Welcome to Sweets N Swings, how many will be playing this evening?"

"Just two." Colton holds up two fingers.

"That'll be fourteen dollars," he wheezes.

"Oh, here," I say, reaching into my mini backpack and pulling out the cash I brought with me, ensuring I count out the right amount before handing it to Colton.

Colton's eyebrows furrow. "What are you doing?"

"Paying my portion of the date," I state, as if it wasn't that obvious.

Colton shakes his head, gently pushing my hand away. "That's not how this works, Sunshine. I asked you out, remember? Therefore, I'm paying."

I shake my head. "No way. I don't like owing people anything."

"It's not about owing me," Colton says. "It's about having fun and living a little. My treat."

"Well, I don't need to be treated," I snap, more harshly than I intended.

A flicker of hurt crosses Colton's face, and I immediately feel a twinge of guilt. Taking a deep breath, I try to soften my tone. "Look, I appreciate the gesture, but I'm perfectly capable of paying my own way."

"I know you can. I just wanted to alleviate that worry for you so we can have some fun together."

Torn between my instinct to be self-reliant and the genuine sincerity in Colton's eyes, I reluctantly put my money away. "Fine. But I'm buying my own food later."

Colton grins, looking far too pleased with himself. "We'll see about that."

He turns back to the man running the booth and hands over his money. "Two, please."

The employee hands us our putters and golf balls—mine is bright pink and Colton's is deep blue.

As we make our way to the first hole, I can't help but feel a little out of my element. I've never been on a real date before, let alone played mini golf.

"So, uh, how exactly does this work?" I ask, trying to sound casual.

Colton inhales sharply, his eyes going wide. "You've never played mini golf before?"

I shrug, feeling embarrassed. "Never really had the opportunity."

Never really had the funds either.

His expression softens. "Well, then, allow me to teach you the fine art of putt-putt."

Colton's face lights up as he explains the basics of mini golf. "Okay, so the goal is to get the ball into the hole in as few strokes as possible. You use the putter to gently tap the ball toward the hole, working around any obstacles on the course."

I nod, trying to absorb his instructions.

"The key is to not overthink it," he says. "Just relax and have fun with it."

He demonstrates with his ball, lining up his shot and tapping it smoothly. The blue ball rolls down the artificial turf, curving around a giant lollipop obstacle before dropping neatly into the hole.

"See? Easy peasy." He grins. "Now you try."

I step up to the tee, feeling slightly nervous under Colton's watchful gaze. I try to mimic his stance, gripping the putter awkwardly.

Swinging the putter, I hit the ball with more force than necessary, and it ricochets off the side of the course, bouncing wildly before rolling to a stop nowhere near the hole.

"Shit," I mutter, and my cheeks heat up.

Colton chuckles, but it's not unkind. "Hey, not bad for your first try. The first ones can be a little tricky. You do have a strong swing, which isn't a bad thing. We just need to work on your aim a bit."

He steps up behind me, gently adjusting my grip on the putter, his hands warm over mine. "Loosen up a bit. You're not trying to choke it to death."

"I'm pretending it's your neck for bringing me here to play this stupid game," I say, smirking.

Colton let's out a soft laugh. "Noted. Now here, try holding it like this," he says, his breath tickling my ear. I'm acutely aware of how close he is, the scent of his cologne teasing my senses. My heart rate picks up slightly, and I silently curse my body's reaction to his proximity.

"Now, just focus on the ball and tap it gently." Colton instructs, his voice and hands still guiding me. "You don't need to hit it hard, just give it a little push. It's all about control and precision."

I try to focus on his words and not the warmth of his body behind me. As I attempt to ignore how flustered I am with him so close, I take a deep breath, line up my shot, and tap the ball. This time my ball rolls smoothly down the green, curving around the lollipop obstacle before coming to rest just inches from the hole.

"There you go!" Colton cheers, stepping back. "See? You're a natural."

I can't help the small smile that tugs at my lips at his enthusiasm. "It's not in the hole yet, Goldendoodle. Don't get too excited."

I walk over and easily tap the ball in for my second stroke.

"Not bad. Not bad at all for your first hole." Colton grins.

"Beginner's luck," I say, but I feel a little proud of myself.

"Baby steps, Sunshine. You'll be a pro in no time."

We continue through the course, with Colton offering tips and encouragement along the way. Despite my initial reluctance, I find myself actually enjoying the game. There's something oddly satisfying about the soft thunk of the ball dropping into the hole.

Colton's easygoing nature and playful banter—teasing me when I miss a shot and cheering enthusiastically when I make a good one—help me to relax. Soon we're laughing and ribbing each other over our shots.

By the time we reach the final hole—a tricky shot that requires getting the ball up a small ramp and through a rotating windmill, my stomach rumbles so loudly I think the people across the golf course can hear it.

"Hungry?"

"I'm starving!" I groan. I was so nervous for this date I skipped eating out of fear I would get sick.

"Care to make a bet, Sunshine?" Colton asks, a playful, devilish smile appearing.

"What would you like to wager?"

"If I make this shot, you have to let me pay for both of our dinners. If *you* make this shot, I'll let you pay for your dinner despite how wrong it feels and how upset my parents would be with me for letting that happen."

I extend my hand to shake his. "Deal. You can go first."

"Nervous, are we?"

"Not at all. I just want to see how you will miss so I know what *not* to do." I smirk at him.

Colton steps up to the tee, lining his ball up, then taps it with enough force for it to go forward. The ball moves up the ramp but just misses the opening, bouncing off the windmill blade.

"Dammit!" he mutters, clearly unhappy he missed.

"Hm, not bad. Let me just show you how it should be done," I state as I line up my shot carefully. With just enough force behind the putter, my ball ascends the ramp, glides through the hole at the windmill, and rolls smoothly down the pathway. Just as it nears the hole, the ball slows and drops in. I did it!

Chapter 16

Colton

After Hollis beat me at mini golf, we head to the restaurant I picked for dinner.

Sapori d'Italia—a small Italian restaurant with a romantic atmosphere.

It's my mom's favorite place to eat and a popular choice when my parents have date night, so it was a no-brainer to bring Hollis here and show her she deserves to be treated like a queen. I want her to know I'm willing to tear down the walls she has built up and to give her a chance to see it's okay to let people in.

"Uh, Goldendoodle. Why are we here?" Hollis leans forward, looking out the windshield at the restaurant in front of us.

"This is where we are having dinner. Do you like Italian food?"

"The closest thing I've had to Italian food is pizza and spaghetti. This place looks … expensive. I'm not even dressed appropriately for this place." I don't miss the anxious undertone in her voice.

"You look … amazing. There's no real dress code for this place. I promise. My offer still stands on paying for the both of us—"

"No!" she exclaims before clearing her throat. "No, I won our bet, and it's fair that I stick to it." She releases a breathy sigh, unsure if it's a good or bad sign.

"Come on, Sunshine. Let's go stuff our bellies full of carbs and sauce." I get out and make my way to her side to hold the door, but she's out before I even get to her.

Locking up the car, I reach out, waiting for her to lace her delicate fingers with my long ones. She hesitates for a moment but relents and takes my hand.

Warmth spreads through me as our skin touches, a fluttery sensation taking over in my stomach. I lead us through the double doors up to the hostess stand.

"Party for two," I tell the blonde-haired hostess. The moment she turns around, Hollis mutters something.

"Colton Reynolds. So lovely to see you tonight," Charmaine purrs, a hint of flirtation in her voice. She leans in, attempting to touch my arm, but I step back and pull Hollis in front of me.

"My date and I will be needing a table for two, please."

Charmaine's eyes move slowly toward Hollis, and I don't miss the sneer she gives her. "You?"

"Nice to see you too, Charmin. How are the nails? Did you get them fixed?"

"Sure did. Granted, Daddy wasn't too thrilled he had to drop an extra five hundred so the manicurist could see me that afternoon, troll—"

"Miss Summers, is there a problem seating our guests?" An older gentleman who looks like he could pass for the don of an Italian mob appears.

"Uh, no, Mr. Bianchi. I was just taking them." Charmaine quickly grabs two menus and asks us to follow her into the dining area.

She leads us to a small round table with a pristine ivory tablecloth draped over it and a lighted candle in the center.

I pull out the chair for Hollis, waiting for her to have a seat before scooting her in and taking my place across from her. Charmaine drops the menus onto the table in front of us, clearly not giving two shits about how unprofessional she is being.

"Alexander will be with you momentarily." She goes to step away, but I reach for her arm, halting her. "You want to try that again?"

Charmaine eyes my hand, then glances at me. Her sour face turns seductive, and I quickly release her.

She leans in close, her expensive perfume making my eyes water. "I always knew there was something between us. Why don't you meet me somewhere after you dump the trailer trash off. I get off at nine, and I can show you how a *real* woman can make you feel," she purrs in my ear.

"What you're going to do is back up off me before I call your boss over and tell him how rude and disrespectful you're being not only to me, but my date as well," I grit through my teeth, ensuring she knows how serious I am.

Charmaine slowly backs away, relieving me of her stinky perfume.

"Enjoy your meal," she sneers but not without having a word with Hollis. She leans down, whispers something in her ear, and with a smug smile, walks back to her podium at the front of the restaurant.

Hollis's jaw tightens, and she clenches the tablecloth, gripping it like a lifeline. Before I know what's happening, Hollis stands and storms out of the restaurant, wasting no time.

A young man in a white button-down shirt, black slacks, and a waiter's apron approaches. "Is ... everything okay with your lady?"

"I sure hope so," I mutter. "I'm sorry for wasting your time, but I don't want to hold your table up. Please inform your boss that he needs to consider firing his hostess for harrassing me, as well as being unprofessional and rude toward my girlfriend."

"Yes, sir. I'll be sure to let him know."

"Thank you." With that, I follow Hollis, hoping to still salvage our date and rectify whatever happened.

It doesn't take me long to find her. She's leaning against my car, arms crossed over her chest, staring off as the sun sets, blasting oranges, pinks, and purples.

I approach her cautiously, unsure of her current emotional state. "Hey," I mutter. "You okay?"

She scoffs, not meeting my eyes. "Just peachy."

I lean against the car next to her, close but not touching, allowing her some space so she can process what she's feeling. "Want to talk about what happened in there?"

Hollis keeps her gaze fixed on some distant point, her jaw clenched tight.

"What did Charmaine say to you?" I press, wanting to know what upset her so much.

"It doesn't really matter. It's nothing I haven't dealt with before."

"It matters to me, Sunshine. *You* matter to me."

She turns to look at me, her blue eyes stormy with anger and something else ... Hurt, maybe?

"Look, can we just go? The night's been ruined, and I just want to go home."

"Sure." I nod, unlocking the car. "Of course."

Hollis sighs heavily and slides into the passenger seat.

I start the car but don't pull out of the parking spot yet. "What did Charmaine say to you?" I ask again, knowing I'm probably irritating her by repeating the question, but I *have* to know so I can help her feel better.

Hollis is quiet for a long moment, staring out the window. Just when I think she's not going to answer, she speaks, her voice low and bitter. "She said I should know my place. That girls like me don't belong with guys like you."

Anger flares in my chest. "That's bullshit. Charmaine doesn't know what she's talking about."

"She also told me not to get too comfortable, that you'd realize soon enough that I'm just some trailer trash and go running back to someone more your speed."

What the hell is wrong with that girl?

I squeeze my steering wheel until my knuckles turn white, pissed off at Charmaine's cruel words.

"Hollis, look at me."

I wait until her blazing blue eyes reluctantly meet mine. "You are not trash. Not even close. Charmaine is just a jealous, spiteful person who likes to tear others down to make herself feel better."

Hollis scoffs. "Yeah, well, she's not entirely wrong, is she? I mean, look at me." She gestures to herself. "I live in a rundown house with my grandmother. I work as a waitress and bust my ass to help pay the bills and make sure my grandmother has her life-saving meds so nothing bad happens to her, all while making sure my schoolwork is done and maintaining my grades so I can graduate and get my diploma in hopes of finding a better job after graduation. I-I don't belong here, Colton. In there, with all those fancy people and their fancy clothes. That's not my world."

My heart aches at the vulnerability in her voice. "Hollis, you belong anywhere you want to be. Don't let someone like Charmaine make you feel otherwise."

"It's not just Charmaine. It's ... everything. This whole date. The mini golf, this restaurant. It's all so ..."

"Normal?" I offer with a small smile.

"A pipe dream," she says solemnly.

Before I can open my mouth to say something, she fastens her seatbelt. "I'm ready to go home now, please."

"Okay," I say, my heart deflating that the night is over far sooner than I had planned.

I drive Hollis back to her grandmother's house and walk her to the front door. The moment she goes for the doorknob, I reach out, stopping her.

"Hollis, wait." I grab her hand, holding it in mine, and place it close to my chest. She looks up at me, and ... Wow, am I goner.

Focus!

"I'm sorry tonight didn't go how I had hoped. You didn't deserve to have it ruined, and I would really like it if we could have a do-over. Let me make it up to you."

"I don't know, Colton. Maybe tonight was a sign that I'm not meant to date or have fun. Maybe I'm meant to be a single old woman who has cats or plants."

"Please?" I make my eyes as big as I can and give the poutiest lip, hoping she'll cave.

"Are you seriously giving me puppy eyes? What's next? You're going to roll over, wanting me to rub your belly?"

"Actually ... I think I would be into that."

"Good night, Colton." Hollis attempts to pull away, but I bring her body into my muscular chest, our faces only inches apart.

"I'll beg if that is what it takes for you to go on another date. Let me make it up to you, Sunshine."

Hollis's gaze bounces from my eyes to my lips, and I have to wonder if I should go in for a kiss. How delicious would she taste if we just give in to the chemistry surging between us.

I lean in closer, staring at Hollis's lips. The air between us is charged with electricity. Just as I'm about to close the distance, her eyes widen. For a moment, I think she might let me kiss her. At the last second, she turns her head, and my lips graze her cheek instead.

"Good night, Colton," she whispers, pulling away from me.

I try to hide my disappointment as I step back, giving her space. "Good night, Sunshine. I'll see you at school on Monday?"

She nods, a small smile playing on her lips. "Yeah, see you Monday."

She slips inside, the door closing behind her with a soft click. I stare at the closed door, feeling a mixture of disappointment and determination.

I may not have gotten the kiss I was hoping for, or the entire date, but I'm not giving up. Not by a long shot. Hollis Whitlock is worth fighting for, and I intend to do just that.

Heading back to my car, I'm already planning our next date in my head. This time, I'll make sure it goes better. I'll prove to Hollis that she deserves all the good things in this life. I have to get her to agree to it first, and maybe, just maybe, I'll get that kiss next time.

155

Chapter 17

Hollis

The moment I close the door behind me, I lean against it, letting out a shaky breath. My heart is racing, and I'm not sure if it's from almost kissing Colton or from the emotional rollercoaster this entire evening has been.

"Hollipop? Is that you?" Grams calls from the kitchen.

"Yeah, it's me," I say, pushing off the door.

I find her boiling some chicken noodle soup on the stovetop. She looks up as I enter, her eyes twinkling with curiosity.

"You're home early. How was your date?"

I shrug, plopping down on one of the dining chairs. "It was ... interesting."

Grams raises an eyebrow. "Interesting good or interesting bad?"

"Both? I don't know." I run a hand through my hair, frustrated. "It started off okay. We played mini golf, which was actually kind of fun. I won, by the way. But then ..."

I'm not sure how to explain the disaster at the restaurant without worrying her. She may not look seventy, but the last thing I want to do is to cause her any stress with my problems.

"Then what, sweetheart?"

"He took me to this really nice restaurant, far nicer than anything I've ever been to, and it just reminded me that we're from completely different worlds. We could never work."

Grams ladles the soup into two bowls, then places them on a tray with some crackers and sets them on the dining table to join me. She passes me a spoon and one of the bowls, with a warm smile directed at me.

"How could you ever think that?"

I shrug. "Face it, Grams. He comes from a loving family, and clearly, they're not hurting to get by."

"Let me ask you something. Did he make you laugh?"

"Yeah, a couple times."

"Did you enjoy spending time with him?"

I slurp some soup off my spoon before nodding, a bit shy to verbally say yes.

Grams eyes darken a little, her tone serious. "Did he do anything to make you feel uncomfortable? Get too handsy?"

"The only times he was *handsy*, as you so eloquently put it, was when he showed me how to properly hold a putter and asked to hold my hand into the restaurant."

The soft smile is back, probably relieved nothing sinister happened to her granddaughter.

"Then I don't see anything wrong. He sounds like a complete gentleman." She pats the top of my hand with hers. "I hope he asked for another date."

"Well ... yeah. But I don't know, Grams. Dating seems kind of pointless. When are we going to have any time together when I work, and when I'm not working, there's football practice or games. Not to mention school."

"Correct me if I'm wrong, but doesn't he play football too?"

"Well, yeah. We both play the same position."

"He's a senior at Bellwood?"

"I would hope so. I mean, if he isn't, then I'd be worried why a random guy is walking the halls and eating lunch in their cafeteria ... Ohh. I see what you did there, Grams."

"I don't know what you're talking about," she says, feigning innocence before taking a big slurp of her soup.

"Right. You weren't just reminding me of all the times I would see Colton or be near him in my hectic, busy schedule."

"Again, I have no idea what you're talking about."

Tilting my head, I stare as my grandmother tries to remain the innocent party before a question comes to mind.

"Why do you want me to give Colton a chance so bad? You've met him like twice."

"Because, Hollipop, he reminds me so much of your grandfather when we were that young. I can tell that boy has a good heart and would do right by you. You just need to stop comparing every male to your father. Not everyone is out to hurt you."

"It's not easy for me, Grams." I spin my spoon around in my soup, trying to force down the truth. She's right though. "But I'll try."

"That's all I ever want you to do, sweetheart. Try to open your heart to others. Allow new people to come in, to breathe life into you before you end up being all alone. No one wants to be lonely until their last breath."

After I help Grams clean up the kitchen, I head to my room to change into my pajamas and crawl under my blankets. As I lie there, scrolling through my socials, I think over what Gram said as we ate.

I close out the app and open my text message thread with Colton. My finger hovers over the box before I say, "Fuck it" and send him a message.

Moments later, the little bubbles appear before his message does.

COLTON

Is this your way of telling me yes to a 2nd date?

HOLLIS

Does Sunday work for you or not?

COLTON

It's perfect. I promise, I'll do better.

HOLLIS

and if you don't?

COLTON

I'm sure you have some interesting ways to punish me.

HOLLIS

Oh, you have no idea. So you better be a good boy and make sure it doesn't go to shit.

COLTON

Plz don't say that.

HOLLIS

???

COLTON

The … ya know. Good boy. It … it does things to me. ⌧

It's been almost a week since our date, and Colton has really been laying on the flirting whenever we see each other. The head nods, the winks, and occasionally, the perusal of my body. I play it off like it annoys me, but deep down, I'm secretly enjoying it. He just won't know that.

We just finished up our Thursday afternoon practice, preparing for the first game of the season tomorrow night against the Redland Devils. As I head toward the locker rooms, ready to shower this funk off me before I have to get to work, I'm grabbed by my waist and pulled to the side of the stadium entrance.

"Hey! What the hell do you think you're doing?" I turn, my fist raised and ready to land a punch when a big hand stops me midair.

"Whoa ... it's just me, Sunshine. Calm down."

I smack him across his muscular chest as hard as I can, but I think it caused me more pain than him.

What's he made of? Stone?

"Are you fucking stupid? Don't you know the serious damage I would have rained down on you had you been anyone else? You can't just sneak up on someone and grab them!"

Colton raises his hands. "I'm sorry! I didn't mean to scare you. I just wanted a moment to be with you."

"Why?"

"So I could be close to you." He steps toward me, getting in my space. I take a few steps back, bumping into the rough brick wall, with nowhere to go.

Colton places one of his hands on my waist and the other by my head, then leans in, our noses just barely touching. I'm encased with his scent, mostly sweat but there's an underlying hint of citrus mixed with notes of sea and earth.

"I have been going out of my mind dreaming of your blue eyes gazing up at me and wondering if your lips are truly as soft as they appear."

I swallow the golf-ball sized lump in my throat, my brain fuzzy from being in our haze of lust. I've been thinking about what his lips would feel like on mine.

"Sounds like you should do something about that," I whisper.

"You want me to kiss you, Sunshine?" His eyes dance back and forth between my eyes.

Is he looking for my consent?

"I mean, if you don't want to kiss me, I guess I could go fi—"

Colton presses his velvety soft lips onto mine, claiming me for himself. His hand on my waist grips me, holding me in place while the other cups the side of my face.

When his tongue presses against my lips, I open for him, tasting him.

The kiss deepens, and I forget all about keeping him at a distance. My hands move of their own accord, sliding up his chest and around his neck, pulling him closer. A small moan escapes me as his tongue dances with mine, igniting a fire deep in my core and sending tingles down my spine.

For a moment, I let myself get lost in the sensation. The warmth of his body pressed against mine, the intoxicating taste of his lips, the gentle caress of his fingers on my cheek. It feels so good, so right.

Colton breaks the kiss, both of us breathing heavily as he rests his forehead against mine.

He pulls back slightly to look at me, his blue eyes dark with desire. "I've wanted to do that for so long, Sunshine. And now that I've gotten a taste, I don't know if I'll be able to stop."

He kisses me again, this time with so much passion my lungs are screaming for oxygen. Just as I'm lost in the moment, a loud whistle pierces the air, making us jump apart.

"Hey! No canoodling on school property!" Coach Watson booms from nearby.

Colton looks dazed, his hair mussed where my fingers had been running through it. I can feel the heat in my cheeks and know I must be blushing furiously.

"Sorry, Coach!" Colton calls out, trying to sound nonchalant and failing miserably.

I peek around the corner to see Coach Watson shaking his head, though I swear I catch a hint of amusement in his expression before he turns away. As soon as Coach is out of sight, I duck under Colton's arm and hurry toward the locker room.

"Hey, wait. Where are you going?" Colton calls out.

I turn around to face him as I walk backward. "Sorry, Goldendoodle. I got to hit the showers and freshen up before work. You're more than welcome to join me," I tease.

For a second, he looks like he's going to take me up on what I'm offering, then pain flashes in his eyes and his whole demeanor changes.

"I should probably head out. I've got some homework to take care of, but, uh, I'll text you later, okay?"

"Yeah, sure. If I don't answer right away, I'm at work."

He nods before taking off toward the parking lot.

Am I imagining things, or did he really do a complete one-eighty? I was teasing him, but if I wasn't, is that how he would have responded to me? As much as I'd like to see what's underneath, to feel his body on mine, I can't help but feel a little hurt at his rejection.

The energy inside the stadium is electric as we prepare to take the field against the Redland Devils. The stands are packed with students, parents, and fans decked out in our school's colors of blue and gold. Cheerleaders are revving up the crowd with their chants and stunts while the marching band plays our fight song.

Standing on the sidelines with my teammates, I look around, taking it all in. My first official high school football game. The nerves I had in the locker room have settled as my adrenaline takes over, coursing through my veins, making me ready to run all over the Devils' defense.

Coach Watson gathers us around to give one final pep talk before we take the field. "Alright, Eagles, this is what we've been working toward. You've put in the time, the sweat, the effort. Now it's time to show everyone what you're made of. Play smart, play hard, and most importantly, play as a team. Now let's get out there and show those Devils what Bellwood football is all about!"

We break on "Eagles" and head to the sideline while we wait for the coin toss. Redland will kick off first, giving us the ball first.

"Hollipop!" comes from somewhere behind me.

I turn around, spotting Grams in the front row of the bleachers with her big foam finger in one hand and cow bell in the other. She came prepared to be my number one cheerleader, not wanting to miss my first game. I wave to her before facing the field in time to see Alora catch the ball at the twenty-yard line and blaze down the field before she gets tackled at the Devils' forty-yard line.

"That's what I'm talking about!" Coach Wells shouts, clapping aggressively. As Alora comes to the sideline, they exchange fist bumps. "Way to move the ball down the field, Alora."

"Starting offense, where are you?" Coach Freeman calls out. "I need Reynolds, Weedon, Davis, Palmer, and Mason on the field. Whitlock, Summers, you girls will go out when I say."

"Yes, Coach," we say in unison.

"Lambert snaps the ball. Minor is looking for an opening, and ohh, he's sacked by Justin Saunders. That will be a loss of yards for the Eagles. It doesn't look like a promising start," the announcer calls out.

"C'mon o-line! You've got to make your blocks!" Coach Watson yells, unpleased with our quarterback being taken down.

I sure hope the next play goes better.

"Second and fifteen on the Devils' forty-five-yard line," the announcer calls out. "Myers takes the snap. He's looking downfield. He's got Reynolds open! He throws and ..."

Colton makes the catch, powering forward for a few extra yards before being brought down. *Yes!*

"The pass is complete for a gain of twelve yards. Eagles get the first down!"

Our offensive coach signals to switch out players before the next play.

"Whitlock, Summers you're in," Coach Freeman calls. "Let's see what you two can do." He hollers for Weedon and Davis to get off the field so Corrine and I can take their places.

My heart pounds as I jog onto the field, taking my position as a slot receiver. Corrine lines herself up in the backfield behind Dylan. I look down the line of scrimmage, catching Colton's eye as he lines up wide. He gives me a quick nod and a wink, setting the butterflies off in my stomach. My mind flashes to our kiss yesterday, and I have to shake my head to bring me back to the game.

"Focus," I mutter to myself.

The ball is snapped, and I sprint forward, cutting sharply to the inside. I see Dylan looking my way as I break free from the defender. The ball spirals toward me, time running in slow motion as I reach out, and the pigskin hits my hands. Once I secure it against my body, I turn upfield and take off.

"Whitlock with the catch! She's at the thirty, the twenty, the ten .... Touchdown, Eagles!!!"

The stadium roars as my teammates swarm me, celebrating our team getting the first points on the board.

We jog off the field to allow the kicking team to get the extra point, and Colton is beside me with pride in his eyes. "Damn, Sunshine. You beat me to the first touchdown of the season. Normally, I get the first one."

"Aw, jealous I beat you to it?" I taunt.

"Maybe." He beams.

We head to the bench for water, and our kicker nails the field goal.

"The extra point is good! The score is now Eagles, seven. Devils, zero."

The game is a back-and-forth battle, with teams trading touchdowns. By halftime, we're tied fourteen to fourteen.

As we head to the locker room for halftime, nervous energy is buzzing through the team. Coach Watson gathers us around, his face serious.

"Alright, Eagles, we've got a real fight on our hands, but I know you've got more in you. We need to tighten up our defense and create more opportunities on offense. Whitlock, Reynolds I want to see you two connecting out there. You've both got the speed and skill to break this game open."

Colton and I exchange a quick glance. Despite the awkwardness after our kiss yesterday, on the field, we're in sync. I give him a small nod, determined to make it happen.

As we head back out for the second half, I feel a surge of renewed energy. This is our chance to prove ourselves, to show everyone what we're made of.

The third quarter starts off slow, with both teams' defenses stepping up, but midway through, we finally get our break.

Our defense forces a fumble, and Alora scoops up the ball to run it all the way into the end zone, putting us in the lead again.

"Touchdown, Eagles!" the announcer yells into his mic, adding to the excitement coming from our home side.

Man, I couldn't be prouder to be a part of this team!

After another intense quarter and a missed field goal by the Devils to try and tie up the game, our team gets the win.

The coaches give their postgame speeches and remind us about practice after school on Monday before dismissing us to go home.

Thank goodness, because I've got food and a hot shower with my name on it!

Chapter 18

Colton

The adrenaline from our win is still coursing through my veins as I head to the locker room. My teammates are all buzzing with excitement, recapping the best plays and celebrating our victory. As I change out of my uniform, I can't help but replay Hollis's amazing touchdown catch in my mind. The way she moved on the field, her determination to get the next first down—it was incredible to watch.

I'm pulled from my thoughts by Jeremiah clapping me on the back. "Great game, man! That last touchdown pass was clutch."

"Thanks." I grin. "Couldn't have done it without the whole team though. Everyone really stepped up tonight."

"For real," Rhett chimes in. "Those girls really proved themselves out there. Alora's fumble recovery was insane."

"And did you see Hollis burn that cornerback on her touchdown?" Anthony adds. "Girl's got some serious wheels."

At the mention of Hollis, my stomach flutters. "Yeah, she was amazing," I say, trying to keep my tone casual.

Zealand gives me a knowing look. "Is someone catching more than just feelings?"

"What? No. I mean ... I don't know."

"Didn't you guys have a first date?" Jeremiah questions. "How did it go?"

"It started out great, but when we went to dinner, things went south."

"What do you mean?" asks Zealand.

"We walked into the restaurant, and Charmaine was the hostess." I check around for my quarterback, Dylan, not wanting him to overhear what I'm about to share with my friends, then lower my voice. "Charmaine was hitting on me in front of Hollis, acting as if she wasn't there. I told her she needed to stop. Then after she sat us down, she was being flirty before I told her I would report her to her boss. Before she walked off, she said some fucked-up shit to Hollis that I couldn't hear, upsetting her, and I had to take her home."

"Man, someone needs to tell Dylan to dump her skanky ass," Anthony says too loudly.

Rhett smacks him on the back of his head. "Would you shut the hell up? You want the whole locker room to hear you?"

"I wouldn't count on those two lasting long. Have you guys seen the way he looks at our new defensive end? What's her name?" Jeremiah snaps his fingers.

"Maisie?" Anthony asks. "The one with all those delectable curves?"

"Yes! Maisie!" He snaps. "You guys, next time they are around each other, just watch them. You'll see what I'm talking about."

"Well, ladies, I'd love to stay and gossip, but I've got to get home. Catch you guys on Monday!"

"Wait ... no Sunday afternoon gaming?"

"Sorry, Anthony. I've got plans with Hollis tomorrow."

No way in hell am I canceling them either.

I've got everything set up and ready to go for my date with Hollis, praying it goes way better than the last one. I don't know if she will be up for another one if this one fails too. As I head into the kitchen for a bottle of water, my phone alerts me to a new message.

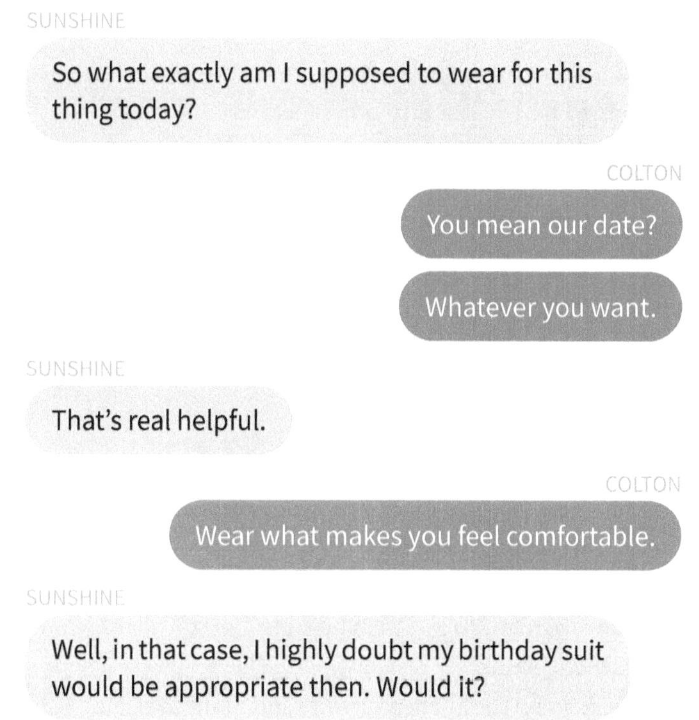

Water shoots out of my mouth and nose, spraying all over the kitchen island.

Jesus! Do not picture her naked, do not picture her naked. The last thing you need is a boner.

A little warning next time, Sunshine. I nearly choked to death and now I've got a mess to clean.

Choking and messes. Sounds like my birthday suit is the right choice.

My dick hardens in my shorts, and I don't have time to take a cold shower. Guess I have to resort to other methods.

"Puppies ... kittens ... haunted houses ..." I mutter, my eyes squeezed tightly, trying to think of anything that will help get rid of my boner.

"Colt, sweetie, have you seen my car ..."

I quickly move to stand behind the island, hiding my tented shorts from my mother's eyes so I don't scar her for life.

"... keys. Honey, are you okay?"

"Just peachy, Mom," I grit out.

"Is your stomach upset?"

"No, no. Just a little bit nervous."

"Oh, I'm sure it will go well. Just be your sweet, charming self and you won't have anything to worry about."

"Thanks, Mom."

She walks toward me to give me a hug, but I'm still not down yet. Oh, god, think, Colt. Think!

I spot her keys on the kitchen counter and point to them. "Your keys are by the coffee maker!"

"Oh, thank goodness!" My mom sighs. "I swear I feel like I'm losing my mind everyday. Sometimes, I despise getting older."

"You're still youthful and beautiful to me, Mom."

Mom clasps her hands over her heart, her lips slightly pouted. "You're the sweetest, you know that?"

"You and Dad raised me this way."

"Alright. Well, I'm off to the store to get stuff for tonight's dinner. Your dad should be back a little later from golfing with his buddies, and Thea should be home from Jules's house before supper. If you need anything, just text or call me."

"You got it."

"Have fun, but not too much fun, if you know what I mean. I'm not ready to be a grandmother just yet."

At the mention of grandmother, I freeze, grief hitting me right in my chest, and my tented shorts are no longer a problem.

"Ahem. Uh, no need to worry about that."

"Enjoy your date," she singsongs on her way out the door. Once the door latches behind her, I relish the silence of the house.

Bzzz. Bzzz.

I grab my phone to find a message from Hollis.

SUNSHINE

Ready whenever you are.

Ah. Perfect timing.

COLTON

On my way now. See you soon, Sunshine.

I pull up in front of Hollis's house to her pacing back and forth outside.

Is she more nervous about this than I am? She seemed way more confident in her texts.

I get out of my car, the door shutting gaining her attention.

"You okay, beautiful?" I ask, my eyes looking over her from head to toe. Loose, dark distressed jeans accentuate her small waist. A tiny white spaghetti strapped tank with a V-cut showcases ample cleavage and her toned stomach, making me groan internally.

"Yeah. Yeah I'm fine." She stops pacing once I'm standing in front of her. "I'm used to moving around because of my job, so I can't really stand still. Ya know?"

"If you say so." I smirk. "Are you ready to go? Do you need to let your grandmother know you're leaving?"

"Grams is nextdoor playing Dominoes with Betty. I'll just check in with her a little later, so I'm all yours."

All mine? I kind of like the sound of that.

"Whose house is this?" Hollis asks when I pull into the driveway of the blue colonial house.

"Mine." I smile at her. "Well, my family's. My parents are out, and my sister is still at her best friend's house, so we have the place to ourselves. I figured we could just hang out, eat snacks, and chill. Is that okay?"

She stares out the windshield, looking at my house. "I could honestly use a chill day, so yeah. It sounds good to me."

She turns to me with a sparkle in her eyes and a soft smile on her lips, a look you don't see often from her. This is already starting off on the right track.

We head inside, and I give her a quick tour of the first floor, leaving our little setup for last.

"The final stop of your Reynolds home tour is where you will be spending the next few hours with yours truly."

I pull the french doors open, revealing one of my favorite places in the whole house.

In the center of the room sits a light-gray sectional surrounded by eggshell-white walls. Two rectangular windows allow for enough natural lighting to fill the room on a sunny day. Between them is a mini fridge stocked with our favorite drinks and a shelf beside it is full of snacks.

Across from the couch, attached to the wall, is our flat screen TV with shelves underneath to store our gaming consoles and video games.

"My sister and I call this the hangout room. It's supposed to be an office, but my parents had no need for it, so they created this space for us. It used to be a playroom until we outgrew our toys and created a space for us to hang out with our friends."

"It sounds like you have amazing parents." She smiles, but it doesn't reach her eyes.

Hollis walks around the space taking in every inch of the room until her gaze locks onto the wall opposite the TV. String lights dangle from the ceiling to the floor with small pictures held up by tiny clothes pins hanging off them.

She moves forward, her eyes darting from one picture to the next, taking in every single face.

"Friends?"

"Most of them, yeah. Thea's friends. My friends. Family is among them as well. Like this one"—I point to a picture of two young twin boys—"those are Payson's twin brothers. Then you have Sadie, Payson's girlfriend. I give it a few years for Payson to pop the question. Those two are endgame."

"Who's this?" My eyes follow to where her finger is pointing. My stomach knots, unease settling in as I look at the picture of Stacey and me.

Stacey's head rests on my shoulder with me looking stupidly like a lovesick puppy at her. The photo was taken the night I told Stacey I loved her for the first time, a time when I thought she would be my person, the one I saw my future with. Turns out I had it all wrong.

"That would be Stacey, my ex-girlfriend. I-I didn't think it was still up there." I snatch the photo off and toss it into the trashcan in the corner.

The room is silent, and I curse that this may have ruined our second date night. Is this a sign that maybe Hollis and I are just not meant to date?

Don't be ridiculous. Just redirect her attention to what you have planned. Focus on her.

"So ..." I clap my hands, causing Hollis to jump a little. "For this chill date, you have two options. Option one, we stream movies and watch whatever you want while snuggled up with each other."

"And option two?"

I hold up two game controllers, smiling like a crazed person. "We video game."

"You got any fighting games?" One of her blonde eyebrows arches, as if to challenge me.

"Mortal Kombat, Street Fighter, UFC, or wrestling? Lady's choice."

"Really? Well ... in that case, let's play some UFC. Just don't start crying when I'm kicking your ass!" She plops her perfectly round booty onto the couch while I get the game ready.

"Are you challenging me, Sunshine?"

"I thought you liked being challenged?"

I grin and hand Hollis a controller, then settle onto the couch next to her, close enough that our thighs are just barely touching. "Oh, I do. Just don't say I didn't warn you when I wipe the floor with you."

"Big talk for someone who's about to get their ass handed to them. Be prepared to get knocked out in the first round." Hollis smirks as she scrolls to pick her fighter.

We select our fighters, and the match begins. Hollis proves to be a formidable opponent, her fingers flying over the controller as she unleashes a flurry of punches and kicks. Her competitive side comes out, and she trash-talks and celebrates each successful move, but I've spent countless hours playing this game with my sister and friends, and my experience shows.

"Ha! Take that, Goldendoodle!" She boasts when her fighter lands a kick to my head.

I get in a few good combos of my own, but Hollis ultimately wins the first round. Her eyes are bright with excitement as she turns to me with a triumphant grin.

"Ready to admit defeat yet?"

"Not a chance," I reply, unable to keep the smile off my face. "Best two out of three?"

After a few intense rounds, I emerge victorious this time. "Yes!" I pump my fist in the air. "Told you I'd win."

Hollis narrows her eyes at me. "Best three out of four?"

"You're on, Sunshine."

We play for the next hour, trash-talking and laughing as we trade wins. It's the most relaxed I've seen Hollis since ... well, ever. Her guard is down, a playful glint in her eyes as she celebrates each victory. This was definitely the right call for our second date.

During an intense match, Hollis leans closer, her eyes focused intently on the screen. I can't help but be distracted by her proximity, the scent of her shampoo teasing my senses. Taking advantage of my momentary lapse in focus, Hollis lands a devastating combo, knocking my fighter out cold.

"Yes!" Hollis jumps up, doing a little victory dance. "Ha! I got you!!"

As she continues to celebrate her win, I'm captivated by the way her whole face lights up when she smiles. It's a rare sight, and I want to see it more often. I can't even be mad about losing when she looks this happy.

I laugh, tossing my controller aside in mock defeat. "Alright, alright. You win this round, Sunshine."

Hollis turns with a smug grin. "Told you I'd kick your ass."

"Yeah, yeah. You got lucky," I tease.

"Oh, please, I totally owned you." She laughs, shoving my shoulder lightly.

"That you did." I laugh. "Clearly, I underestimated you. I bow to your superior gaming skills." I raise my hands and bow a few times.

"A mistake you won't make again, I hope," she says, her eyes twinkling with mischief.

"Never," I promise solemnly, though I can't keep the smile off my face.

She plops back down on the couch closer to me. "So, what's my prize?"

As I turn to face her, our eyes meet, and suddenly, I'm acutely aware of how close we are. "What did you have in mind?"

We fall into a comfortable silence, the game's menu music playing softly in the background. Hollis bites her lower lip, her eyes flicking down to my mouth before meeting my gaze again. The air between us is charged with electricity, much like that night on her porch.

"I have a few ideas," she murmurs.

The playful atmosphere shifts, tension crackling between us. My gaze drops to her lips, remembering how soft they felt against mine when we kissed.

"Hollis," I whisper, leaning in slightly, giving her time to pull away. "I'm really glad you agreed to give this another shot."

Her breath catches, her blue eyes wide with a flash of vulnerability before she quickly masks it. I think she might pull away, but then she surprises me by closing the distance between us.

Our lips meet in a soft, tentative kiss. It's gentle at first, a stark contrast to our heated kiss by the stadium. I cup her face with one hand, deepening the kiss as she sighs against my mouth.

She shifts closer, her fingers tangling in my hair, and the kiss grows more passionate. I wrap my arm around her waist, pulling her flush against me onto my lap and reveling in the feeling of her body against mine. My dick hardens, and I have no doubt she feels it. She rubs her core over my bulge, a small moan escaping her and sending a jolt of desire through me.

When we finally break apart, we're both breathing heavily. Hollis rests her forehead against mine, a small smile playing on her lips.

"Me too," she mutters.

Her hand slides down my stomach, her nails leaving goose bumps in their wake, and inches closer to the top of my basketball shorts.

As her fingers move beneath my waistband, I grab her wrist, stopping her. "What are you doing?"

"I want to make you feel good," she says, her voice husky and full of lust. God, the way she says it has my dick ready to tear through my shorts.

Not realizing I released her wrist, her small hand wraps around my cock and strokes my aching erection, eliciting a moan from me. "Don't you want me to make you feel good?"

My brain is caught up in a lust-filled haze, not sure how to respond to her.

"Y-y-yess," I moan when her thumb brushes over the head of my penis, swiping the precum and massaging it into the tip.

"Good boy," she whispers, and I swear on mother earth, more precum leaks out.

Hollis pulls my cock out of my shorts, getting a better angle to stroke me. My balls tighten, and I'm certain I'm about to bust a load all over myself and her hand.

Stacey flashes in my head, the memory of a time we were in this very predicament, abruptly pulling me from the haze and back to reality.

I can't put myself in another situation like that again.

"Hollis, wait," I gasp out, gently grasping her wrist to still her movements. As much as my body is screaming at me to let her continue, I know we need to slow things down. "We should stop."

Confusion flashes across her face, quickly replaced by hurt. She pulls her hand away and moves off my lap. "I'm sorry, I thought ... Never mind. I should go."

"No, please don't," I say, keeping my arm around her waist to stop her from leaving. "I want you, Hollis. God, do I want you, but ... I don't want to rush into anything physical before we really know each other. You're something special to me, Sunshine, and I really want to do this right."

Hollis stares at me for a long moment, as if trying to decipher if I'm being truthful. Finally, she nods slowly. "Okay. So, what now?"

I smile softly, tucking a strand of hair behind her ear. "Now we keep getting to know each other. Maybe watch a movie? And if you're up for it, I'd really like to take you out on a proper date next weekend."

A small smile tugs at her lips. "I'd like that."

Just as our lips are about to touch, the sound of the front door slamming echoes through the house followed by my sister's voice.

"Colton? You home?" Thea calls out.

We spring apart, and Hollis smooths down her hair while I tuck myself back into my shorts.

"Yeah, in here!" I call back, my voice slightly hoarse.

Thea appears in the doorway a moment later, her eyes widening slightly when she sees Hollis. "Oh, hey! I didn't realize you had company."

"Uh, yeah. Thea, you remember Hollis, right?" I say, trying to sound casual.

"Of course! How are you?" Thea asks brightly.

"I'm good, thanks," Hollis replies, her cheeks still slightly pink.

"Cool, cool." Thea nods, her eyes darting between us with a knowing smirk. "Well, Mom just pulled in and could use a hand with the groceries."

"Okay, I'll be there in a second," I say.

As soon as Thea disappears, Hollis stands up abruptly. "I should probably get going," she says, not quite meeting my eyes. "I'm ready whenever you are."

"Hey ..." I reach for her hand and pull her back down onto the couch beside me. "You don't have to go just yet. Why don't you stay for dinner? My mom's making her famous lasagna."

Hollis hesitates, and I can see the walls starting to go back up. "I don't know, Colton. I should probably get home to Grams ..."

"Come on, Sunshine. It's just dinner. I promise my family won't bite, and you can call your grandmother to check in on her."

She looks at me for a long moment before sighing. "Okay, fine. But only if you let me help clean up afterward."

"Deal." I grin, pulling her in for another kiss.

Chapter 19

Colton

After I help my mom with the groceries and inform her Hollis is joining us, I return to the hangout room where Hollis and I watch a movie until dinner is ready.

The sound of laughter drifts from the kitchen as I lead Hollis down the hallway. My mom's voice carries over the others', regaling everyone with some funny story from her day. As we approach, Hollis tenses beside me.

"Hey." I give her hand a reassuring squeeze. "It's just dinner. You've got this."

She takes a deep breath and nods, squaring her shoulders. "Right. Just dinner with my ... whatever you are and his family. No big deal."

I chuckle at her phrasing. "Whatever I am, huh? We'll have to figure that out soon."

We enter the kitchen to find my family gathered around the island. Mom's at the stove putting the finishing touches on her lasagna while Dad and Thea set the table. They all look up as we walk in.

"Well, hello there!" Mom says brightly, wiping her hands on a dish towel. "You must be Hollis. I'm Charlotte, Colton's mom. It's so nice to finally meet you!"

"It's nice to meet you too, Mrs. Reynolds," Hollis says.

"Oh please, call me Charlotte," Mom insists, coming over to give Hollis a warm hug. Hollis stiffens before awkwardly patting my mom's back.

"This is my dad, Richard," I say as Dad steps forward with a friendly smile.

"Nice to meet you, sir," Hollis says, shaking his hand.

"Please, Richard is fine. We're glad you could join us for dinner."

"And you've already met my sister, Thea."

Thea gives a little wave. "Hey again."

"Alright, everyone, grab a seat," Mom says, carrying the steaming lasagna to the table. "Dinner's ready!"

We all take a seat around the table, with Hollis sitting next to me. Mom pulls out all the stops, serving up generous portions of her homemade lasagna with garlic bread and a Caesar salad. As we eat, I can feel the nervous energy coming from Hollis.

"So, Hollis," my dad says between bites, "Colton tells us you're quite the football player. That touchdown in last night's game was impressive."

Hollis blushes, swallowing a bite of lasagna before answering him. "Thank you, sir. "

"I love that there are so many more girls this year on the team," my mom chimes in. "It's about time girls got the chance to show what they can do on the field."

"Same!" Thea exclaims. "I mean, have you seen Maisie on defense? She's a beast!"

"All the girls are impressive," Hollis adds. "They each definitely bring their own talent to the team."

"Well, I'm looking forward to the next game. I'll have to make a fan sign just for you, Hollis."

"You really don't have to do that."

"Nonsense! I want to!"

Thea leans in closer to Hollis. "Just a tip of info for you. Once my mom has her mind made up, there's no telling her no. She's going to be your biggest fan in the stands, next to Colton's. Maybe bigger since you play better than him."

Hollis quietly laughs, but me? I'm a bit offended.

"Hey! You better take that back!"

"We know it's true. Hollis has more talent than you, if last night's game was any indication."

"Alright, that's it!" I jump from my spot and go toward my sister, who bolts from her seat before I reach her. We chase each other around the table like we used to do when we were little.

"Alright, you two. Settle down and park your butts!" Mom commands, her tone somewhat serious. "It's dinner time. Chase each other when you're done."

"But mom—" I whine.

"No buts, Colton Reid. Sit down and eat your food," mom demands, and I listen to my mother.

"Thank you," my mother says once the two of us are seated again. "That's no way to act when there is a guest in our house." Mom glares at Thea, then me before softening her gaze on Hollis.

"So sorry for the behavior of my children. I'm sure you get it though with your siblings?"

Hollis tenses and her eyes gloss over, as if she is about to cry.

"Excuse me," she whispers, quickly wiping her mouth and storming down the hallway. A moment later, the front door opens and slams.

The table is quiet, my parents and sister looking at each other confused.

"Did I say something wrong?" my mom asks, a hint of guilt in her voice.

"No, Mom, you didn't. I think family is just a sensitive topic for her."

"Oh. I had no idea. Maybe I should go talk to her?" My mom stands, but I stop her.

"Let me go talk to her. You guys finish dinner," I say before going outside, hoping like hell Hollis hasn't gotten too far away.

As soon as I'm outside, I spot her walking down the street, her arms crossed over her chest.

"Hollis!" I shout as I run after her. "Hollis, wait!"

I race after her, her pace picking up the moment I call out to her.

As soon as I catch up, I reach for her arm. As if sensing me, she jerks her arm to the side, dodging me, and walks even faster.

This time, I jog until I'm within reach and grab her waist, pulling her into me.

"Get off of me, Colton!" she shouts, but I refuse to let her go, knowing she's upset. Turning her around so we are face-to-face, I see tears streaming down her cheeks, tinged black from her mascara.

"What happened back there, Sunshine?"

"It was nothing."

"If it was nothing, then why did you just abandon the table and storm out? Why are you crying? You wouldn't be crying if it was nothing."

"You wouldn't get it." She stares off into the distance, not wanting to look at me.

I reach for her chin, and she attempts to move it away, but I grab it and guide it 'til we make eye contact.

"Then explain it to me so I do get it. Help me understand what it is you're going through so I can be here for you. All I want is for you to let me in."

She stares into my eyes, nostrils flaring. I see the hurt and turmoil, and when I think she isn't going to say, I release her.

"Look, if you don't want to tell me, that's fine. But I think I deserve to know why you just up and left, making my mom feel guilty that she somehow said something to hurt you. The last thing my mother ever wants to do is hurt some—"

"Do you know why I keep people out?" Hollis finally breaks her silence.

I shake my head, allowing her to express herself, wanting to understand her.

"I don't let anyone in because I'm afraid if I do, if I allow someone the chance to know me, the *real* me, they'll end up leaving me just like everyone else in my life."

My brows pinch together. "What are you saying?"

She takes a moment to herself before she speaks again. "My mom was married to another man when she had an affair with my dad. From what I know, her husband was a player, and she caught him a few times with different women. She was hurt, and my dad, who happened to be best friends with her husband, comforted her. One thing led to another, and I was the byproduct of said affair. She left her husband for my dad, thinking that she would finally have her happily ever after. But then my dad got hurt, a career-ending injury, and he spiraled so bad that he developed a gambling and drinking problem."

"Is that why you reacted the way you did when I was hungover?"

"It triggered me, I won't deny that." She glances over at me. "Sorry for being such a bitch to you that day."

"It's okay. It actually worked in my favor."

"How so?"

"It drew me to you." I shrug. "Your feisty temper is actually kind of hot."

She lets out scoff, the tension dissipating a bit. "You're weird."

"I prefer the term charming." I wiggle my brows, earning me a beautiful smile. "So, what happened with your mom?"

She releases a sigh. "My mom was heartbroken seeing the second man she loved become a stranger. He would disappear for a while, leaving her to raise me by herself, and I guess she was tired of it. All I know is one day I'm a five-year-old little girl going to grandma's house for what I thought was for the summer, only it ended up being permanent. I have no clue where my mother is or what she's doing with her life. All I know is, she left me with no intention of coming back."

Her jaw clenches, and there's pain in her voice. She's been abandoned by the two people who brought her into the world. No wonder she's always got her defenses up.

"Seeing your family like that, how you guys are with each other? I didn't have that. I don't have siblings to pick on, loving parents to show up for me or prepare amazing home cooked meals that we eat together around the dinner table." Hollis uses her arm to brush away a few tears that escaped her eyes. "You have no idea how fortunate you are."

"I'm so sorry, Sunshine," I say. "Come here." I pull her into me and wrap my arms around her. She hesitates, but then her arms surround me, and I just squeeze her, putting all the comfort I can into the hug.

I hold her close, allowing her to feel what she needs to feel. My heart aches for her, for the little girl who was abandoned and the walls she's built up to protect herself.

"I hope you know that even though you don't have that family, you have people who care about you," I say, still holding her close. "Your grandmother loves you fiercely. The team has your back. And I ..." I pause, not wanting to overwhelm her with too much too soon. "I'm here for you too, Hollis. Whatever you need."

She pulls back slightly to look at me, her eyes shimmering with unshed tears. "Why? Why do you care so much?"

I cup her face, wiping away a stray tear with my thumb. "Because you're worth caring about, Sunshine. I see how strong you are, how hard you work. You've been through so much, but you keep pushing forward. It's inspiring."

Hollis looks down, shaking her head slightly. "I'm not … I'm just surviving."

"Hey," I say, tilting her chin so she meets my eyes again. "You're doing more than surviving. You're thriving. Look at how well you're doing in school, on the team. You're amazing, Hollis."

She stares at me for a long moment, as if searching for any sign of insincerity. Finally, she lets out a shaky breath. "I'm not used to this. People caring about me. Opening up. It's … scary."

"I know, but I'm not going anywhere, okay? You can trust me."

Hollis nods slowly. "Thank you," she whispers, her blue eyes still watery.

Leaning down, I press a soft kiss to her forehead. "Anytime, Sunshine."

We stand there for a moment, my hands resting lightly on her waist. "Do you want to go back inside? My mom's probably worried sick about you."

Hollis hesitates, biting her lip. "I don't know if I can face them after running out like that. I kind of made a scene."

"Trust me, they'll understand. And if you're not comfortable, we can always call it a night. No pressure."

She takes a deep breath, seeming to steel herself. "No, I … I think I'd like to go back. If that's okay?"

"Of course it's okay." I smile, taking her hand in mine. "Come on, Sunshine. Let's go finish that lasagna before Thea eats it all."

As we walk back to the house, I give her hand a gentle squeeze. "Thank you for sharing that with me, Hollis. I know it couldn't have been easy."

She glances at me, a vulnerability in her eyes that I haven't seen before. "Thank you for listening."

When we reenter the house, my family looks up from the table, concern evident on their faces.

My mom immediately stands. "Oh, Hollis, sweetheart. I'm so sorry if I said anything to upset you."

Hollis shakes her head. "No, Mrs. Reynolds ... uh, Charlotte. You didn't do anything wrong. I just ... needed some air. Sorry about that."

My mom's expression softens. "There's no need to apologize. We're just glad you're okay."

"Why don't we sit back down and finish dinner?" my dad suggests, trying to ease the tension. "The lasagna's still warm."

We retake our seats, and I'm relieved to see Hollis actually take a bite of food. The conversation resumes, but this time my family is careful to keep things light, sharing funny stories, mostly the embarrassing ones involving me. As the meal progresses, Hollis slowly relaxes. She even laughs at one of my dad's terrible jokes, which is a miracle in itself.

By the time we've finished dinner, our bellies stuffed, Hollis and I excuse ourselves so I can take her home before it gets too late.

I walk her to her front door, the epitome of the gentleman my parents raised me to be.

"Got to say, I enjoyed spending time with you today. Just you and you with my family."

"Even the part when I ran out on them like some kind of drama queen," she mutters.

I lift her face to look at me. "No one saw it that way, I promise you. You're allowed to feel those feelings, Hollis. It's what makes you human."

"You're ..."

"What?" I ask, wanting to hear what she has to say. "Handsome? Funny? The best football player on the team?"

Hollis smacks my chest before letting out a giggle. "No! You are not the best football player because that title belongs to me."

"So you think I'm funny and handsome?"

Hollis shoves me the best she can, but I don't budge. She makes another attempt, but I grab her and pull her into me, wanting her close, not ready to say good night just yet.

"You're not denying those things, so it must be true," I say.

"Whatever." Hollis rolls her eyes and shakes her head. "Thank you for today, Colton. I really enjoyed myself with you."

"Does this mean you'll go out with me again next weekend?"

She pretends to think about it for a moment. "I suppose I could pencil you in," she says with mock seriousness before breaking into a grin.

I laugh, leaning in to kiss her good night. It's a soft, sweet kiss full of promise for what's to come. As we pull apart, I'm fighting against everything to walk away from her.

"Good night, Colt," Hollis says before walking through her door and gently closing it behind her.

"Good night, Sunshine." Once I hear the lock on the door, I head back to my car on cloud nine.

Chapter 20

Hollis

The next few weeks go by in a blur, or at least that is how it feels when you are constantly on the go day in and day out.

We're halfway through September, and classes are in full swing. Practices have been kicking my ass, I've been battling it out on the field with my teammates once a week, and I'm working as many hours as my boss will let me between it all.

Colton and I try to make time for us when we can, squeezing in quality time with each other in my chaotic life. I'm not sure how he tolerates my busy schedule, but he finds any way he can to make sure we get some alone time.

Lately, he's ingraining himself into my thoughts. Now I think of him when I wake up and before I go to bed. When I'm not with him, I sort of miss him and feel like I'm anxiously waiting for the next time I get to see him and spend time with him.

God, what is this boy doing to me?

He isn't like anyone I've met. The patience, the chivalry and how understanding he is with me ... How did I end up with someone like him?

Everything with him is great. The only part of our relationship, although we never officially stated we were a couple, is that he won't go past kissing with me despite me initiating a few times.

Every time I make a move to go further, he always stops me, telling me he doesn't want to rush things. I can respect that, and I never guilt him or force him to do anything he isn't comfortable doing, but is it weird that I'm wanting to be more intimate and he isn't? Is something wrong with me?

Sure, I've had a few one-night stands in my past, but that was before Colton showed me someone could care about me the way he does.

I've been opening myself up to him, showing him pieces of me I showed no one before, and if I'm being honest with myself, I may even be falling in love with him.

Is it scary to admit that to myself? Fuck yes, because loving someone means the chances of it not working out, and the pain of that heartbreak would shatter me, and I'm afraid what a broken Hollis would look like. I can't help but feel like Colton is worth the risk.

My phone buzzes with a text, pulling me from my thoughts.

COLTON

> Hey Sunshine, you free tonight? I was thinking we could grab dinner and watch a movie at my house?

I smile at his nickname for me. At first it annoyed me, but it's slowly growing on me.

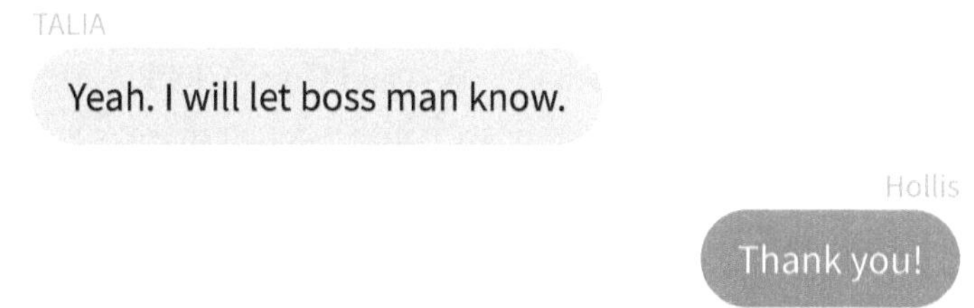

It's a bye week for our team this weekend, and I had Mr. Munson put me on the schedule to work the Friday dinner shift to close. This was before things between Colton and me grew to what it is now.

I quickly shoot a text to Talia, asking her if she would be able to switch my shift tonight for her shift tomorrow.

I pull up my text thread with Colton to let him know I'm available for this evening.

Grabbing my backpack, I close my locker and head to the student parking lot, excitement coursing through me at getting to spend Friday evening with the boy I'm falling for.

I pull into Colton's driveway around five o' clock after I went home from school to take a head-to-toe shower and figure out what the hell to wear.

Oh, God. I've turned into one of those girls who worries how she will look for a guy. Only, Colton isn't just some guy. He's ... special.

Tonight, I decided to step out of my comfort zone and surprise Colton. I chose a short blue floral dress with thin straps that tie on the shoulders, and paired a white long-sleeve top underneath with my black and white Converse.

I even went the extra mile to pull my hair halfway up and added a cute ivory bow to accessorize it, leaving the rest of my hair in loose curls.

The door opens as I'm about to knock, and Colton, looking as handsome as ever, stands before me with his wavy hair messy, a white muscle tee showcasing his mouthwatering biceps, and baby-blue shorts.

My panties dampen just looking at him. *Maybe tonight we can finally cross that line I've been wanting to cross.*

"Wow ... you look ... Wow." Colton's gaze takes in every inch of me. "You are stunning, Sunshine."

"You look good yourself," I say, checking him out the same way he did me.

"I'd look good on you," he whispers, and I bite my lip to muster the groan that wants to escape my mouth. My cheeks warm and my panties dampen a little more at the mere thought of his body on mine.

Dear god, Hollis! Get a grip! You're like a cat in heat!

"Don't bite your lip, baby. I want to do that." He smiles, pulling me into him until my front presses with his. His thumb tugs my bottom lip, and I don't miss the opportunity to suck it in my mouth.

His eyes flash with want, and I silently pray he takes the hint of where I want things to go.

Colton takes his thumb from my mouth before claiming my lips with a hot, scintillating kiss.

His hand gradually slides down my back toward my ass, then squeezes, a groan escaping his lips.

A car alarm sounds, making us break apart, my heart racing at the noise.

"You've got to be kidding me," Colton mutters, his eyes looking off in the distance.

"What?" I turn, trying to see what he's looking at.

"It's my nosey neighbor, Mrs. Garrett." He spins me toward the blue colonial next door. He leans over, his mouth beside my ear sending shivers down my spine. "See the big bay window and how the curtain is pulled to the side?"

I squint, as if that will help me see any better. "Yeah?" I look a little harder before I finally see what, or should I say who, he is waving at.

An elderly woman is shooting daggers in our direction, her car's lights going off in her driveway. Obviously someone wasn't a fan of our little public display of affection.

I raise my hand and shoot up my middle finger, sticking my tongue out, giving her a visual representation of how I feel about her nosey ass ruining our moment. The car's alarm stops, and the old woman quickly disappears out of the window.

"I hope that doesn't come back to bite me on the ass," Colton says, more to himself than me.

Turning around, I grab his hand and lead us inside, ready to forget nosey granny and spend this evening with my man. "If she didn't like you groping my ass, she shouldn't have been watching. Now, c'mon, big fella. I've missed you and I'm starving."

Colton follows, wrapping his arms around my waist the moment the door shuts behind him and pressing a kiss to the side of my neck before he breathes me in. "Mmm ... I love the smell of Sunshine."

"If you keep doing that, I'm going to have my way with you," I tease him. Colton pulls away, and I'm not sure if I should feel hurt by his response. Maybe his family is home?

He grabs my hand and leads me straight for the room where we spent our second date. This time, the curtains are closed, darkening the room from the evening summer's rays, the only light coming from the twinkling string lights above.

On the coffee table in front of the couch is a box of pizza, a bowl of chips, two sodas, and what appears to be a few battery-operated candles to add a romantic vibe to this evening.

"You really went all out, didn't you?" I taunt, knowing I'm perfectly fine with simple dates like this.

"Only for you, beautiful."

I blush at his compliment, relishing the fact he's the only man to ever call me that.

He grabs my hand and guides me over to the couch, pulling me onto him as he lies down. His arms wrap around me, holding me close as he nuzzles his nose into my neck and shoulder.

"Mmmm ... so much better. This is all I ever need to be happy."

My heart leaps into my throat at his words. The sincerity in his voice and the way he holds me so tenderly is almost too much. I'm not used to feeling this cherished, this cared for. Part of me wants to run, to protect myself from getting hurt. But a larger part of me wants to melt into his embrace and never leave.

I turn my head to look at him, finding his blue eyes gazing at me with such tenderness. "You're such a sap," I tease, trying to lighten the intensity of the moment.

Colton chuckles, the vibrations rumbling through his chest against my back. "Only for you, Sunshine." He leans in and presses a soft kiss to my lips.

When we part, I can't help but smile back at him. "So, what movie did you pick for us?"

"Well, I thought we could watch that new horror movie that just came out. You know, the one about the killer clowns?"

I wrinkle my nose. "Ugh, clowns? Really?"

He laughs as he reaches for the remote, turning on the TV. "I'm kidding. I know you're not big on horror movies. Actually, I was thinking we could watch that new action movie you've been wanting to see. The one with the car chases and explosions."

I smile, touched that he remembered. "Sounds perfect."

As the opening credits roll, Colton grabs the pizza box and offers me a slice. We eat and watch in comfortable silence, with him occasionally running his fingers through my hair or tracing patterns on my arm. It feels so natural, so comfortable being here with him like this.

About halfway through the movie, I get distracted by his proximity. The heat of his body against mine and the way his breath tickles my ear when he leans in to whisper a joke makes it hard to concentrate on anything else.

I shift slightly, turning to look at him and the way his chest rises and falls with each breath, the strong line of his jaw, the fullness of his lips. God, those lips.

Without thinking, I close the distance between us, pressing my lips to his.

He responds immediately, deepening the kiss as his hand comes up to cup my cheek. I turn my body to straddle him, and the kiss grows more heated. My hands tangle in his hair, and his move to my waist, gripping me tightly and pulling me closer. He hardens beneath me, so I grind, eliciting a groan from him.

When we finally break apart for air, we're both breathing heavily. Colton's eyes are dark with desire, mirroring my own. "God, Hollis," he breathes against my lips, his voice husky with desire. "You drive me crazy."

Encouraged by his reaction, I trail kisses down his jaw to his neck. "Then let's do something about it," I whisper against his skin. "I want you, Colton. All of you."

I drag his hands to the bottom of my dress, ensuring they go under the material and feel the bare flesh of my ass peeking out from my lacey thong.

The moment he groans, my restraint snaps, and I'm unsure how much longer I can take the sexual tension between us.

For a moment, I think he's going to give in. His thumbs graze the sides of my breasts, eliciting a moan from my throat. Just as my hand slips under his shirt, his body stills and he gently grasps my wrists, stopping me. "Hollis, wait."

He closes his eyes, taking a moment for himself.

"Don't," I say, pulling back, confusion and hurt flooding through me.

His eyes fly open, and his eyebrows furrow. "Don't what?"

"I know what you're going to say. You're going to say you don't want to rush things. That we should take our time, or let's get to know each other before we get physical. Right?"

He swallows deeply, not denying what I'm saying, and I realize I'm right.

I climb off his lap, frustration building inside me. *I need to get out of here before I have a breakdown in front of him.*

As I go to leave, my foot catches on the coffee table and I go down, knocking over the drinks and spilling over my outfit.

"You okay?" Colton gets up quickly, pulling me to my feet.

"Does it look like I'm okay?" I scowl at him. "I'm a sticky mess."

"This is something I can fix. Why don't I show you my bathroom? You can use my shower to clean off, and I can grab you something to wear from Thea's room since my clothes would swallow you up. The last thing I want is for you to go home in my clothes. I don't need Grams calling up that crazy uncle of yours to hunt me down."

Rolling my eyes, frustrated both sexually and emotionally, I extend an arm. "Show me the way."

I follow him up the stairs to the second floor into his bedroom. His bedroom has to be twice the size of mine.

A queen size bed sits between two windows. Beside it, tucked up against the wall across from the bed is a walnut-stained desk, and beside it, a shelf of medals and trophies, no doubt from his little league years.

It's definitely a room designed for an athletic eighteen-year-old.

"Here," Colton says. He hands me a navy-blue towel and directs me into a bathroom attached to his room.

I'm not jealous.

"If you want, I can put your clothes in the washer and clean them up for you." The way his eyes are full of guilt, or sorrow, I'm not quite sure, is making it very hard to be mad at him.

"Sure," I say. I pull my dress and top off before he even steps out of the bathroom, not bothered that I'm basically stripping down to my birthday suit in front of him.

"W-w-what are you doing?"

"What's it look like I'm doing? Can't exactly shower with my clothes on, now can I?" I raise an eyebrow, keeping my eyes on him as I remove my bra and let my thong hit the bathroom floor.

"N-n-no ..." His throat bobs as he takes in my naked body.

I scoop up my sticky clothes and shove them into his arms. "I'll be quick," I say before turning on the shower to my liking and climbing in.

Colton stands there unmoving. I grab his loofah from the hanging rack, squirt some of his body wash, and lather it all over my body.

"Colton?"

"Yeah?" he says, still not moving from his place.

"I'm going to need something to change into."

"Hmm ... oh. Right. I'll be back," he says, shaking his head and exiting.

I scrub my body down quickly, not wanting to waste too much water. When you're constantly having to save every nickel and penny, you learn how to shower fast.

After drying myself off, I wrap the towel around my petite figure and walk into Colton's room, taking in everything. Posters of big-name NFL stars are framed neatly along the walls, some with autographs on them.

I make my way over to the shelf with all of Colton's medals and trophies. Baseball, soccer, track, basketball, and a slew of a few different ones, but the vast majority? Football. Not surprised though.

Quite the athlete, aren't we?

My eyes drift over to the poster by the desk, a man in a Patriots jersey with the name Whitlock on it. The infamous one of my very own father.

As I go to move closer to the picture, a paper falls to the carpeted floor from the breeze I created as I walked by.

I pick it up and place it back on the desk, then notice it's a letter written to Colton.

From Stacey. *His ex?*

I glance back at the door, unsure where Colton is before looking back at the letter in my hand.

Read it. Maybe you can find out what went wrong so you don't make the same mistake.

Don't read it! It's an invasion of his privacy!

The devil and angel are at play.

I shouldn't. He would be so upset with me.

Then read it fast and put it back before he gets back. He'll never know. He won't even have sex with you.

The reminder of his rejection earlier reignites the frustration I felt, and I forget about the stupid angel's words of reason.

Fuck it.

Chapter 21

Hollis

Dear Colton.

I never wanted to break your heart the way I have, but it was the only way I could save you from a future you didn't want. Or deserved. I know I told you that it was due to me going away to college. I have to admit, that was a small truth to the real reason for our breakup.

The full, honest truth is that just shortly after prom, I found out I was pregnant with our baby. I know we were being careful all the times we slept together, but condoms aren't always foolproof, and I guess we had a defective one.

I'll be honest, I freaked out. I didn't think it was accurate, but after five tests coming up positive on top of the symptoms, there was no denying the truth.

After my appointment with the doctor for one final confirmation, I decided I was going to have the baby but give him/her up for adoption when they were born. Because of this decision, I decided it was best and easiest to leave you in the dark about the baby, so I broke things off with you, using me going away to college as the best excuse.

To be fair, did we really think we would work long distance? With you in your senior year of high school and me in my freshman year at a college hours away? I couldn't make you put your life on hold for me, for us. You deserved to live out your senior year single and having fun.

I know you're going to be upset or angry with me now that you know the truth. I deserve that. But this baby? Deserves to have a family that will love him/her and be able to raise them properly. I'm not ready to be a mom, and you're not anywhere ready to be a dad. A baby would take away your chances of a scholarship and you chasing your dreams to play in the NFL. I don't want to be the reason you never got your dream.

Please try to understand why I made this decision. It was never to hurt you.

-Sincerely,

Stacey

There's another piece of paper underneath dated for a few weeks after this one.

Hey Colton.

I tried a thousand times to send you the first letter, and every time I came close to doing so, I chickened out. I couldn't bring myself to do it. I was afraid you may find a way to prevent the adoption from happening, and I just couldn't let that happen.

I was going to save the letter until the adoption was completed, signing away all my rights and not naming you on the birth certificate, claiming it was a drunken one-night stand.

But life can be scary, and plans can change.

About a week after I wrote the first letter, I had the worst pain of my entire life and was concerned about the pregnancy. I rushed myself to the ER and had an ultrasound done, showing that the baby was developing in my left fallopian tube.

The doctor recommended that I should end the pregnancy before the fetus got any bigger and ruptured my fallopian tube, putting my life at risk.

I was in shock and struggled with what she was suggesting. I had to call my mom to come be with me because I knew I couldn't put you through this pain that I was feeling emotionally. Once my mom arrived, I had to finally confess to her about the pregnancy and made her promise to never speak of it to you or your family until I was ready.

The doctor explained the risks to both my mother and I, saying I could die if I allow the fetus to grow and develop. For me, it was really eye-opening. I have always been pro-life. Someone who could never see how a person could end a pregnancy, but here I am in this position where my only option is to have an abortion or I'm going to die.

And I had the abortion.

I've cried a million tears for the loss of this little life. How unfair it was to him/her and how unfair it was this all happened this way.

The only reason I'm sharing this with you is to help me grieve and heal from this whole experience. Keeping you in the dark was holding me back, and I needed to release the guilt to move forward with my life.

I'm so sorry for everything, and I hope that one day you can forgive me.

-Sincerely,

Stacey

"So I grabbed you one of Thea's older shirts she doesn't really wear anymore and a pair of her cheer shorts. I can give you a pair of my boxer briefs since your undergarments are in the wash, because there was no way in hell I was going to go through my sister's underwear drawer."

I slowly turn around to face Colton, so many emotions swirling within me that I can't pick which one is the most prevalent.

"You all right, Sunshine?" He sees the letter in my hand, and his face pales. "Why do you have that?"

Colton

My heart drops at seeing the letter in Hollis's hand. The same letter I've read over and over, trying to process everything Stacey went through. The same letter that explained why she really broke up with me.

The secret I haven't shared with anyone is in the hands of the woman I'm falling head over heels for. Judging by the look on her face, though, I'm not sure what will come of this confrontation.

"Hollis," I say, stepping toward her. "I can explain."

She holds up a hand, stopping me. Her blue eyes flash with hurt and anger. "Explain what, exactly? Why you still have a letter from your ex?" Her voice cracks slightly. "Or why you really won't be intimate with me?"

"No, it's not like that," I state, my mind racing.

"Then explain to me what it's like, Colton," she grits out.

I take a deep breath, trying to gather my thoughts. "The reason why I still have that ... I only kept it because ... because it was closure, I guess. A reminder of why things ended with Stacey." I pause, struggling to find the right words. "And maybe ... maybe as a reminder to be more careful in the future."

Her eyes widen slightly at that. "Is that why you won't sleep with me? You're afraid I'll get pregnant?"

Her words hit me like a punch to the gut. "No, that's not it at all," I say, even as I realize that maybe subconsciously, it has been affecting me.

"Well, not exactly." I run a hand over my face. "It's more complicated than that."

"Then make it so it's not," she demands, her voice rising slightly. "Because from where I'm standing, it looks like you're still hung up on your ex. Or maybe I'm just not good enough for you to fuck. Is that it?"

"That's not it at all." I step toward her. "Hollis, I care about you. So much more than I've cared about anyone in a long time, including Stacey."

She scoffs, shaking her head. "And you didn't think this was something worth mentioning to me? We've been seeing each other for weeks, Colton. I've opened up to you about my shitty past, about my family, something I've never told anyone else before. God, I thought we were being honest with each other."

Guilt washes over me. She's right. I should have told her about all this when she was finally open with me about her past. "I'm sorry," I say, running a hand through my hair. "I just ... I didn't know how to bring it up. It's not exactly easy to talk about."

"Oh, like it was so easy for me to talk about my gambling, alcoholic father abandoning his partner and his child to go chase some fucking addiction. Or ... or for my mother to just give me up so easily because she couldn't stand the fact I look like the man who left her for booze and money? Yeah, so fucking easy, let me tell you." Her voice shakes, her anger evident.

"I just wanted to take things slow, to do things right with you."

Hollis laughs bitterly. "Right. Because clearly I'm so different from Stacey, but you had no problem sleeping with her."

"That's not fair," I say, frustration creeping into my voice. "After everything that happened with Stacey, I realized how easily things can go wrong, even when you're being careful. I care about you, Hollis. Way too damn much that I don't want to risk messing things up between us by moving too fast. God! Don't you get it, Sunshine? I'm not willing to risk making a mistake because I lo—" I catch myself, realizing this is definitely not the right time for that confession.

Her eyes widen slightly at my near slip, but she masks it with anger. "You know what? I think I should go," she says, grabbing the clothes I brought for her. "I'll change, and then I'll get out of your hair."

"Hollis, please." I reach for her arm. "Can we talk about this?"

She jerks away from my touch. "I think you've said enough," she snaps. "Or rather, not said enough."

With that, she storms into the bathroom, slamming the door behind her. I stand there, feeling helpless and angry with myself for not being honest with her from the start.

A few minutes later, she emerges from the bathroom dressed in Thea's clothes. Without a word, she brushes past me and heads for the stairs.

"Hollis, please don't go. Not like this."

"I have nothing else to say to you!"

She jogs down the stairs, grabs her shoes, and darts for the front door, not sparing a moment to put them on.

"Hollis!" I rush after her, catching up to her, thanks to my long legs, closing her car door before she has the chance to get in.

"We need to talk this out, Sunshine. Please!" I practically beg, wanting nothing more than to go back to when our date began.

"I need some time to process this," Hollis breathes out, refusing to turn and face me.

"Okay. How long do you need?"

"I don't know, Colton, but I'd really appreciate it if you would let me get home so I can check on Grams."

I hesitate but relent, allowing her to get in the car and drive away, hoping like hell I just didn't fuck up and lose the girl I'm falling in love with.

Chapter 22

Hollis

My hands shake, and I grip the steering wheel, overcome with so many emotions. Tears blur my vision as I drive, but I refuse to let them fall.

I won't cry over him.

The rational part of my brain knows I'm overreacting. That I shouldn't have read those letters and I'm jumping to conclusions. But the hurt, angry part of me doesn't care about being rational right now. All I can think about is how could he keep something like that from me? After everything I've shared with him, all the walls I've let down, and he's been holding onto this huge secret the whole time?

I pull into my little driveway and dart inside the little white house that is home.

The moment I open the door and cross the threshold, something feels off.

"Grams!" I shout into the quiet house, but she doesn't respond. My heart begins to beat rapidly, my pulse thumping in my eardrums as I run to the kitchen before I head down the hall to our bathroom and her bedroom, where I find Grams lying on the floor, not moving.

No. No, no, no!

I rush to her side. "Grams!" I shout, and shake her to get her to wake up, but I don't get a response. As I check for her pulse, her skin feels super warm. She is breathing, but it doesn't sound like it should.

Fuck! What do I do!? Why wasn't I here when she needed me?

I grab my cell phone and do the only thing I can to help my grandmother. We can't afford an ambulance ride, but I don't care. There's no way I can lift her into my car by myself and drive her to the hospital, and all I know is I can't lose her.

"Nine, one, one. What is your emergency?"

I give her the address, explaining what's wrong with my grandmother, and she assures me an ambulance is on the way.

"Thank you," I tell the dispatcher while clinging to Gram's hand as we wait for the paramedics to arrive.

"Please don't leave me, Grams. I need you to stick it out a little while longer. You're all I have left in this world."

I drag myself into school Tuesday morning, exhausted, ready to go home and crawl back into my bed.

The only reason I'm in school today is because Grams insisted I go now that she's finally been discharged from the hospital after spending the weekend there. Her blood sugar levels had spiked dangerously high, and she didn't have enough insulin to lower them—a miscalculation on my part since they raised the price of her medication again last month.

The guilt is eating me alive for not keeping an eye on her meds, but also for not being there when she needed me, even though Grams keeps assuring me it's not my fault.

My mind drifts to Colton and how badly things turned prior to my grandmother's diabetic episode. I shake my head, pushing thoughts of him away. I can't deal with that on top of everything else, or I may have a full-on meltdown right here in this hallway.

As I make my way to my locker, I spot Colton down the hall. Our eyes meet briefly before I quickly look away, my stomach twisting with a mix of emotions. Part of me wants to run to him, to let him hold me and tell me everything will be okay, but the hurt and anger from Friday night is still fresh in my mind, creating a wall between us.

I haven't responded to any of his texts or calls since that night. I know he says we need to talk, but I just can't bring myself to do it yet. I'm not ready to face everything.

I feel a presence beside me and tense up, thinking it's Colton, but when I turn, it's Maisie.

"Hey, are you okay?" she asks, taking in my disheveled appearance. "The girls and I missed you at practice yesterday. We tried messaging you on your socials since you weren't in school, but you never got back to any of us. No one had any way of contacting you except Colton, and he said you weren't responding to his texts."

I sigh, closing my locker. "Sorry, it's been a rough few days. My grandmother was in the hospital over the weekend, and I was with her. The hospital has crappy cell service."

Maisie's eyes widen. "Oh my gosh, is she all right?"

"She's home now, but it was pretty scary there for a while," I admit. "Thought for sure I almost lost her." Tears well up in my eyes before I quickly blink them away.

Don't let anyone see you cry.

Maisie pulls me into a hug. "I'm so sorry, Hollis. Why didn't you reach out? I could have been there for you."

I shrug as we pull apart. "I didn't want to bother anyone. Plus, I was kind of a mess and not in the right headspace to talk."

"But that's what friends are for," Maisie says, lightly punching my arm. "Next time, let me know, okay? Even if it's just to bring you some coffee or simply sit with you."

I nod, a lump forming in my throat at her kindness. "Thanks, Maisie. I really appreciate that."

The warning bell rings, signaling we need to get to class.

"Are you sure you're all right?" Maisie asks as we walk toward our first classes.

"Yeah, I'll be fine," I say with a small smile.

I catch sight of Colton again. He's looking at me with concern and takes a few steps in my direction, but I shake my head to get him to understand I need my space. I have enough on my plate without adding relationship drama to the mix, if what we were can even be considered a relationship.

I turn away, my heart aching as I push myself to follow Maisie and focus on getting through this day one step at a time.

Football practice after school doesn't go well. With my head everywhere else, I'm missing passes and fucking up my routes.

"Whitlock, hit the bench and take five!" Coach Freeman yells.

I plaster my ass to the metal bench and remove my helmet and toss it to the turf. My anger isn't directed at the coach. He has every right to pull me because I'm not playing my best. I'm angry at everything in my life going to hell and feeling like I'll never be able to fix it all.

"You okay, Hollis?" Corrine asks.

"No, Cori. I'm not, at least at the moment. Maybe one day I will be."

"You know the girls and I are here for you, right? We care about you."

"You shouldn't care about someone as pathetic as me. I'm nothing special. You will all forget about me. You guys will be off into the real world and do amazing shit with your lives, live out your dreams. Meanwhile, I'm going to be stuck in this godforsaken town, busting my ass working two or three jobs to take care of myself and all the cats I'll probably end up having."

"How can you say that? You are far from pathetic, Holls. You're smart, athletic, gorgeous … Do you know how badly I wish I had your don't-give-a-fuck attitude so I could finally tell my sister to fuck off and stop trying to make me into her clone? To let me be my own person?"

"To don't give a fuck, you got to quit giving a fuck," I state. "No one is stopping you but you, Cori. You want to be your own person? You gotta make the changes yourself, big or small."

"What do you mean?"

"You say she wants you to be like her, right?"

Corrine nods.

"Well, I hear changing your hair can be quite liberating. Ever wanted to change up your hair?"

Her face lights up when she realizes what I'm saying. "It's brilliant. She would totally spazz out and … This could work." I see the wheels turning in her head, and I hope she has the balls to go through with it so I can watch it piss her stuck-up sister off.

Corrine leans in, giving me a hug, catching me off guard. My arms awkwardly wrap around her and pat her shoulder pads.. "See, Holls. You're an awesome person. Whatever you're going through? You're going to overcome it. Just know you don't have to do it alone." She pulls away, and her green eyes bore into me. "Maisie, Alora, and I are here for you, not just as your teammates, but as friends. Remember that, okay?"

I nod, my eyes welling with tears and my throat swelling from holding back all my emotions.

"Summers, I need you out on the line!" Coach Freeman yells.

"Yes, Coach!" she shouts before putting her helmet on and racing onto the field.

Just as she leaves the bench, Coach Watson takes her place. "How you doing, Whitlock?"

"I'm okay, Coach. Just dealing with a lot of stuff."

"Yeah, I figured, seeing as how crappy you're doing out there today." He chuckles, which I do too. He's not wrong. I've been playing like shit. "What's up, kiddo?"

I swallow the lump in my throat. "My grandmother had a medical emergency and was in the hospital all weekend. It's just her and me, and I've been a wreck because I could have lost her. She's the only family I've got."

"Why don't you head home and take this week off. Don't worry about our game against the Lincoln Knights. Alright?"

My head swivels to look at my head coach. "W-w-what? No! Coach, I can play. You guys need me—"

He raises his hand to stop me. "What I *need* is for my kickass wide receiver to get her mind right so she can be ready to take on Wimbleton next week. I hear you're familiar with them."

Fucking Wimbleton. My old high school and Bellwood's biggest rival, next to Greystone Academy.

"Can you do that for me, Whitlock?"

"Yes, sir," I grit out, picking up my helmet off the ground. I go to head to the lockers when a tall ass dude steps in front of me. Dark hair, long on top. Probably six feet tall. Our eyes meet, and I stare in them, something vaguely familiar about the shade of his eyes.

"You know, if you took a picture, it would last longer," the big ogre speaks, his deep voice breaking the stareoff.

"Nah. Your ugly ass face would just break the lens," I retort, shoving past him for the locker rooms.

"Whitlock!" Coach Watson shouts, and I turn to face him. "It's just one game. Get your head right so we can be ready for them Wildcats."

I nod, glancing at the tall guy standing next to him. His eyes focus on me, as if he is trying to place me somewhere, but I roll my eyes and storm off, ready to go home, check in with Grams, and forget this day.

Colton

"Hey. What's Brady doing here?" I tip my head toward where Coach Watson and Hollis are standing.

"No clue, man," Zion says.

"I don't know." Dylan shrugs.

We toss the ball back and forth, but my eyes laser focus on the interaction between Brady and Hollis, and for a moment, a possessive anger courses through me. Jealousy?

I mean, how is he getting her attention, and I can't even get a text back?

"Nah, your ugly ass face would just break the lens," Hollis tells Brady before she shoulder-checks him on her way to the lockers. I grin at the old fiery attitude of hers laying into him.

Hold up. Wait. Why is she leaving?

"Hey, Coach." I jog over to where he and Brady are standing. "Is Whitlock okay?"

"You said her name is Whitlock?" Brady asks, but I ignore him, solely focused on what Coach has to say.

"She's not playing like herself, so I told her to go home and get her mind right so she can be ready for Wimbleton. Her mind's elsewhere. Said her grandma was just in the hospital this weekend."

"What!?" I exclaim, feeling more like an ass than I did after Friday. No wonder she looked like she hadn't been sleeping. God, I need to fix things so I can be there for her. Help out in some way.

"Don't worry, Reynolds. We will be all right without Whitlock for the Knights game."

I'm not worried about that. The Lincoln Knights record is one in three, and I have no doubt we will be fine. I'm more concerned about how hard this is on Hollis. Her grandmother is the only family member she has left.

I glance in Brady's direction and squint at how he's looking after Hollis. I've seen the way this guy has checked out girls, but this look? It's more like he's figuring out a puzzle, trying to piece it together. My brain thinks back to what Hollis told me about her past and the research I've done.

Maybe Grams isn't the only family member she has left.

Chapter 23

Hollis

I lie in my bed, tossing and turning, sleep avoiding me. Without football practice, the stress of my life is swarming me, and I have no way of releasing it.

Grabbing my phone from my nightstand, I check the time.

1:40 a.m.

Ugh. I will be dragging for school in the morning.

Pulling myself out of bed, I go into the kitchen for a glass of water and grab a notebook. Since Grams was hospitalized, I've got to do better tracking her medications and our finances. I can't let another mishap like that happen again. We got lucky this time, and I don't want to chance her life on a second mishap.

I sit at the kitchen table, scribbling down numbers and calculations in the dim light. Between Grams's medical bills, her medications, our rent and utilities, and just basic necessities like food, the numbers aren't adding up. Even with my job at the diner and Grams's social security, we're barely scraping by. Add in the ambulance ride and the hospital stay, we'll be even further in the hole.

I run my hands through my hair, frustration and fear bubbling up inside me. How are we going to make this work? Maybe I can pick up more shifts at the diner or find a second job, but when would I have time for school and football?

Football. The thought of it sends a pang through my chest. As much as I love the game, as much as it's been healing and is possibly my ticket to getting into college with financial help, it feels like a luxury I can't afford. Maybe Coach Watson was right to bench me for the next game. Maybe I should quit altogether and focus on working more hours.

Then I think about my teammates Corrine, Maisie, and Alora. About how they said I was their friend, that they cared about me. The thought of letting them down and walking away from the team makes my stomach churn.

My mind drifts to Colton, to the fun times we shared and how I opened my heart to him before I pushed him away with his secret. Now the walls I've spent years building are firmly back in place. This time I'll be stronger and make sure no pretty boy has the capability to destroy it.

Yeah, right.

I glance at my notifications of his missed calls and unread texts. The guy is relentless, I'll give him that. With a sigh, I swipe them away, not wanting to be tempted to read or hear what he has to say.

"Hollipop. What are you doing up?"

I quickly close the notebook, covering it the best I can. "I, uh, couldn't sleep, so I'm catching up on my homework."

She eyes me suspiciously, pulling the notebook from under my arms and looking over my math.

"Really? Since when did bills become a part of high school homework?" She gives a pointed look, calling my bluff.

"Since ... recently?" I shrug. I sigh, laying my head on the table and let out a frustrated growl.

I feel Grams's presence in the chair next to me, and she finger-combs my hair. "Hollipop, you are too young to be stressing over this stuff. It's not healthy."

"Then what else am I supposed to do? It almost cost you your life! I-I-I can't chance it happening again. We may not get lucky next time." I lift my head and stare into my sweet grandmother's face, tears blurring my vision.

Grams cups my face, her thumbs brushing under my eyes as a few tears descend my cheeks. "I'm a strong woman, sweet girl. I've survived so many things in my life meant to destroy me, and you know what always helped push me through?"

I shake my head.

"You," she says, pressing her lips to my forehead. "You, my dear, have been my greatest strength, my guiding light through any storm."

I wrap my arms around her, clinging to her and breathing her in, needing her hugs like I need my next breath. I cry into her shoulder, letting the dam break and my tears flow freely.

"Shh ... everything is going to be all right," she whispers, squeezing me tightly.

Once the tears have stopped, I pull away from Grams, swiping my hands under my eyes.

"Now, why don't you take your cutie patootie behind to bed and get some rest for school."

"Yes, Grams." I kiss her on top of her head before putting my glass in the sink and heading to my room.

"Oh, and one more thing, Hollipop."

"Yes?"

"Stop being so stubborn and go talk to that boy. Hear him out instead of pushing him away."

"How do you—"

"A grandmother just knows." A sly smile works its way across her face. *What the hell?*

We wish each other good night, and I head to bed.

As I lie there, waiting for sleep to come, I think over everything I calculated and realize the only way to be sure Grams has her insulin is with money I can make fast.

With Coach sidelining me this week, I may be able to get in a few fights. Without second-guessing, I unblock Rowan and send him a message.

Colton

How the fuck did we lose to Lincoln Knights!?

The bus ride back to Bellwood after Lincoln beat us twenty-four to twenty-one is quiet, many of us beating ourselves up mentally at how we let the team with one of the most horrible records kick our asses.

"You need to fix things with your girl, pronto!" Anthony says, leaning across Jeremiah. "This moping shit you've been dealing with is affecting your ability to play, and it showed tonight."

"Trust me, I'm trying! I've called, I've texted. Hell, I even left notes in her locker, but she's completely shutting me out! At this point, I don't know what else to do?"

"What caused her to freeze you out?" Jeremiah asks.

For a moment, I think of what excuse to come up with, but with Hollis knowing, my secret already out there with one person, it is time to share it with my friends.

I pull up the group chat and text the guys, not wanting the whole team to know my personal business.

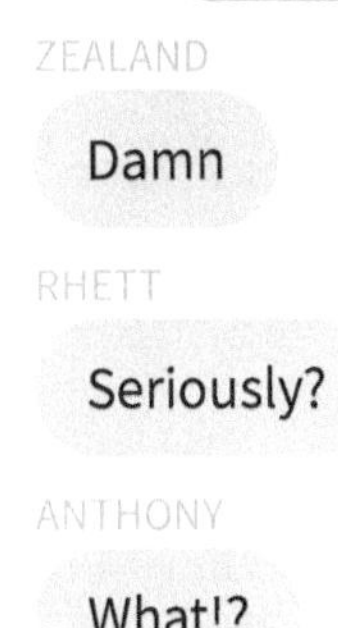

COLTON

This was why I was acting out most of summer, what I was struggling to deal with. I was angry she hid something from me and was keeping me out of this stuff and then I saw the word abortion, and I don't know, I guess I was grieving. I mean, it was my baby. It was a part of me.

JEREMIAH

I'm sorry bro.

ZEALAND

Yeah, man. I'm sorry.

ANTHONY

So why is Hollis shutting you out?

COLTON

She had tried to have sex with me a few times, and I shut her down.

ANTHONY

Excuse me?

RHETT

You're joking.

Please tell me you're joking.

All my friends turn to stare at me, and I shake my head.

ANTHONY

Have you lost your ever fucking mind!? She wanted to put out and you refused????

JEREMIAH

Hate to say this, but I'd freeze your ass out too. Girls don't like being rejected. But to find a letter, knowing you have had sex with your ex? :|

RHETT

How are you going to reject that fine piece of ass?

COLTON

Talk about Hollis like that again, and we will have problems.

RHETT

Calm down, Romeo. It was just a compliment.

ZEALAND

So she is refusing to let you come to her and won't respond to you?

COLTON

Basically.

ZEALAND

Then it's time you went to her and make her listen to you.

COLTON

How do I do that?

> We're going to get dinner at the diner tomorrow night.

My friends and I pull into the parking lot of the diner, and I'm starting to feel nervous. What if this doesn't work?

"Are you sure this is a good idea, Z?" I ask my best friend.

"It's got to be. She can't technically leave here until she gets off work, and I have it on good authority she closes tonight since there is no football."

"And what happens when we are all done? We have to leave, otherwise we are hogging tables from the servers. That gives me approximately an hour and a half to work with."

Jeremiah comes up and slaps my shoulder. "Relax. You're forgetting we have Anthony and his bottomless pit of an appetite."

"Mm-hm, and I've been starving myself all day for this!" Anthony says enthusiastically.

I peer into the windows and catch sight of Hollis wiping off a table. *She's here.*

Relief and nerves settle in, hoping like hell I can get her to listen, to let me back in. As she goes to lift a tray, she winces, quickly grabbing her right side.

The nerves I had moments ago transform to anger and worry, wondering if someone dared to lay a hand on her.

"She's hurt," I grit out, my teeth clenched, unable to take my eyes off her as she struggles with pain.

The guys all stop and watch, noticing as well.

"Alright, let's try to not get ahead of ourselves," Zealand says, speaking in a calm tone. "You want to talk to her, we are going to have to approach this cautiously. Alright? The key is to get you and her alone so she can hear you out."

He's right. If I go in there and demand to know what happened, she will only shut me out, and I may lose her for good.

"Let's go inside, then," I say, following behind Jeremiah.

The brunette girl with glasses, the one who sort of reminds me of Stacey, approaches us.

"Hey, guys." She beams with joy. "You're usual booth?"

"Actually, we were wondering if you had any availability in your section." Jeremiah winks at Talia, making the girl blush.

"Follow me," she says, and leads us to a booth. I look around but don't spot Hollis anywhere.

After we order our drinks and appetizers, the guys and I settle into conversation regarding our upcoming game against Wimbleton, ensuring we don't repeat the mistakes we did against yesterday's team.

Occasionally, I glance around, waiting for Hollis to make an appearance, but she hasn't been out into the dining area in a while.

I hope she didn't leave because we showed up.

Just as my mind swirls, thinking she saw me and decided to cut out early, she pushes through the kitchen door, a woman on a mission.

As if sensing my very presence, our eyes briefly connect before she makes her way to a booth of guests that were seated a few moments ago. She has a beautiful smile on her gorgeous face as she takes their orders.

The bell above the diner door chimes, and someone enters, the familiarity of their presence making me uneasy. Blonde mullet and blue eyes. A cockiness in his stride. The new guest walks up to the counter after Hollis puts the order in, his sole focus on her as if she is a target. Only then do I remember why this guy seems familiar. He was here before, with a friend. A friend who was being aggressive toward my sunshine when she wasn't mine.

My jaw clenches, not liking how he's leaned in close, too close for my liking. From this angle, it looks like they are sharing some intimate moment, and my heart cracks.

"You good, man?" Zealand says, my hands are balled tightly into fists. His eyes follow my line of sight to see what I'm staring at. "Alright. It's not what you think it looks like. Okay? She's definitely not flirting with him. It looks like they're having a heated conversation about something." He says it so calmly, as if it will calm me down.

News flash. It won't.

I watch intently, noting his body language, my nerves on edge. This feels all too familiar. Almost like déjà vu.

In one swift motion, the guy latches onto the front of Hollis's top.

I. See. Red.

I'm up out of my booth in a flash, heading right for him, consequences be damned.

You don't ever, *ever* put your hands on *my girl*.

Chapter 24

Hollis

The timer on my cell phone goes off, alerting me my fifteen-minute break is over.

"It was fun while it lasted," I mutter to myself. After taking one last deep breath of the outdoor air, minus the greasy smells coming from my place of employment, I head through the kitchen, making my way toward the dining room.

"Hollis, booth eighteen needs to be picked up," Janet says.

"Got it!" I shout back, securing my apron around my waist. *Let's hope I make some good tips tonight.*

I head out to the dining area, pausing momentarily when I spot Colton and some of the guys in one of the booths, grateful they're not in my section.

Thank you Talia for that.

As if we are two magnets, my body always seems to know whenever he's around. My eyes seek his, only this time when they lock for a brief second before I'm off to tend to my newly seated guests.

I take their orders, and as I place it in the window, a throat clears from the countertop seats behind me.

"Well, if it isn't just my luck." I freeze, knowing who that voice belongs to. "Hello, Pixie."

"What do you want, Rowan?" I turn to glare at him, his presence unnerving. "If you're planning to eat, Janet covers the countertop seating, not me."

"Just here on business." He smirks. "Got another fight lined up for you against Colossus—"

"Pass," I state. "I work till close tonight."

"We don't have any fights for tonight. However, we are planning something big next week, something to lure the crowds in. How's next Friday night work for you?" he asks, crossing his arms over his chest. "That fight last night made us bank, and people are already paying double to watch you take on Colossus. That means a big payout for you. What do you say?"

"Let me make this clear to you," I grit out, leaning so I'm super close to his face. "I'm *not* fighting Colossus, or anyone else in the foreseeable future. The fight last night was a one-time deal because I needed the cash desperately. I'm not a permanent resident to your stupid little club, so find someone else, and fuck off!"

I go to move back, but Rowan grabs the collar of my shirt, yanking me forward, our faces close enough it would appear somewhat intimate to anyone else.

"Let me put it to you this way. You don't have a choice here," Rowan growls, his grip tightening on my shirt. "You owe me, Pixie. Don't forget who helped you out when you were desperate. I own you now until that debt is paid off."

My heart is pounding, a mix of fear and anger coursing through me. "I never agreed to that," I hiss back. "One fight. That was the deal."

He chuckles darkly. "Oh, sweetheart, you should know by now that deals can change. Besides, do you really want me to tell your dear old grandma about your extracurricular activities? I'm sure she'd be so proud."

The threat hangs heavy in the air between us. I want nothing more than to punch that smug look off his stupid face, but I know I can't afford to lose this job.

"Fine," I grit out. "I'll do the fight against Colossus. But after that, I'm done. I want out, for good this time."

"Tell you what. If you win your fight and make me enough money to cover your debt, I'll consider your debt paid in full and you can leave. I'll never come tracking you down again. How's that sound?"

"Sounds like I'll beat his ass until he's unrecognizable. Is that good enough for you?"

Rowan's lips curl into a satisfied smirk. "That's my girl. I'll text you the details later."

Before he gets the chance to pull away, a large hand clamps down on Rowan's shoulder.

"If I were you, I'd remove your hand from her shirt," a deep voice says from behind Rowan.

Rowan releases his grip before he turns slowly to face Colton, their heights damn near the same. Colton and Rowan stare each other down, the tension between them palpable. Colton's jaw is clenched tight, his normally friendly blue eyes are cold as ice as he glares at Rowan.

"This doesn't concern you, pretty boy," Rowan sneers. "Why don't you mind your business elsewhere?"

"That's where you're wrong. You see, when you put your hands on someone, especially a female, then it becomes my business. *Particularly* when that someone is her." Colton doesn't budge, doesn't flinch. "So I'm not going anywhere until your ass leaves. And I would suggest that be right now."

Rowan looks like he's considering throwing a punch, but he glances around the diner, noticing the attention they're drawing. With a scowl, he turns back to me.

"Remember what I said, Pixie. I'll text you the deets."

He brushes past Colton, shoving him with his shoulder as he exits the diner. As soon as he's gone, Colton turns to me, concern etched on his face.

"Are you okay? Did he hurt you?" He looks me over from head to toe.

I straighten my shirt, trying to regain my composure. "I'm fine. I had it handled."

He raises an eyebrow. "Didn't look that way to me. And what was that about? What deets does he need to give you?"

"Like Rowan said. It's none of your business!" I move away from the counter to get my customers their drinks and drop them off at their booth. Colton follows behind me, in step with me like some lonely puppy.

"If you're in some kind of trouble, I can help."

I stop in my tracks, turning on Colton. "I thought I made it perfectly clear that I needed some space. I don't need nor want your help! So do us both the favor and fuck off!"

I say that last part too loudly, causing the whole diner to go dead quiet. My cheeks warm with embarrassment, so I dash through the kitchen, racing for the exit.

"Hey, you can't be back here!" Al shouts somewhere from behind me.

Not bothering to turn around, I rush through the exit. As soon as I'm outside in the warmth of the late September sun, big hands snatch my waist, turning me around. I'm gently pushed back against the side of the building, the rough exterior scratching my back.

"Hey, shhh. It's just me," Colton says, putting one of his hands over my mouth, preventing me from screaming.

"What the hell, Colton?" I snap, pushing against his chest.

He steps back, giving me some space but not letting me bolt. "I'm sorry, I didn't mean to scare you. I just ... I couldn't let you run off like that, not away from me. Not when it feels like you're in trouble that I don't know about."

I cross my arms over my chest. "Why?"

He runs a hand through his hair, frustrated. "I know you said you needed space but ... damn it, Hollis. I can't take you shutting me out. I can't just stand by watching you suffer over your grandmother's health and whatever else is going on with you. And I damn sure won't watch you get into trouble with a guy like that. Something isn't right about him. I don't know what it is, but he gives me bad vibes."

"You don't know anything about it," I mutter, looking away.

"Then talk to me! Help *me* to understand," he pleads. "Who is he? What kind of trouble are you in?"

"It's complicated. Okay?"

It's quiet for a moment, and I battle how much I should say or if keeping him in the dark would be best, not wanting to bring him in the middle of my problems. Remembering how I had gone off on him for his secret, the reason why I've pushed him away this past week, I relent, deciding it is time he knows.

I take a deep breath.

"His name is Rowan Hall. He's very well known around Ravenwood's campus. Not only does he have connections, but he runs the underground fight club."

"So the masked ring announcer is Rowan?"

I nod. "About a year ago, my grandmother's insulin was getting extremely low, and I wasn't really working. Grams was barely able to make enough money for bills and groceries, sacrificing her meds for our necessities. When I found this out, I knew I had to do something because she needed her insulin, otherwise it put her life at risk."

Colton nods and waves for me to keep going.

"You know, I used to attend Wimbleton?"

He shakes his head, so I continue. "Got kicked out for beating the literal shit out of one of their star defenders, who was three times bigger than me. He thought he could just get away with sexually assaulting the girls in my school, like he was untouchable. Well, I made sure to let him know he fucked with the wrong one the day he thought he could reach up my skirt and grab my ass. Grams was proud of me for it too."

I smile at remembering her pride, knowing she supported me in that moment and made sure I got right into that lame ass virtual school so I wouldn't get behind.

"Anyway, word got around, and next thing I knew, some college girl was giving me a ride to meet with Rowan. He heard what I did and was impressed. He began to talk about his underground fight club business, wanting to add me to his roster of fighters, stating I would be offered a lot of money to fight and win against my opponents. Since I would be a newbie, I may not make as much starting out like one of his more well-known fighters. I'd have to build my reputation up and gain the crowd's support. When I had asked how much the fighters typically make, I was shocked, knowing that money could help get us through. After I won my first match, Rowan was impressed, said he saw good things for me and started putting me in several matches, as many as five or six in a night. I wasn't making much though, and I desperately needed money, so I explained to him about my grandmother, how she needed this medicine to survive, so he cut me a deal.

"He would use his connections to get me insulin, but I have to fight for him, no questions asked. I didn't take him seriously until he showed up with a few months worth of insulin. Since he was a man of his word, I became a woman of mine. Once I received his help, I was in his debt. I kept fighting for a while, making good money, but it started to take a toll. The bruises, the injuries—I was worried Grams would figure it out. So I tried to quit, but Rowan wouldn't let me go that easily. He said I still owed him. I fought for him for almost a year before one of the fights got busted by the cops. I thought for sure I was going to get arrested, but I managed to sneak away. That night was a reality check for me. So ... I blocked Rowan on everything and made sure I kept a low profile in hopes I'd never have to go back. Until he somehow managed to find me when he came in with his buddy, offering me a fight."

"So you took him up with the fight against Titan?"

I nod. "I needed to get my alternator fixed and didn't want to have to owe Nathan anything, so I took the fight, telling Rowan it would just be that time. Apparently that fight was a huge deal, so he started blowing up my messages for other fights until I blocked him. I heard from Talia he's shown up here a few times, but I wasn't working because of football practice or a game. I held out hope that he would think I no longer worked here, but I was wrong. He must've followed me last night."

Colton's jaw clenches as he processes this information. "So that's why you were wincing earlier? You fought last night?"

I nod, wrapping my arms around myself. "Grams's hospital stay put us in a tight spot financially. I reached out to him, desperate for quick cash. I told Rowan I would do last night's fight if he promised to leave me alone if I won, but now he's going back on his word, saying I owe him, that I have to keep fighting to pay off my debt."

"Hollis, this is serious," he says, his voice filled with worry. He gently tilts my chin so I'm looking at him again. "This isn't okay. You shouldn't have to put yourself in danger like this. There has to be another way."

"I don't have a choice," I reply, frustration evident in my tone. "If I don't do what he says, he'll tell Grams everything. She would be so disappointed in me. Not only that, he's willing to pin the stolen insulin on me, and I could go to jail. I can't let that happen."

Colton takes a step closer, his hands coming to rest on my shoulders. "There's always a choice, Sunshine. Let me help you. We can figure this out together."

I shake my head, pulling away from his touch. "No. I got myself into this mess, I'll get myself out of it. I just need to win this next fight and make enough money to pay him off. Then I'm done for good."

"And what if you get seriously hurt? Or worse? What then?" Colton argues.

"I don't know ..."

"There has to be another way—"

"There isn't!" I snap, my emotions getting the best of me. "Don't you get it? This is my life, Colton. It's messy and complicated and full of impossible choices, one you don't belong in."

Hurt flashes in his eyes at my words. "I *want* to be in your life, Hollis. All of it—messy parts included. Why can't you see that?"

Tears prick at the corners of my eyes, but I refuse to let them fall. "Because everyone leaves eventually, remember? It's easier this way."

His expression softens, and he cups my face in his hands. "I'm not everyone, Sunshine, and I don't plan on going anywhere."

For a moment, I lean into his touch, craving the comfort and security he offers. Then reality comes crashing back in, and I pull away.

"I should get back to work," I say, avoiding his gaze. "God knows how long we've been out here, and it's our dinner rush. They probably need me in there."

Colton sighs, dropping his hands to his sides. "Okay. But just so you know? This conversation isn't over, Hollis. I'm here for you, whether you want me to be or not."

"Sure, Colton."

I don't expect his hand to wrap around my throat as he takes a few steps closer to me. My panties may have dampened a little.

"I mean every word of it, Sunshine. I don't know what I have to do to prove it to you, but I will spend every minute, every second of every day until you get it through that beautiful head of yours how much you mean to me because I love you."

My breath hitches. "You ... what?"

"You don't have to say it back, but I want you to know. I love you," he says with conviction, staring into my eyes. "There isn't a single thing about you that could make me want to go anywhere without you. Not even you demanding some space. Do you have any idea how tortuous it's been to not touch you, to not hear your voice? I'd rather burn in the pits of hell than you keep me at a distance."

A small smile tugs at my face. "To be fair, it was tortuous for me too."

"Good. I hope it was," he says, a dimple popping in his cheek. "Now, I'm going to let you get back to work, and I'm going to be waiting for you outside when you get off, and then you and I? We need to discuss the letters. Got it?"

I nod, swallowing deeply as I fight how turned on I am by his bossy attitude.

"Good girl." He smirks, and I'm nearly a goner. Then he plants a soft kiss on my lips before pulling away. "I'll see you after work."

"Okay," I mutter, and make my way back inside, my head reeling from the roller coaster of events that played out.

Chapter 25

Colton

I pull into the spot next to Hollis's car and wait for her to get off work for us to finally sit down and talk things out. This past week, I've done nothing but replay our fight over and over in my mind. It wasn't until I finally opened up to my friends that I realized how badly I had messed up by not being honest with her from the start.

As I wait, I think back to our conversation outside the diner earlier. Learning about Hollis's involvement with the underground fight club and this Rowan guy has me on edge. I don't like her putting herself in danger like that, but I understand why she felt she had no other choice. Still, there has to be a better way to help her grandmother without her risking her safety.

The diner door opens, and Hollis emerges, looking exhausted after her long shift. When she spots my car, she hesitates for a moment before slowly making her way over.

I get out of my car to meet her. "Hey. Thanks for agreeing to talk."

Hollis nods, tucking a strand of hair behind her ear. "Yeah, well, I figured it was time for us to clear the air."

"Do you want to go somewhere to talk? Or we could just sit in my car if you're too tired."

She considers for a moment before sighing. "Let's just sit in your car. I'm beat."

"Of course. Whatever you're comfortable with."

We climb into my car and sit in silence for a few moments. The tension between us is thick and uncomfortable. Finally, I take a deep breath and turn to face her, but we start speaking at the same time.

"I'm sorry—"

"I shouldn't have—"

We let out small laughs, some of the tension easing.

"You go first," I say.

Hollis takes a deep breath. "I'm sorry for how I reacted when I found those letters. I shouldn't have read them in the first place; it was a huge invasion of your privacy. And I'm sorry I just shut you out without giving you a chance to explain. That wasn't fair."

I nod, grateful for her apology but needing to offer my own.

"I'm sorry too. I should have told you about Stacey and everything that happened. I was in the wrong to keep that from you, especially after you opened up to me about your past. The truth is, after what happened with Stacey ... I was a mess," I admit. "I felt guilty, even though I didn't know about the pregnancy at the time. Betrayed that she wanted to keep me in the dark about it so she could give our baby up, just like that, not even taking my feelings into consideration. And then I was sad, knowing that she had to abort our baby, something that was a part of me, because it could have killed her. I was dealing with so many emotions, I had no idea what to feel ... how to process it all." I look at Hollis, willing her to understand.

"That sounds awful. Did you confide in your parents?"

I shake my head, surprising her. "I never told them. Truth is, I never told anyone and just kept it to myself."

"Seriously? Colton, that is some heavy shit."

"Which is exactly why I couldn't tell them. I didn't want to disappoint them or bring them shame. What's worst is, as angry as I was with Stacey, I couldn't allow anyone to think of her differently, so I kind of did it to protect her character."

"That's honestly admirable of you."

"Yeah, I guess."

Hollis is quiet for a beat. "Why didn't you tell me?" Her voice is soft, almost vulnerable. "Did you not trust me?"

"No, that wasn't it at all," I say quickly. "I trust you completely, I do. I guess I was just ... ashamed. And scared. Scared of how you might react, of dredging up all those feelings again. Scared you might see me differently or think less of me somehow."

"Colton," Hollis murmurs, finally meeting my gaze. "Nothing could make me think less of you. But finding out the way I did ... it hurt. It made me feel like maybe you didn't see me as someone you could confide in."

"I'm sorry," I mutter, understanding the hurt she felt.

"And I get being scared to open up, hell, probably better than anyone, but Colton, I shared things with you that I've never told anyone else. Do you know how hard that was for me? How much trust that took?"

"I know," I say, guilt washing over me. "And I'm so sorry I didn't reciprocate that trust. You deserved better than that."

She is quiet again, her gaze fixed on her hands in her lap fidgeting with the hem of her shirt. When she finally speaks, her voice is barely above a whisper. "Is that why you wouldn't sleep with me? Because of what happened with Stacey? To me, I thought maybe you just didn't want me that way."

The vulnerability in her voice breaks my heart. I reach out, gently taking her hand, pulling her to sit on my lap, grateful she follows.

"Sunshine, look at me," I say, locking my eyes with hers. "I want you in every way I can have you, every way you will let me have you. Believe me when I say that. But I also want to do this right. You're special to me, and I don't want our relationship to be just about sex or rush things and mess this up. I want to build something real with you, something that is going to last."

She stares into me, looking for the lie. "So you're not rejecting me? You do want me?"

"God, yes," I say. "Do you have any idea how much I want you? But I also want all of you, not just your body, but your heart too. I want to earn your trust, to show you that I'm not going anywhere."

I see a flicker of vulnerability in her eyes before she masks it. "And what if I'm ready? Because, Colton, you do have my heart. You've had it for a little while in fact, I've just been afraid to admit it to myself. I love you, and I want to be with you, all of you. I want to experience us on a deeper, more intimate level."

My heart beats against my ribs like a drum, emotion clogging my throat at her telling me she loves me.

I pull her into me and kiss her with every ounce of love and desire I feel for her. She responds eagerly, wrapping her arms around my neck as she deepens the kiss. The passion between us builds quickly, and soon we're both breathing heavily.

I reluctantly pull back, resting my forehead against hers. "I love you too, Sunshine. So much. And believe me, I want nothing more than to be with you right now. But not like this, not in my car in the diner parking lot."

She lets out a soft laugh. "Yeah, I guess that's not very romantic, is it?"

I brush a strand of hair behind her ear. "You deserve better than that for our first time together. I want it to be special."

"I want you now, Colton." Her voice is husky, filled with lust for me, and the final strand snaps.

Fuck it.

"Listen to me, Sunshine," I say, holding her face in my hands. "I want you to get in your car and drive home."

I don't miss the hurt and anger that appear on her face. "I swear to you I'm not rejecting you, baby. Just listen to me before you get fired up. I'm going to follow you to your house and let you check in on your grandmother. Then you're going to get in my car, and we are going to sneak into my house, up into my bedroom where I will make love to you in my bed."

Her eyes widen slightly at my words, a mix of surprise and desire flickering across her face. She bites her lip, considering for a moment before a slow smile spreads across her face.

"Okay," she murmurs. "Let's do it."

I give her one more quick kiss before she climbs off my lap and heads to her car. As promised, I follow her home, my heart racing with anticipation and nerves. This is really happening.

I wait in my car as she goes inside to check on her grandmother. A few minutes later, she emerges and climbs into my passenger seat, a small overnight bag in hand.

"Everything okay?" I ask.

She nods. "Grams is asleep. I left her a note saying I'm staying at a friend's house tonight."

The drive to my house is filled with a charged silence, the air between us thick with anticipation.

We quietly make our way into the house and up to my room, our hands intertwined, careful not to wake my family. Once inside my bedroom, I close and lock the door behind us.

We stand there for a moment, just looking at each other in the dim light from my bedside lamp.

"Are you sure about this?" I whisper, giving her one last chance to back out, letting her know there is no pressure. She is in complete control of what happens between us.

She steps closer, wrapping her arms around my neck. "I've never been more sure of anything," she says before pressing her lips to mine.

The kiss quickly deepens as weeks of pent-up desire come rushing to the surface. My hands roam her body, and hers tangle in my hair.

Slowly, we start undressing each other, taking our time to savor each revealed inch, pressing soft kisses and nipping at each other's skin.

When we're both naked, I drink in the sight of her beautiful body. "God, you're gorgeous," I whisper.

Hollis blushes slightly but doesn't look away. Her eyes roam my body as well, desire evident in her gaze. "You're not so bad yourself," she says with a smirk.

I go to reach for her, but she shoves me back, and now I feel like I'm the one being rejected.

"Oh no. You got to be slightly bossy earlier. Now it's my turn."

She crawls onto my bed, a devilish smirk playing on her lips, then props the pillows up before leaning back and beckoning me with a dainty finger.

I grab my cock, stroking my hardened length, and walk to the goddess lying in my bed. "What do you want me to do?"

"You're going to crawl up here and straddle my head and fuck my face."

My dick jumps at her dirty language, precum leaking from my tip. I follow her instructions, crawling over her gorgeous body before placing a thigh on either side of her face.

Once I'm settled, my cock in front of her face, she smiles up at me. "Good boy."

I groan, the praise making my dick throb.

Her warm hands grab onto my thighs and glide up and down before sliding toward my balls. She gives a small tug, eliciting a moan from me.

"Shh. We don't want to wake your family," she whispers.

She massages my balls before using her other hand to grip my hardened length.

"God, you're so perfect. Just the right size, the right girth. I can't wait to taste you." Hollis grabs my cock, guiding it to her mouth, taking me in as far back as she can. My eyes nearly bulge out of my head when she doesn't gag as my tip hits the back of her throat.

She moves back and forth slowly, her nails digging into my ass, guiding me to move on pace with her mouth. She pulls back, her blue eyes locked on me as she makes a show of her tongue swirling around, licking the swollen head.

"Sunshine, if you keep that up, I'm not going to last very long, and I don't plan on coming before you do," I grit out.

"Don't worry. I won't let that happen," she whispers before shoving me all the way into her mouth again and hollowing out her cheeks. She sucks me faster, harder, and soon, my hips thrust in time with her, and I grab my headboard for support.

I can feel myself getting close, and Hollis must sense it too because she pulls back, releasing my cock from her pretty mouth, a string of saliva dangling from her lips.

"Colt, I need you inside of me. I want to feel you," she rasps.

I freeze, panic taking over.

Fuck. I need a condom.

As if reading my mind, she climbs off the bed and grabs the bag she brought with her. She pulls out some condoms, tearing one off before making her way back.

"You thought of everything, didn't you?" I tease.

"Wanted to make sure you didn't chicken out on me," she taunts. She tears the golden foil, tossing it to the side. "Lay back, handsome."

I lean back, resting in the spot she was in not long ago and watching as Hollis glides the condom onto my penis.

She crawls over top of me, her perfect breasts gently taunting my muscled chest. She straddles me, placing her core above me before slowly gliding down onto me.

I pull her toward me, my mouth swallowing both of our moans at the sheer pleasure of finally being inside of her. Hollis takes a moment adjusting to me before she grinds down on my pelvis, taking her pleasure.

Wrapping my arm around her slender waist, I flip us so she's lying beneath me, needing to have those eyes looking up at me.

"You are so beautiful, Sunshine. I've got to be the luckiest guy in the world."

"You're not so bad yourself," she says, leaning up and kissing me softly.

We move together, finding our rhythm as we whisper words of love and devotion. It's passionate yet tender, everything I hoped our first time would be.

"Colton," she breathes, arching into me.

"I love you, Sunshine."

She smiles up at me, her eyes shining. "I love you too."

And with that, we come together, allowing ourselves to fully express our love for one another.

Afterward, we lie tangled, Hollis's head resting on my chest, and I run my fingers through her hair.

Hollis

I wake up slowly, feeling warm and content. It takes me a moment to remember where I am, but as I blink my eyes open and see Colton's sleeping face next to mine, the memories of last night come flooding back. A smile spreads across my face, and I think about everything that happened between us.

Carefully, so as not to wake him, I prop myself up on my elbow and just watch him sleep for a few minutes. He looks so peaceful, his long eyelashes resting against his cheeks, his lips slightly parted. I resist the urge to trace my finger along his jaw, not wanting to disturb him.

Part of me still can't believe this is real. That I'm here in Colton's bed after spending the night making love to him. It feels almost too good to be true.

Then he stirs, his eyes fluttering open. When he sees me, a sleepy smile spreads across his face.

"Good morning, Sunshine," he mumbles, voice still rough with sleep.

"Morning," I whisper.

He tugs me closer, and I go willingly, snuggling into his warm embrace.

"How are you feeling?" he asks, pressing a kiss to my forehead.

"Good ... Really good."

We lie there for a while, just enjoying being close to each other. Colton's fingers trace lazy patterns on my back while I listen to the steady beat of his heart.

Eventually, though, reality starts to creep back in. I need to get home soon to check on Grams. Plus, I don't want to risk running into his family and having to do the walk of shame.

With a reluctant sigh, I start to pull away. "I should probably get going."

He tightens his hold on me. "Five more minutes," he pleads.

I laugh softly. "Okay, five more minutes, but then we really do need to go."

He nods, pressing another kiss to my forehead. We lie in comfortable silence for a few moments before I ask the one question that's on my mind.

"So ... what happens now?"

He looks at me, hopefully seeing the mix of hope and uncertainty in my eyes. "What do you mean?"

"I mean ... with us. Are we ... like officially together?"

Colton cups my face, dragging me in close and kisses me softly. "Well, let's see. We've been on several dates already. I love you and you *finally* admitted you love me too. And well, after last night, I would say that makes you and I officially Mr. and Mrs. Reynolds."

I smack his chest, his gloriously toned and muscular chest. "That's not how that works."

He pushes out his bottom lip, the cutest pout on a grown man I ever did see. "Why not?"

I roll my eyes. "Because it just doesn't."

"Fine. I guess I can settle for boyfriend and girlfriend, but mark my words, Hollis Whitlock, you will be Mrs. Reynolds one day."

My heart flutters, the mere idea of him talking about us being endgame does something to me.

"You don't have to say that just because I sucked your dick and you got pussy."

"I'm not." His tone takes on a serious tone. "I meant what I said before. I want to make this work between us, and I will do everything in my power to fight for us, to see to it that we last. You're it for me, Sunshine. If you need me to prove it? I'll prove it. Walk over fire? Done. Climb the tallest skyscraper, let me take a climbing class first, but I'll do it. If you—"

"Okay, okay. You've proven your point." I giggle. "I want to believe we will last, Colton. I don't think I can picture myself with anyone else. I just need you to have a lot of patience with me. Okay?"

"Okay. As long as I got you, that's all that matters to me."

That's all that matters to me as well.

Chapter 26

Colton

"You sure this is the right address?" Brady asks, looking up at the brightly painted café in downtown Ravens Rock. No doubt we are both thinking the same thing. Out of all the places to have this meeting, this was the last one I was expecting.

I glance at the text thread, double-checking the address. "Yeah, this is the place. Prism Perk Café."

"Well then, after you," Brady says, motioning for me to go first.

We head inside the colorful small business, a quaint little coffee shop with walls lined with hundreds of books. There are small round tables, some with two and four chairs surrounding them, sporadically placed around except for the area where two floral sofas sit across from each other, a coffee table in between them. Quickly, I spot the person we came to see.

Rowan Hall.

Brady and I stand before him, watching as he drinks from the big ass coffee cup in his hands, waiting for him to acknowledge our presence.

"Well ... if it isn't the pretty boy who can't mind his business and ... You are?"

"Just a tagalong," Brady answers. We agreed on the way here to not reveal his name until necessary.

"Well, pretty boy and tagalong, have a seat. Seems we have some things to discuss." He motions to the couch across from the one he's sitting on.

"For someone who runs an underground fight club," I say, keeping my voice low to not draw any unwanted listeners, "this doesn't quite fit your vibe."

"Precisely why I chose this location," he says. "So what can I do for you fellas?"

"For starters, we need Hollis pulled from her fight tonight," I say point blank. The sole reason for this meeting is to get my girl out of this mess. Permanently.

"Who?" Rowan asks.

"Pixie to you," I say, growling out her arena name.

"Ah, Pixie. My most valued fighter." He says it with the smuggest face, making me want to throat-punch him. "What's the matter, pretty boy. Her fight interfering with you tapping that ass later?"

I stand up, ready to charge his ignorant ass for disrespecting my woman, but Brady grabs my arm, pulling me back down.

"Sit your ass down, Reynolds. He's just provoking you." Brady glares at Rowan.

"Yeah, and it's working." I stare Rowan in his eyes. "Watch how you talk about her," I growl out.

"Oh. Did I hit a sore spot?"

"Anyway," Brady says a little louder, trying to get this conversation back on track. "Pixie, as you call her, cannot partake in her fight. She has a football game to play this evening."

Rowan cracks up laughing, earning a few disgruntled looks from the few customers in this place. "You're kidding. They actually let guys smash girls on the field these days?"

I'm so close to smashing this asshole's face into the coffee table. "She actually runs all over them," I state, speaking with pride. My girl can ball better than most of the guys we go against.

"Sorry, boys. No can do. Hate to break it to the two of you, but people are already paying double the money for her match, which means I'm going to be making bank!"

"Listen here, dipshit," I growl, leaning forward. "I don't give a damn about your stupid profits. Hollis has worked her ass off to earn her spot on the football team, and she sure as hell deserves to play in that game tonight."

Rowan leans back, a smirk playing on his lips. "And I should care because ...?"

"Important people are coming—"

"Because if you don't pull her from the fight, we'll go to the police about your little underground operation," Brady threatens.

Rowan's eyes narrow. "You're bluffing. Why do you think we change the locations frequently? This operation has been going on for the past three years. We've managed to evade the police this long, what makes you think you can expose us? You've got no proof."

"Maybe not," I say. "But I'm sure they'd be very interested in checking out that abandoned warehouse you use. Who knows what they might find?"

For a moment, Rowan's cool facade cracks. He laughs, but it sounds forced. "Nice try, boys. But Pixie signed a contract with me. She fights when I say she fights."

"A contract she signed under duress," Brady points out. "Which wouldn't hold up legally."

We watch his whole demeanor change when he realizes the seriousness of Brady's words.

Rowan's jaw clenches. "What do you want?"

"Cancel her fight tonight. And tear up whatever contract you have with her. She's done, for good."

"And why the hell would I do that?" Rowan sneers.

Brady leans forward. "Because if you don't, not only will we go to the police, but I'll personally make sure every college in a one-hundred-mile radius knows exactly what kind of operation you're running. I'm sure the administration at Ravenwood would be very interested to hear about one of their students running an illegal fight club."

Rowan's eyes widen slightly as he looks at Brady more closely. "Who the fuck are you?"

Brady smiles coldly. "Brady Thomas. My father is Russell Thomas, former NFL quarterback. I'm sure you've heard of him. He's got quite a few connections in both the sports and academic worlds. One phone call from him, and your little operation is done for good."

As Rowan processes this information, his face goes through a range of emotions before settling on resignation.

"Fine," he spits out. "The fight's off. I'll tear up her contract."

"And you'll leave her alone," I add. "For good."

Rowan glares at me but nods. "You have my word. Besides, she's more trouble than she's worth anyway."

Relief washes over me. No more fighting to pay off a debt. Hollis can focus on football and her future without this hanging over her head.

"Pleasure doing business with you," Brady says sarcastically as we stand to leave.

"Yeah, yeah," Rowan replies, shooing us away.

As we exit the café, I turn to Brady, appreciative of his help despite how much we never got along before. "Thanks, man. I really owe you one."

Brady shrugs. "Don't mention it. I'm just glad we could help her out."

Me too.

Now that Rowan and this mess is officially taken care of, it's time to head back to Bellwood. I've got a girl to see and a game to prepare for.

Chapter 27

Hollis

The energy of tonight's rivalry game can be felt all the way in the locker room. The girls—Alora, Corrine, Maisie, and I—finish getting our game gear on, ready to take the field, making a name for ourselves before we head out to the sidelines to meet the rest of our team and coaches.

With us being a co-ed football team, protocol is that we must change in separate locker rooms, and to be honest, I don't mind. Those guys get really smelly after a game.

"You nervous, Holls?" Maisie asks, working on tying her shoulder pads over her busty chest.

"Nope. If anything, I'm ready to stomp all over those fuckers."

"Got a lot of animosity against your old school, do you?" Alora questions.

"You have no idea," I state.

"Anything we should know about these guys before we head out?" Corrine asks.

"Yeah. Watch their hands when it comes to tackling. They'll use any excuse to cop a feel," I warn them. "But if you really want to get under their skin? Just use your bad ass athletic skills against them. They really don't like it when a female can one up them."

"Good to know," Alora says, a sly smirk on her face. She loves nothing more than to show up guys, especially since she has two brothers.

As we jog out onto the field to meet with the rest of our team, the roar of the crowd hits us. The stands are packed, a sea of blue and gold on our side, and burgundy, gold, and black on Wimbleton's. I scan the crowd, easily spotting Grams in her usual spot near the fifty-yard line. She catches my eye and gives me a thumbs-up, beaming with pride.

Coach Watson looks around at all of us, his expression serious. "Alright team, this is it. Our biggest game of the season so far. Wimbleton may be our rivals, but tonight, they're just another opponent standing in our way. I know you've all worked your asses off to get here, and I expect nothing less than one hundred and ten percent effort out there."

His eyes land on me. "Whitlock, are you ready to show your old school what they're missing?"

I nod firmly. "You bet, Coach."

He continues addressing the whole team. "Remember what we practiced. Stick to the game plan, watch each other's backs, and play smart. Myers, I'm counting on you to lead this offense. Wallace, lock down that secondary. And ladies"—he looks at the four of us—"show these boys what you're made of."

We all nod, determination written across our faces.

"Alright, bring it in," Coach calls. We all put our hands in the middle. "Eagles on three. One, two, three!"

"Eagles!" we shout in unison.

As we break apart to get ready for kickoff, a gloved hand latches onto my wrist.

"Hey, before we go out there, I need to tell you something."

My heart drops into my stomach, unprepared to hear what he has to say. "What is it?" I ask defensively, bracing myself, preparing for him to say something along the lines of not wanting to be with me anymore.

"Hey," he murmurs, and pulls both my hands into his. "It's not whatever is running through your head, I swear. It has to do with Rowan."

At the mention of Rowan's name, my eyes snap to his. "Rowan?"

"Yeah. You don't have to worry about him anymore. No more fights, no more debt, nothing."

"Are you fucking with me right now?" I'm not sure if I'm elated or if I believe it's possible.

"Not a joke. That's where I went earlier, Coach Thomas and I." He nods to our new quarterback coach. The one who shares the same shade of amber eyes as my mother.

"Why did you take him with you? Weren't you two like enemies last year?"

"Let's just say, he and I? Not the best of friends, but I respect him a little more. I think fatherhood has helped him become a slightly better person."

"How did you guys manage—"

"Not important right now. We'll tab that discussion for a little later, okay?"

"Sure."

"You ready to go show these suckers what you can do, Sunshine?"

I grin back at him, feeling a surge of confidence. "Oh, I plan to, Goldendoodle."

The coin toss goes in our favor, and we elect to receive. The kick soars through the air, and Alora catches it cleanly at the five-yard line. She takes off running, following her blockers as she weaves through Wimbleton's special teams. Alora breaks free around the thirty, picking up speed and racing down the sideline. Logan Putterman, a defender on Wimbleton and the boy whose ass I beat, is closing in fast. Just as he's about to make contact, Alora cuts back sharply, leaving him grasping at air as she sprints the final twenty yards into the end zone.

"Alora Lewis with the touchdown!" the announcer shouts into the microphone, the crowd going crazy.

The kick for the extra point is good, and now it's time for our defense to put in the work.

The game is intense with both teams trading touchdowns. Wimbleton's offense is tough, but our defense gets some key stops when it counts. By halftime, we're up twenty-one to seventeen.

The third quarter starts off strong. Our defense is doing the damn thing, holding off the Wildcats and getting us the ball back. On our first possession, our quarterback does a fake handoff, making sure it looks like I have the ball, fooling many defenders who give chase. I'm taken down, the defender thinking he made a big stop. When I stand in front of him, revealing I'm not the one with the ball, I point over my shoulder at Corrine, who's scoring us the next touchdown.

"Corrine Summers is in the end zone for another Eagles touchdown!"

With the extra kick, we are now up twenty-eight to seventeen.

The rest of the game is a back-and-forth battle. Wimbleton scores again, closing the gap to twenty-eight to twenty-four. With just under two minutes left, we're trying to run out the clock and secure the win.

On third down, Dylan passes the ball off to Colton. As Colton is about to catch the ball, he's hit excessively hard by Logan. The refs throw their yellow flags, whistles are blown, and every Eagles player drops to a knee.

"Folks, it looks like number eighty-two, Colton Reynolds, has been injured on the play."

The stadium is quiet, watching with bated breaths as our coaches and medics surround Colton.

Please be okay.

A few moments later, the crowd claps when Colton stands and walks off toward the sidelines to sit on the bench.

"Folks it appears the ruling on the field is a personal foul, unnecessary roughness on Wilmbeton's number sixty-one, Logan Putterman. The result is a fifteen-yard penalty."

Cheers echo from the blue and gold side while boos pour from the opposing side.

With Colton out for the rest of the game and only a minute left on the clock, Coach Watson calls a timeout to regroup. As we huddle up on the sidelines, I can see the concern on my teammates' faces.

"Alright, listen up," Coach says. "We're still up, but it's too close for comfort. We need one more first down to run out the clock and seal this win. Whitlock, you're our best option right now. Think you can handle it?"

I nod firmly. "Absolutely, Coach."

"Good. We're going with Jet Sweep Left on my signal. Offensive line, I need you to hold that block for just a few seconds. Give Whitlock the room she needs. Dylan, I need a clean handoff. Whitlock, you get that ball and run like hell. Got it?"

We all nod in understanding.

"Alright, let's finish this. Eagles on three. One, two, three!"

"Eagles!" we shout in unison before jogging back onto the field.

As we line up, Logan glares at me from across the line of scrimmage.

"Watch yourself, Whitlock. I'm gunning for you next," Putterman spouts.

"Awe, really?" I say it with fake enthusiasm. "You do know you would have to actually catch me first."

"Not only will I catch you, but I'm going to enjoy tackling that ass almost as much as I enjoyed groping it."

The memory of what he did to me when I was a student there flashes in my head, and I see red.

"Prepare to eat those words, Pukerman," I grit out.

The ball is snapped, and Dylan fakes the handoff to Zion before turning to hand it off to me as I sweep across. I clutch the ball tightly to my chest and sprint toward the left sideline.

Out of the corner of my eye, I see Logan break through our offensive line, charging straight for me. Time seems to slow down as I plant my foot and cut sharply back toward the middle of the field. Logan's momentum carries him past me as I accelerate through the gap.

I'm in the open field now, sprinting as fast as I can. I can hear footsteps pounding behind me, but I don't dare look back. Ten yards to go for the first down. Five yards.

Just as I cross the first down marker, arms wrap around my legs, tackling me to the ground. But it doesn't matter. I've got the first down.

The whistle blows, and the crowd erupts into cheers. With only a few seconds left of the game, our fans know there isn't anything the opposing team can do.

My team lines up on the line of scrimmage. After the snap, Dylan holds the ball and takes a knee. We repeat the snap, our quarterback taking a second knee. Game over. We won!

After the game, everyone heads home to shower and clean up before we meet at Munson's for celebratory milkshakes.

Colton and I take a booth across from Alora and Corrine while everyone else squeezes into a booth or chair nearby so we can talk among each other.

"How's your shoulder feeling?" I ask, noticing he's still moving it gingerly.

"It hurts a bit, but I'll be fine." He shrugs. "Nothing a little ice and rest can't fix. How's your head?"

"My head?" I quirk an eyebrow at him.

"Yeah. I don't need your ego being inflated after the way you played tonight."

I shove him, making sure to touch his injured shoulder. "Ow, ow. Okay, okay. I shouldn't have said that." He puts his hands up in front of him, surrendering. "I'm sorry, beautiful."

At that moment, Janet and some servers working tonight come out with trays upon trays filled with various milkshakes. The moment mine is placed in front of me, a tasty cookies and cream coated in chocolate sprinkles and whipped topping, I notice it's different.

What … the …

My milkshake, delivered on a white plate, and in beautiful, cursive chocolate is a little message.

It would be sweet if you went to homecoming with me?

My head slowly turns to look at the handsome man beside me. "Is this … a hoco proposal?"

"Yeah. I wanted to make it a memorable one, and I don't think any other time would have been more perfect than this moment. So, what do you say, Sunshine? Wanna go to homecoming with me?"

"Would you take me if I had nothing but rags on?"

"I don't care what you have on as long as I'm with you."

"Good answer," I say right before I press a soft, chaste kiss to his lips.

"Look at 'em," Anthony says, sitting in the booth across from us. "And to think, Reynolds, you almost missed out on this happiness with that lame ass bet."

The room goes quiet, so quiet you could almost hear a pin drop.

"What did you say?"

"Jesus Christ, Anthony," Colton mutters.

My heart beats a little quicker, embarrassment flooding my body. "I'm … are you saying I'm a bet?"

"No!" Colton jumps in to say. He looks to his friends, pleading for them to help him.

"Listen Hollis," Zealand speaks up. "Before you ever came into the picture, Colton was going through a very hard time with … something. That morning when we came in, Colton made a comment about taking the senior year off from dating, a rule his cousin Payson made last year. Basically, he was betting with us guys he could go the whole year without dating or falling in love."

Jeremiah speaks up next. "When he was falling for you, though, he made sure we knew the bet was off. He didn't want it to come off like you were the bet."

"And we were doing so good until blabbermouth over there spoke up," Rhett chimes in.

"Don't ever say anything you don't want shared to Anthony. He can't keep shit to himself," Alora adds.

"So I was never a bet?" I ask, making sure I'm understanding what they are saying.

"Sunshine, I swear to you on everything, you were never once a bet. I was not in a good spot when we made that bet. Hell, I was hungover. I think."

"It's a shame. He lost to his own bet, and now we don't get to see him streak at graduation."

"What!?" everyone says as I almost choke on my milkshake.

Anthony continues. "You see, I bet him that if he fell in love with a girl, he had to streak at graduation. But that was before he actually broke it."

"Ohhh ... really?" I could have some fun with this. I turn to look at this man, the one who has torn down my walls piece by piece, his love for me seeping into my skin. "I say the bet is back on." I tilt my head.

"Sunshine ..."

"Oh, don't you Sunshine me, mister. A bet is a bet, and you need to pay up come graduation."

Epilogue

Graduation Day

Colton

Standing in the girls locker room, I hand Hollis my blue graduation cap and gown.

"Sunshine, are you sure you want to share all of this with our graduation class?" I ask, undoing the buttons on my dress shirt.

She pauses, glaring up at me. "You're not chickening out on me now, are you?"

"What? No! Of course not. I'm just saying, you know, all of this is for you, and there are so many people out there, *other girls* who are going to be getting a good look at the goods." I point to my crotch for emphasis. "I just don't want you to feel some type of way, ya know."

Hollis bends her arms, her hands at her armpits, and starts flapping them like wings. "Bawk. Bawk, Bawk. Bawk."

My mouth falls open from disbelief that she is trying to mock me. "I *know* you're not calling me a chicken."

"Exactly what I'm doing." She smirks. "Look, you're the one who likes to make bets. If you weren't going to see this one through, you shouldn't have shaken hands on it."

"To be fair, I believe I was hungover."

"Doesn't matter. A bet to Colton Reynolds is a bet he sees through." She pulls me down toward her, planting a soft kiss. "Now, lose the bottoms, handsome. You're still not completely naked yet."

Fucking Anthony and his blabber mouth. He had to say something in front of her.

Once I'm in the nude, Hollis hands me back my cap and gown. I don't miss the way she bites her bottom lip, lust in her eyes, probably thinking of all the ways she wants me right now.

I grab her throat, gently guiding her toward me. Moving my hand up her throat, I use my thumb to pull down on her bottom lip, releasing it from her teeth. Leaning forward, I suck her bottom lip into my mouth and nibble it, relishing in how Hollis's body shivers. A soft moan escapes her lips, making my dick harden.

"Don't bite your lip like that, Sunshine, unless you're planning to fulfill whatever dirty thoughts are running through that beautiful head of yours."

I look down, my penis full erect. "Look what you did. How am I supposed to go streaking with a hard-on?"

Hollis moves to sit on the bench in front of me, her face leveled with my erection. "I can fix that. You just gotta keep your voice down. Can you do that?"

"Yes," I say, my voice husky.

"Good boy," she praises before swiping her tongue up my length, maintaining eye contact with me the whole time.

"God, I love when you look at me like that, Sunshine." I groan when her hand massages my balls while her tongue swirls the tip of my cock.

She sucks me into her mouth, and it feels like heaven, the way she takes me. Every inch of me.

"Just like that, baby," I rasp. I pick up the pace a little, not wanting to go too rough, the way she likes. Wouldn't want to ruin all that pretty eye makeup before she got her picture taken with her diploma and family.

"You're doing such a good job. I'm so close …" I praise her, letting her know I'm ready to come down her pretty little throat.

Hollis adds her other hand, stroking me while her face bobs on my shaft, and within seconds, my orgasm hits, a burst of pleasure coursing through my body, and I release into her mouth and watch her take every single drop of me down her throat.

It's the hottest thing I have ever witnessed in my life. And she's all mine.

I pull Hollis up to me, wrapping my arms around her, staring into her eyes where I see our future play out. The both of us graduating from Ravenwood University together. Starting our careers, whether I'm an NFL superstar or mastering my skills in cybersecurity. Her walking down the aisle to me, probably in a dress that isn't white. Maybe a few kids. I want it all, and I want it all with the woman in front of me. She is still weary about the future, the fear of abandonment still in the back of her mind, but I never stop showing up for her. Proving to her that I have no plans of leaving her. She's stuck with me.

I lean forward and plant a feathery kiss on the tip of her nose. "Mm … you're incredible. You know that?"

"You remind me everyday." She smiles, kissing me softly on my lips. "Now, put your stuff on so we can head out there. I'm ready to see a full moon at graduation." She winks, a playful smile on her face.

"You see this full moon every time we have sex, and you can see it anytime you want. Why does our entire graduating class have to?"

"Again. *Your* bet."

"Remind me never to speak to Anthony ever again once graduation is over."

"Yeah, yeah. Come on, crybaby. The ceremony will be starting soon."

I pull on the cap and gown before Hollis grabs my hand, and we head toward the field hand in hand where everything is set up for graduation. We kiss each other quickly before departing to our seats, ready to close this chapter of our lives to start on the next one.

Principal King makes her way to the podium, and the ceremony is underway. Once we get to the part where we are called to walk across the stage, the nerves begin to kick in.

Each row that goes up, getting closer to the one I'm in, my heart picks up its pace, beating like a caged animal, until finally, it's our turn.

We walk in a single file toward the ramp next to the stage, waiting for our names to be announced. It goes from feeling like hours to minutes to a mere few seconds, then ...

"Colton Reid Reynolds."

Guess it's show time.

Hollis

I stay focused on Colton, wondering if he is going to go through with the bet or if he's going to chicken out at the last second. My phone vibrates, and it's the group chat.

JEREMIAH

Taking bets now. $5 he chickens out. $10 he goes through with it.

ANTHONY

Ain't no way goldilocks is going to pull this off. He's definitely chickening out.

ALORA

Way to have confidence in your bro, bro.

ANTHONY

Does she have to be in here?

HOLLIS

Yes because she's my friend. So suck it, buttercup!

RHETT

I say he chickens out.

ANTHONY

You go suck Colt's dick :p

ZEALAND

I want to believe he's going to pull this off, but he looks super nervous so I'm going to say he's out.

MAISIE

He won't do it.

CORRINE

Yeah, I'm not so sure he will pull this off you guys.

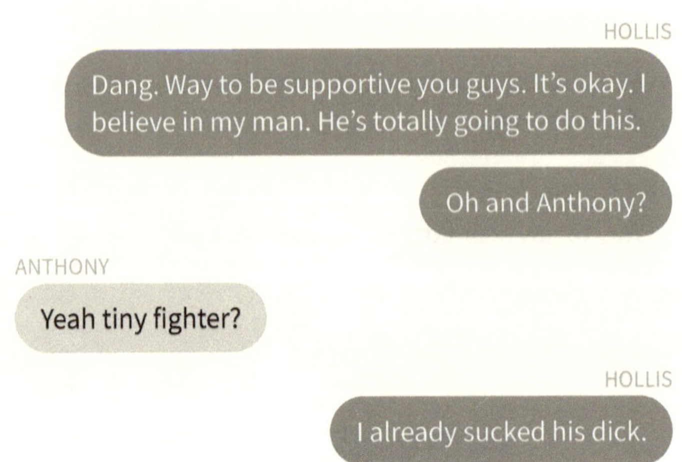

I return my phone to my pocket, putting my attention on the new row of students walking toward the stage. Colton is the sixth person in line. He's biting his lips, shifting from one foot to the other, just a bundle of nerves.

Poor guy. Maybe he will chicken out of this.

Keeping my eyes focused on him, I wait to see if he feels me out. When his pretty blues land on me, I mouth *I love you* to him.

He raises his hand, holding up four fingers before turning it sideways, tucking his pinky. He raises both of his hands to form a heart over his chest; his little hand signal of forever.

Our little exchange distracts him, making him visibly more at ease before Principal King announces his name.

"Colton Reid Reynolds."

Whistles, claps, and shouts from friends and families go off, excited cheers of love and pride ring out over the stadium as he crosses the stage to receive his diploma.

I place two fingers in my mouth and whistle. "That's my man!" I shout as loud as I can, hoping he hears me over the noise.

As he walks off stage down the other ramp, I wait with anticipation to see if he goes through with it.

He looks around, probably checking for any signs of security, before he dips behind the fake plant pot and pulls out ... a mask? Wait, is that a ski mask?

He pulls on the ski mask, unzips his graduation gown, then takes off.

His beautiful, athletic naked body runs through every student row before he takes off toward the stadium entrance, his white ass cheeks a sight to see.

"Can we have security get that streaker, please?" Principal King shouts into the microphone.

Officer McCarty runs after Colton, but he's no match. Colton has endurance and speed, his many dedicated years of youth sports on his side.

"Alright, alright. Let's all calm down now that the incident is out of sight. We have more diplomas to hand out, so let's get back to it and get you guys out of here. Shall we?" Principal King says.

The ceremony continues, student after student receiving their high school diplomas, a surreal moment for me. So many times, I almost dropped out to work full-time, but Grams put the pressure on me, telling me she would be disappointed if she didn't get to watch me walk across the stage. It was because of her I pushed myself to continue with my education, to make her proud, to see this moment happen right here, right now.

And thanks to football, I was granted a full-ride scholarship to Ravenwood University, where I'll be attending in the fall, getting my degree as a pharmacist.

Dealing with everything regarding my grandmother's medications opened my eyes to the world of pharmaceuticals. Maybe one day, I can find a way to make life-saving medications more affordable for people who struggle in poverty.

Being a student at Ravenwood means I'll be close to Grams, able to check in on her and visit her often.

I've grown so close to Colton's family; they've practically accepted me into the family. We have family dinners every Sunday, Grams included.

It's become a favorite tradition for me and something I look forward to every week.

Brady and I are slowly working on our relationship, taking it one day at a time. It's still hard to wrap my head around that I have a half brother. After one of our conversations, I learned after my mom's affair with my father, Brady's dad made sure he got sole custody of Brady, forbidding my mother to have any contact with her son, leaving him to be raised by numerous nannies, out of pure spite and hatred toward my mother. With his fame, Russell Thomas wanted to ensure this didn't cause a scandal that would tarnish his name. Despite him having numerous affairs, he would ensure she looked like the wrongful one. Brady did some digging, angry at his father for the reason he grew up without our mother, and it was discovered there was a contract. Due to the prenup in place, my mother was basically flat broke. Russell, however, was willing to give her a couple grand as hush money, to walk away from her son and never mention him to anyone. It's safe to say, she kept her word, but I guess I will never know why. Maybe one day, Brady and I can track her down and get the answers to our questions.

I'll forever be grateful for his help with Rowan and Grams, more so with Grams. Having her on a better health insurance plan that covers her insulin has lifted so much stress off my shoulders.

Oh, and when I found out what Brady did to sweet Sadie, I made sure he gave an authentic apology. His ribs were bruised for about a week, but hopefully, he will think twice about pulling stupid shit like that. Especially since he's the father of an adorable little girl, Savannah Rose Thomas. Not only do I have a brother, I have a niece! And I cannot wait to teach her some of my skills so she knows how to protect herself.

After the ceremony, we gathered our caps and set out to look for our parents, and I search for Colton.

Just as I'm about to text him, strong arms wrap around me from behind.

"Looking for someone, Sunshine?" Colton's deep voice rumbles in my ear, sending a slight shiver down my spine.

I turn in his arms, wrapping my arms around his neck. "As a matter of fact, I was. There was a really hot, naked man wearing a mask running around here, and I wanted to get his number. You wouldn't happen to know where he went, would you?"

"I'm pretty sure he's spoken for."

"Damn. I really wanted a better view of that ass," I tease.

"Well … we could cut out of here and head to your house before everyone shows up at mine."

"As fun as that would be, Grams needs her graduation picture with me and my diploma."

"Ugh, fine. But I get first pics."

"What? She's *my* grandmother!" I exclaim, gently shoving him away.

"She's mine too."

"How so?" My eyebrows quirk, curious to know his answer.

"C'mon, Sunshine. We've been over this. We'll both graduate from Ravenwood, I'll put a ring on your finger, wedding bells will ring, followed by the sweet, sweet cries of our two to three little babies."

"Still thinking we're endgame, huh?"

"I *know* we're endgame. Besides, Thea's got a head start on the wedding planning."

Joking or not, I wouldn't put it past his sister. We've really bonded these past few months, and she's already calling me her sister-in-law.

Lacing our fingers together, Colton and I walk to find our families.

"So, uh, where exactly did you run off to?" I raise an eyebrow.

"Let's just say I had a very good hiding place." He winks. "Can't have Officer McCarty arresting me on graduation day, now can we?"

"No, we can't. That wouldn't go well with your graduation present I have in store for you lat—"

We're interrupted by Anthony's booming voice. "There's the man of the hour! Dude, that was epic!"

The rest of our friends crowd around us, a mix of shock and awe on their faces.

"I can't believe you actually went through with it," Jeremiah says, shaking his head. "Props, man." They do that hand grab, chest bump thing all guys do.

"Thanks." Colton grins, so pleased with himself.

"Oh, good. Since all of you are here, you can pay me." I smirk, holding out my hand. "I was the only one who believed in my man."

There's a chorus of groans as money starts changing hands. Colton looks at me, eyebrows raised. "You bet on me?"

"Of course I did." I grin. "I'll always bet on you."

His smile is radiant as he leans down to kiss me. It's soft and sweet, making me feel loved and wanted. I kiss him back, this time with a little more passion, a kiss full of promises for our future together.

Acknowledgements

First and foremost, I must thank my wonderful husband. From the moment the idea of becoming an author first touched my heart, he's been by my side, making sure I saw it through every step of the way. His unwavering love and support, and the way he's been my rock when I needed it most, mean more than words can express. Whenever I doubt myself or question whether this dream is truly worth the struggle, he's always there—reminding me that it will all pay off, and that I should never let anything convince me to give up. Having a supportive partner like him is everything, and I'm endlessly grateful he's mine.

To my four, beautiful children ~ If there is anything I want you to take from watching me write my books, it's this: go chase your dreams. Never let fear hold you back or the doubts hinder what you are capable of. With patience, hard work and support, you can do anything. And I'll be behind you, cheering you on in support!

To Ganny ~ Every morning you would sit down to drink your coffee, eat your cinnamon sugar, peanut butter toast as you read a Nora Roberts romance book. I may not have known it then what you were reading, but what I would give to have you here today, to share this love of romance stories with you. To hand you a copy of one of my own books and hear what you thought of my own stories. How proud would you be of me? Thank you for being an amazing woman, full of love and spunky humor. You will never be forgotten.

To Grandma Timmons ~ Diabetes may have shorten your life, but your spirit lives on through me. To help where I can, to give back, and just be a decent human being to spread a little kindness and light to everyone I cross paths with. And that same spirit is what I am passing down through my children, so they too can bring more light, more kindness in a world that feels dark most of the time. Thank you for showing what love, empathy and humanity looks like.

To my family and friends ~ Thank you for all the love and support you have shown me on this newfound journey of mine. Whether you are telling people about my books, reading them or just buying my work to support me, I am so appreciative that you are showing your love for me and it does not go unnoticed.

To Maria ~ Thank you for the All Write Well program and your always positive feedback as I stepped foot into the writing world. I would not be turning this dream into reality if it wasn't for you and the program you have created. I hope I make you proud! I will continue to use what I learned from AWW to help me build this author dream of mine.

To my editor, Dee Houpt ~ Thank you for your time and work that you put into editing my manuscripts. Thank you for always being so positive, understanding, reassuring and always giving your honesty. I knew the moment I saw your website, you were the person I wanted to work with and I'm so glad I took the chance. This book wouldn't be what it is today without you. Thank you truly doesn't seem to be enough!

To my book cover designer, Dee Garcia ~ You always have the magic touch when it comes to designing book covers. When I feel like I can't fully express my vision, you somehow manage to put together my visions and make them reality. The number of compliments I get in regards to the covers make me proud to showcase your talent for the world to see. Thank you for the amazing work you do!

Finally, to the readers who took the time to read this book. Thank you for taking a chance on a new indie author. It means the world to me that you chose to read my story. Whether you loved it or felt it could have been better, I appreciate you and thank you! If you could leave an honest review on Amazon and any other social platform, I would greatly appreciate it! Reviews help indie authors such as myself get our books out to more readers.

About the Author

Dev Hahn is a new indie author, learning as she goes and ready to bring her notebook of story ideas to life and share them with the world. Reading has always been an escape for Dev when her depression became too much or when she just needed to escape reality for a few chapters. She hopes she can do the same for anyone willing to take a chance on her books. Besides reading romance and falling for fictional characters, Dev enjoys watching American football, singing karaoke with her family, iced coffee all year round, and spending quality time with the people she loves most. She's a stay-at-home mother who writes around her children's busy schedules. She resides in Maryland with her husband, two fur babies and their four children who make life fun, chaotic and entertaining.

DEV HAHN

272

Also By Dev Hahn

<u>Standalones</u>
Beyond Broken Colors

<u>Bellwood Lady Baller Series</u>
Coming Out on the Sidelines
Catching Feelings in the End Zone
Tackling Temptations on the Line
Opposing Hearts on the Field, *Coming Fall 2025*

Connect With Me

Be sure to follow me on my socials for updates and new releases!

Bookbub: bookbub.com/profile/dev-hahn
Facebook: facebook.com/authordevhahn
Goodreads: goodreads.com/author/show/47750634.Dev_Hahn
Instagram: instagram.com/authordevhahn/
Pinterest: pinterest.com/authordevhahn
TikTok: tiktok.com/@author.dev.hahn
Threads: threads.com/@authordevhahn